D1301631

# The Devil's Cohort
## A Vampire's Vault Novel

Stephen Mills

## Dedications

For Dad, Mom, and Lupe
One, the best proofreader I could ask for
Another instilled in me her love of reading
The last puts up with me

-and-

To all my friends in this intimate community of writers,
who are always ready to lend a hand, a bit of advice, and
invaluable encouragement

# Prologue

Wallachia, Romania
December, 1476

"All of this would be so much simpler if you'd just allow me to help you," Cosmin said flatly. A warm night breeze tickled the castle's ramparts, the slight wind carrying his words away as if Vlad had never heard them. "They are knocking on the door, son, and my army is positively hopping at the chance for blood," he continued, but the Drăculea ignored his father still. The vampire sighed audibly and Vlad worked his jaw in annoyance, the joints clicking and popping.

"Help," Vlad said flatly. "What an interesting choice of words, Cosmin the Wicked…Cosmin the Terrible," Vlad whispered through clamped lips. He knew the damnable secret that his father carried. "You certainly live up to your monikers."

"Do I?" the vampire shot back. "Your orgies of blood-letting make my crimes seem infantile by comparison."

Another click sounded from Vlad's jaw, another pop. Cosmin was a charismatic son of a bitch. Simply telling his father "no" felt nearly impossible, as if the words themselves were a betrayal of sorts. Still, the offer he had laid on the table was tempting. Turkish armies had crossed the Bosporus and swept up from the south to threaten Wallachian borders. Vlad's armies were strong, but not strong enough to stop the flood that was carrying the southern enemy this way. Still, Vlad wondered how steep of a price his father would demand for the assistance of his savage army.

"All we need to do is open the door," the vampire crooned in a soft voice.

"What would that take?" Vlad snapped, suddenly short of temper.

"One life, son. Just one life. Imagine what one more life could accomplish!"

"Whose life would that be, Father?"

"Is that really so important?"

Vlad frowned deeply, his brows carving a furrow until they touched. Cosmin had an agenda, he always had an agenda. Wallachia's predicament was merely the vehicle for his father to seize more power. Cosmin the Wicked was a cunning bastard, and the Drăculea did not know everything, but he was certain that Cosmin's motivations were driven only by his perpetual, selfish wickedness. "Nothing comes for free," he said at length. Deep brown eyes, that sat nearly hidden in his ruddy face, studied Cosmin's pale skin and black pupils. Vlad knew what his father was, he knew that the vampire had once been a man. That changed long ago, though. Something lurked within that body, a horror which had created the monster that stood before him. Cosmin had kept the secret close. Vlad, however, was nothing if not resourceful. His spies had teased out the details, they had sleuthed about until the horrible secrets had been exposed, yet Vlad suspected the secrets had been discovered all too easily. It was as if the vampire wanted his son to know the worst of it.

Cosmin threw his arms wide to encompass the dark landscape laid out before them. "All this could be yours!

An empire, son." He fixed a knowing eye on Vlad, his head cocked and brow peaked. "Nothing can stop us. Nothing can stop *you*. I mean this in the most literal way possible: you can rule the world."

Another deep sigh rattled from Vlad's breast. "Why would I want to do that?" he asked, unwilling to meet the vampire's intense gaze. "*This* is my land. These are my people."

No sooner than the words left Vlad's mouth the vampire's lip wrinkled into a sneer. "*Everyone* can be your people. You wouldn't even have to put forth any effort! Whoever opposes you would be…"

"…killed," Vlad interrupted the vampire.

"Torn to bits! Fed to my beasts! Only the loyal would be left! Does that really sound so bad?"

Vlad knew the real answer to that question. All the blood that had already been spilled, all the death that had already been dealt, was a consequence of holding Wallachia together and resisting the might of the invading Turkish armies. Despite the fierce reputation he had earned, Vlad Drǎculea hadn't enjoyed the wholesale slaughter. Nor did he particularly care to rule a far-flung empire won by dubious allegiances.

*Besides*, he thought, *how long until the Devil's Cohort turns against its puppet master?*

"I know what you're thinking," Cosmin offered with an air of helpfulness, which was no great surprise to Vlad. The old monster's tricks far outstripped the primitive abilities of Wallachia's resident strigoi, those canny undead who weren't mere ghouls, and Vlad knew the vampire could peak into people's minds and see glimpses of their thoughts. "There is no risk, Vlad. You are my son. Even the worst of them wouldn't dare to harm you."

Incessant clicking and popping in Vlad's jaw snapped to a suddenly booming laugh. "You can't be serious," Vlad said, a finger wiping the humor from his eye. "Those foul things you call your army are even less trustworthy than you. I can't bear the cost, and you know it."

"Why would you say that?" Cosmin asked, feigned hurt paining his face.

"Because you still haven't told me whose life is forfeit."

"You already know the answer to that question."

Vlad spun, a fierce gaze spearing Cosmin. "If you know who it is, why torment me?" the half-breed dhampir spat, his furious voice gaining an octave.

Cosmin's eyes narrowed. "Because we need each other, son. I will keep the army in check, and you will lead them."

"Why me?" Vlad despaired. "Why can't you leave me alone?"

"Because I am tied to these mountains. My power will wane if I travel too far. Besides, it's hard to get around when daylight drives me to sleep. I need you, and you need me."

Vlad's explosion of humor had quickly soured into a festering anger. Cosmin was right. The vampire needs his son, and Vlad did know who the sacrifice would have to be. The Drăculea only wanted confirmation from his demonic, vampiric father, and he spun away in anger, stalking his way from the castle's ramparts.

\*\*\*\*

László knocked, timid raps on the thick oak door. Taps, really, so quiet one could easily confuse him with a coward. Vlad Drăculea knew better, though. László Dăneşti was his cousin, one who had kept faith with the House of Drăculeşti, and he was a fearless warrior and captain who led a contingent of Vlad's army.

He was also Adina's father, and she had been revealed as the Navă, the vessel who had been randomly blessed with a fate both terrible and exhilarating. She was tiny, a black-haired imp who reveled in mayhem, and through her would flow either salvation or damnation.

At least, that's what Father Vasile had said, and when the wizened old priest spoke, wise men listened.

Vlad ushered the man into his chamber. Candles spluttered in the door's sudden movement, their jumping flames causing the shadows to dance.

"My lord," László wheezed. He had rushed here as soon as the summons came.

"Cousin," Vlad said as he embraced the man, relief making his voice breathy. Night had surrendered to harsh daylight, but the chamber was windowless, dark and stale and stifling. All the better for surreptitious encounters. Cosmin's offer was a recent memory whose foulness cloyed in his brain and time was of the essence. The day was still young which meant László had ridden his horse hard to get to the castle so quickly. "We have to talk."

"Of course," the man said with exhaustion. "Can I just…"

"No," Vlad whispered, the urgency in his voice cutting László off. "The attacks have grown more frequent, more brazen, and I know why."

He wasn't talking about the Turkish army, who had been predictable and lackadaisical. Vlad was talking about something else. People had disappeared, only for their bodies to turn up, half-eaten and desecrated. Animals, they were told, feral animals from the wilderness. The Old Families in the mountains knew better. They had lived with the tales and the folklore and the evil itself for many generations. Now that same malevolence had awoken, as it always did when the Navă was coming of age. Her power was growing, and as its fingers worked their way about the countryside, foul things had risen to seek it out.

Stress creased Vlad's chiseled features, and as a consequence the words came tumbling out thick and fast, full of improbable stories that drained the blood from László's already pale face. At the end of it all, after the fantastical tales of the macabre and the demonic, László agreed to take his family and flee. If they stayed to face the coming Turks, then Cosmin the Wicked would do what Vlad could not. Little Adina would become an offering, and the demons of Hell would be released to flood the land.

Preparations took some time, but later that day, when life-giving sunlight still burned evil from the land, László Dăneşti fled with his wife, with his sons and daughters. It was a journey fraught with danger, for if Cosmin was able to sniff out the conspiracy then all would be lost. First they went south, but before long the caravan turned east away from the slashing rays of the sun, their little procession of wagons and horses and oath-sworn men trundling along well-worn paths. Time was what they needed. Time and distance, because if they were given enough time, they would be able to put plenty of distance between themselves and the ungodly evil that haunted the land around Cetatea Orașului.

Vlad Drăculea had proven himself a good friend and a faithful ruler, one who demanded the utmost fidelity but gave the same in return. Why else would he warn László of Adina's fate should they stay?

Impossible thoughts prowled the man's mind, and László refused to believe the truth of it, but he acquiesced to Vlad's demands. Adina must go, she could not fall prey to Cosmin and the Old One. Even though he and Vlad were kin and bound by marriage and blood, she was the Navă and so the girl was at risk.

Over a distant horizon, the sun dipped under mountain ridges, its dying corona singeing high ridges as shadows grew long and the sky deepened to an inky blue. Night was coming. Soon, so very soon, the day would die, and the slow carriages hadn't traveled nearly fast enough. Now a thick mist seeped its way out of the forest floor, and László cursed. "We make camp!" he yelled against his better judgment. Forests were dangerous at night, even more so for any caravan which was foolish enough to try and wind its way through dark trees across a moonless land. Bandits and worse inhabited these woods and the best defense would be to circle the wagons and settle in for a restless night. László wanted to continue on, he yearned to be away from this cursed place, but there was nothing to be done.

All they needed to do was survive the night.

****

Sullen embers glowed weakly in the chill night air. Smoke rose lazily from the dying fire, a slight breeze diffusing the acrid stench of the burnt wood, and a lone wolf circled the caravan camp, its ears flat against its head. The bitch was tense and anxious, but hunger drove her forward into the camp of the travelers. She sniffed the air, a scent of food on the night's slight breeze. A pang in her empty belly drove the bitch deeper into the dangerous circle of carriages.

Mist had risen from the forest floor, its musty soil imparting an earthy scent into the air. The fog lifted, swirled in the breeze, grew denser until the forest's details were obscured into a distant memory. The bitch wolf hesitated as the vaporous mist grew nearer, a thin whine escaping as she bared her teeth. Slinking back, she made a slow and hesitant retreat. Hungry as she was, a primal instinct of survival overcame the threat of starvation. She looked back, whined again, and loped deep into the forest.

The fog circled, creeping around the camp to envelope the wagons, its vaporous touch smothering the fire's remaining embers. It probed, drifting about the wagons. László and Simion had fallen asleep, their flask of liquor long emptied, and the mist crawled across their legs, caressed their faces before moving on, flowing beneath and between the ornate wagons.

Ileana's tears had dried long ago. She was too tired to cry, too exhausted to sleep. She sat next to her daughter's bed and stroked the little girl's black hair that shimmered in the lamplight. Adina was finally asleep, her hysterical shrieking silenced for the time being. She was paler now, as if the blood had left her, as if she were wasting away.

"Poor child," the woman whispered, "poor, sweet Adina." Ileana stood to stretch, her tired eyes oblivious to the tendrils of mist that seeped under the wagon's cover. A sudden thirst came over her, an unquenchable desire for water. Her mouth was inexplicably parched, as dry as tinder before the match, and she groped about for a waterskin. She found one, only one, but it had sprung a seam and was dry, as parched as her throat. Ileana silently cursed her husband's oversight. He was a good man, her László , but since he had returned from Cetatea Oraşului earlier in the day he had become distant. He had become cold and angry and turned to drink to settle his fears. She turned to her daughter, caressed the girl's forehead and frowned, then left the wagon to slake her thirst.

****

The fog grew thicker, unnaturally so. It enveloped the wheels of Adina's wagon, crept up the sides and tickled the cloth of the wagon's cover. Adina whimpered in her sleep. Her fingers clawed involuntarily at the blanket and her jaw worked, teeth clicking as they ground together. She suffered from nightmares, hellish dreams that haunted the night. The girl wanted to cry out, to leap into her mother's arms, but she couldn't move. It was as if she were frozen in time and the nightmares played out, over and over, in the deepest recesses of her mind.

This dream was different, though. She had descended into a wood, a forest thick with fog, their camp long disappeared, her only defense against the cold a simple night dress. Vapor swirled about as if it were searching, creeping back and forth across the forest floor, until it slowed to a stop, and the mist began to coalesce before the little girl's eyes, twisting and turning and piling up ever taller until it was the height and shape of a tall man. Adina became aware of details of the man, his arms long and lank at his sides, his eyes glowing a fierce red. His skin was flushed, lips crimson. He flicked his tongue along a row of sharp teeth.

"Hello, Adina," he hissed.

Her heart clenched tightly in her chest. He took a step closer.

"Do you know me?" he asked in his serpent-voice.

Adina tried to scream, but she was paralyzed. She knew his face instantly though she had never seen him before. It was a face of evil, of pitiless horror. Tears streamed down the stricken girl's cheeks.

"You know my mother, don't you?" he crooned to her. "She has been visiting you all these nights. I was there too, sometimes as a beast, other times as something else. Now I present myself how I *truly* am."

She stared at him, wide-eyed and fearful. "Your mother is the old woman, isn't she? The witch." Snot bubbled from her nose to mingle with salty tears.

His smile widened, crimson lips stretching to show even more of those pointed ivory fangs. "Yes! You remember. Regrettably, she is a crone, isn't she? I admit it, my mother isn't easy on the eyes. Never mind her, though. *I* am the important one. I am the one that gave your family life. I delivered them from persecution, helped them to thrive all these years, I protected them for all of these centuries." The wide smile quickly disappeared, his face darkening. "What did I receive in thanks? Betrayal. I sheltered your family. I brought them under my wing and in turn, I was deceived by them. By your *father*." He drew closer, or rather the forest shrank away so the gap between man and girl disappeared. "Now, you will help me. If you help me, I will make you a solemn promise: I will not harm them. Doesn't that sound good?"

She nodded imperceptibly, too scared to move.

"Say it," he said.

Adina swallowed deeply, trying to choke back briny terror.

"Say it, girl. Say it! Say you will help me."

More tears cascaded down her cheeks. She clutched at her night dress, and Cosmin felt Adina wishing him away. She was wishing the cold and the evil and the all of the horrid nightmares away. "Please, darling girl," he whispered as she teetered. "You must help me. If you do not I will be forced to hurt your family. All of them. I don't want to do such a thing! So, you must help me. If you refuse me, then your mother and father and brothers and sisters must be disciplined, so they do not betray anyone else. Don't you see the importance of this?" the man pleaded wolfishly.

She let out a small cry, the howl of a tortured soul, and palpable anguish radiated off the girl. Adina was ready to burst out of adolescence, to become a woman, and the power within was near its peak though she didn't know how to control it. If the girl knew what God had placed within her, then she could have banished him from her world, from this realm, sent the demon within him tumbling back into his own dreary land of red and black, of wan light and sulfurous air. "All of this will end, little princess. All of this can end, you just have to do one thing for me. Just one thing. Can you do it?"

Adina's eyes, large and brown and full of fear, stared at him, but he could see the courage begin to well up in her chest. She was small for her age, he noted, yet that diminutive frame belied a profound mettle. That inner strength gave her courage, yet she was powerless to resist the inevitable acquiescence that was building within her.

"I can see it in your eyes, Adina. You will help me, won't you? Say you will, say it."

She swallowed again. "I will," she said solemnly.

A relieved smile washed across Cosmin's face, blood-red lips again splitting into a wide grin. "Excellent," he whispered. "Then come with me, little one. Come with me and your family will be saved."

Adina nodded assuredly. "Where are we going?"

"Back to my home, where you will sleep. And when you sleep, your family will be safe. They will be safe from their own duplicity and even from the Turks themselves, because you will help to raise my armies."

Adina's brow furrowed as her brain processed what the strange man was saying. "I will go to sleep, and that will help your army fight the enemy?"

One corner of his lip raised higher, amusement dancing in his dead eyes. "You understand! That is wonderful. Now, we must go." With or without his son, Cosmin would bring his horde of demons through the void, and given enough time he would figure out a way to lead them to war.

\*\*\*\*

Simion heard Ileana's screams first, and even after Simion kicked his brother awake, it took László a moment to rise from the depths of his drunken slumber. Her cries were an agonizing sound, the visceral wail of subconscious pain. Ileana's shrieking was the sound of a parent mourning her child. The men raced towards the haunting shrieking noise that reverberated through the makeshift camp. Other members of the small clan clambered down from their wagons, but László ignored them as he leapt into the cart that Adina slept in. His heart seized in his chest, limbs frozen in time, his wife's incessant screeching stabbing at his eardrums.

Adina, his dear, sweet little girl, had the pallor of a corpse. Her skin was gray, her brown eyes rolled back so he could only see the vitreous whites. The girl's hair was lank, and where it had always been black, it was now white as sun-bleached bone. Her hands were hooked into claws, toes bent painfully under the balls of her feet, animal-like grunts and howls erupting from her frail little body.

She was levitating just below the ceiling of the wagon, suspended by some black magic, her teeth gnashing at them.

"Adina!" László bawled, aghast at the evil that had seized his daughter, but then his hand was guided by pain and fear and torment to raise his heavy iron sword, its razor edge glinting in the lamplight, ready to deliver his luckless daughter's spirit from the demon's clutches.

# 1

Saarbrücken, Germany
November, 1938

Nationalists had taken over the city, and the riots that followed paralyzed industry and services. It all made Charles's travels from Saarbrücken tricky. He had made it, though, despite the political dangers, and now throngs of hungry men and women demanded food, and it was through these unwashed masses that Charles fought his way. He had wisely exchanged his usual aristocratic dress for the rags of a pauper, all the easier to navigate the city's streets, itself brought to its knees by striking workers and destitute people. *I must make this quick*, Charles thought, *before the city burns.* Hunger was a dry tinder-bundle, waiting impatiently for a spark that would engulf the city in a conflagration.

Charles hurried through the streets, glancing at signs to ensure he didn't miss a turn or lose his way. Concern of injury, even death, was foreign to him. Through war and famine and heinous injuries, he had lived when others had died.

When he should have died.

Instead, Charles was worried for Bekhmoaram's safety, because Bekhmoaram was a Jew who had the bad fortune to live in Germany. He was a wise man, though, because he chose to live on a nondescript road, his unmarked, modest home hiding in the shadow of the synagogue.

All the better for him.

The Pharmacist, just before he had been murdered, had told Charles that Bekhmoaram stayed shut inside his unmarked shop, that he was always afraid of being identified and singled out. While Jews were no longer banished per se, men like him weren't welcomed by most Saarlanders. Those who followed the Hebrew faith were always on the verge of persecution and so lived in a perpetual state of fear, and it was this knowledge that drove Charles on.

The Jew had knowledge that Charles needed, and at any moment the spark would alight the tinder, and the city would go up in flames.

He chewed anxiously on his lip as he looked for the synagogue. Rumors abounded regarding Germany's Jewish population and the persecution they suffered, and now recent times had become even harder for them. Since the nationalists had taken to the streets the followers of Moses were in ever increasing danger. Charles blithely wondered why Bekhmoaram hadn't fled back to Alsace, where the larger French Jewish community would shelter him, but then he forced that thought from his mind. It wasn't his concern.

Rising monolithic from the street, the synagogue's white stone façade boasted a huge Star of David, a beacon for the wrath of the German Nationalists. Charles knew that Bekhmoaram's unmarked home was near, but he had to hurry. The reek of impending violence had stained Saarbrücken's air, and he didn't want to be in the city when stones began flying.

The man was a rabbi, or rather had *been* a rabbi, at one time. Charles had learned that he was also an accountant, for that was one of the few professions available to a man such as him. Bekhmoaram was also, within certain circles, a noted hunter of monsters, which had caused Charles to pause.

Only a slight pause, though. Overcoming such a threat was a necessity, and Charles had also learned the rabbi held information that Charles needed to complete his quest.

*Shit*, Charles chastised himself silently. *I missed the street.*

Backtracking, he found the unmarked alley that shot arrow-straight with two dozen flats lining each side of the old, cobbled road. He ran a hand down his face, wiping away mist and trepidation.

He had found Bekhmoaram's flat, and its brass door knocker beckoned.

\*\*\*\*

A knock sounded on the door, quiet yet sharp. Bekhmoaram looked up, a hiss escaping his lips, and wondered if he should answer its summons.

He smiled sadly. *What times we live in, where a man should be afraid to answer his own door.*

Bekhmoaram rose and arranged a kippah on his head, adjusted the payot that hung on either side of his face, and stroked his beard thoughtfully. *If they come for me, would they knock?* he considered. *Surely not.*

The old man hobbled to his door, knees aching and feet shuffling across the oak planks. Those old floorboards were worn smooth from innumerable feet. *What stories these walls could tell*, he thought morosely. This story would be the last for the walls to whisper, as Bekhmoaram's fear galvanized his resolve to flee to his adopted home. Alsace may not have been the community of his birth, but it would undoubtedly welcome him back. Perhaps he would once again lead prayers at the synagogue, maybe once more take up the familiar mantle of a rabbi. His hand, joints swollen from arthritis and pale skin traced with a map of bluish veins, reached for the door's latch. A visitor should not be kept waiting.

Gritty shrieks of protesting metal sounded from the knob as it turned in its brass plate. Bekhmoaram pulled the door open with deliberate slowness, its hinges protesting audibly, so that he was met by the intense stare of brown eyes in the ruddy face that stared back at him through the door's crack.

"May I help you?" the old man asked in French.

"I am looking for the Jew," Charles answered in Aramaic.

Bekhmoaram said nothing for a moment. He returned Charles's intense stare, trying to place the stranger's face. He was clearly not Jewish, yet he spoke the ancient tongue flawlessly, though with a foreign accent. A familiar accent.

His visitor shifted with an uncomfortable air. "I will not hurt you," he said, "nor will I tell anyone you are here. I merely come looking for answers."

"Answers?" Bekhmoaram asked warily.

"A family affair. I come searching for truth, and I have been told that you are the man to enlighten me."

Bekhmoaram thought for a moment more, weighing the dangers this stranger presented in these strange times, before opening the door wide. "You are welcome in my home," he said. "How should I address you?"

Charles nodded, a slight smile on his face. "I am honored," he said. "You may call me Charles. Charles Resseguie."

\*\*\*\*

The men faced each other. Charles, stoic and stone-faced, looked at a bemused Bekhmoaram. The old rabbi scratched at his beard and Charles was not sure what to make of this complex man. He had lit an oil lamp, its flame flickering in the dark room, the lamp shade raised high to expose its light.

"Rădescu?" he asked, a confirmation that his old ears had heard the visitor correctly.

Charles nodded. "I was told that you can help me on my quest."

"Who would tell you such a thing? Not many people know of me, and even fewer know where I live."

"It doesn't matter," Charles frowned. "I just need to find out about my father."

Bekhmoaram waved away Charles' petulant dismissiveness. "There are many Rădescus. And you said his name is…"

"I did not. In fact, I don't know his name. My mother never spoke of him. He went by Rădescu and he lived near Pitești, that's all I know."

The old man peered closely into Charles's eyes, who steeled himself against the rabbi's intensity. "You're not telling me everything, are you?" he asked. A brief moment of silence stretched uncomfortably long, then Bekhmoaram gestured at a tired stool. "Please, sit." It was not an offer so much as a demand.

Charles shifted uncomfortably on the old stool, its protesting legs creaking angrily. It was ancient, this chair, near to collapse from age and exhaustion. *Much like Bekhmoaram must be*, Charles mused as the retired rabbi fussed about the room, clearing a place for himself to sit. Clutter was everywhere. Not trash, but books. Stacks of tomes, ancient and new alike, covered in thin dust. Rolls of parchment had been stashed in the nooks formed by all sizes of the books. "Pardon the mess," Bekhmoaram muttered. "As you can imagine, I don't receive much in the way of visitors these days." He paused, a smile's faint trace under the trimmed beard. "One wonders how I was able to amass such a collection! I certainly wonder at it. Perhaps it is a consequence of a long life?" Satisfied that his hasty arranging was sufficient, the old man sat down. "Now, then. Where were we?"

*How much should I tell him?* Charles wondered, but despite his best efforts, he had taken a liking to Bekhmoaram. Rotund and jovial, with a manic mind reflected in the clutter of his home, for a hunter he was fairly personable. To boot, Bekhmoaram seemed a rare treat in the otherwise gloomy city of nationalists.

The rabbi leaned back and let an exhausted sigh escape. "You were saying that your father was a Rădescu near Pitești, and I'm sure there is more you're not telling me. However, if that was all to the story you would have just gone there and asked around, wouldn't you? So please, tell me more, and I will help you if I'm able."

"All I can remember is that we fled when I was young, we fled the flames and the bodies. My mother was frantic, she would scream nonsensical things about monsters and cannibals…and undead men…" Charles trailed off, losing himself in the mists of time.

"How old were you?" Bekhmoaram asked lightly.

Charles shrugged. "I'm not sure. Five or six years old, probably."

"And how long ago was that?"

He chewed at a pursed lip. *How much can I tell the old man?* he thought. *How much should I tell him?*

"Honesty is always the best policy," the rabbi chided Charles softly.

"It was a long time ago," Charles said at length. "I don't remember exactly when."

"You don't look that old. What, mid-thirties? Yes, mid-thirties. I would say no older than thirty-six. Which would mean you were born…sometime before 1910?"

"I was born before 1910," Charles confirmed.

"My estimation is wrong, isn't it?"

Charles simply grunted in surly reply. The Jew certainly seemed to enjoy this back-and-forth.

"I'm not just a retired rabbi, book-keeper, and historian, Mister Resseguie. You already knew that, though. It's why you're here. I had another occupation that gave me a deep knowledge of the things we refuse to talk about except in the tiniest whispers." His hand rested on the lampshade, a curious construction of thin crystals in hues of blue and green. "It was obvious. I saw what you are as soon as I laid eyes on you. Your ruddy complexion, for instance. Then there is the ancient haunt in your eye and an immense strength and rage that you are barely able to contain. It's obvious to me, and perhaps the two dozen or so others like me."

"Others like you?" Charles asked, his words edged with menace.

"Yes, Charles, the others who are just like me. Hunters of the undead," he said flatly, then colors burst across the room as his hand pressed the shade down over the lamp's flame.

****

Charles stumbled backwards, his stool clattering across the floor. For the first time in his long life, he felt fear. Not fear for the curse that plagued his soul, but an acute terror that his revenge would go unfulfilled. Charles's hunt was all-consuming, a fire of vengeance that had flared years before, and it burned deep within to keep him warm on the coldest of nights. But now, in Bekhmoaram's home, it all seemed to be slipping from his grasp.

Bekhmoaram guffawed out loud as Charles skittered like a spider across the room. It was funny to the old man, who was as much a threat to the half-breed vampire as a newborn pup.

"Relax, Charles," the Rabbi said. "Let your anger go. I'm retired. I have no desire to hunt the spirits and vampires and wolfmen and ghouls through dark catacombs and dank vaults. I'm quite happy to tally numbers and tend my flock these days and peruse tomes of the occult. Besides, you're not a vampire. Not completely. You've nothing to fear from me if I have nothing to fear from you."

Charles was in the corner of the little room, paralyzed with dread. He loathed the pharmacist at this moment, that miserable little shit who sent him here. Somewhere within him, somewhere hidden beneath the acute dread and loathing, Charles coddled a satisfaction that the man was dead.

To find *this* man, this old Jewish vampire hunter. Hate roiled within Charles, a violent storm of hostility. He hated them both, the pharmacist and the rabbi. Frowning, he ground his teeth and grasped frantically for his next move, yet his mind raced and his muscles were seized as if the rigor of the dead afflicted him.

"You are not relaxing," chided Bekhmoaram. "I do not want to hurt you, but you mean malice. I have your answers and offer them in trade for my safety. All I require is the truth from you. No more secrets, Charles."

Charles glared at him, his eyes half-closed in a seething distrust. Grunts and growls spilled from him like an animal.

"Tsk. It was you that came to my door, not the other way around. And it was you sat in that chair, spouting half-truths with muscles tensed as if you were ready to pounce. If I wanted to kill you I would have done so at the door. Stop acting so juvenile," the rabbi said curtly. "I will tell you what I know about your father, but I honestly do require more information. First, you must come and sit and have a glass of wine with me. If you can't manage that, then you can leave. It's your choice, Charles. Can you do it?"

He gritted his teeth but nodded in fits and starts, his eyes mere slits.

"Very good. I'll release you, but if you try anything…"

With extreme effort, Charles forced himself to rise, to force his fear down, deep down into the pit of his stomach. The last time he had felt such horror was when his wife and children had been murdered by the Turkish hoards, their poor broken bodies huddled together in the muddy courtyard. He choked back the memory and stalked rigidly toward the old man.

"Good, Charles. I know it must be difficult. Most creatures of your ilk aren't accustomed to common men being unafraid of them, however I'm no normal man myself."

"What do you mean?" Charles managed to croak, his voice a hoarse rattle. Whatever magic Bekhmoaram practiced had a power unlike any he had experienced.

"I come from a long line of healers, of rabbis…and of hunters of the undead. My father, my uncles and grandfathers, they all taught me much about the profession when I was but a child. Not much scares me, not after I've experienced what this world has done to my fellow man. Now, first, before I tell you about the Rădescus of Pitești, what specifically do you want to know? Ask me anything at all."

Charles shook a thick fog from his mind. It took him several long moments to clear his head, yet still he struggled to form coherent thoughts, as if they were fleeting memories that would appear and disappear at will. Concentrate as he might, he could not form a sentence beyond just a few words.

"Oh!" said Bekhmoaram. "My apologies, Charles, it's just a parlor trick. Old habits die hard," he said sheepishly. The old Jew rose from his chair and plucked the shade from the oil lamp, its diffused colors falling into a golden glow. "There, all should be better now."

Charles's mind had cleared, the rabbi's magic veil lifted from his thoughts. His face flushed with anger. "What did you do?"

Bekhmoaram stared keenly into Charles's eyes, his glare a burning brand that seared the soul. "You don't survive in my line of work without learning a trick or two. Now unclench your fist and tell me your story."

Charles sat back. his anger slowly melting away so that his fist loosened, and then he felt suddenly drained. There was no tension in his chest, no anger or sorrow, just an emptiness that yearned to be filled. He took a deep breath, then another. "I grew up in München with my mother's cousins, only we didn't call it München back then. I wasn't born there, though. Some of my earliest memories are fleeing the fires and the battles. My mother was hysterical, talking about cannibals and things crawling from their graves. Worse, even, but I was a child and thought it was all folktales."

"Do you know where you were born?"

Charles shook his head. "Maybe Târgoviște or one of the other towns near Pitești. Wallachia, anyway. That is what I know for certain."

"An area with a long history of bloodshed and conquest. You really don't know your father's name?"

"That was not a lie," Charles said with a shake of his head. "My mother never talked about him and when I would ask, she would shush me. She would say that to speak the devil's name would be to summon him."

Bekhmoaram tensed his lips so the corners turned downward, giving Charles an expression of deep thought. "How long ago was this? No half-truths, please."

Charles's muscles tensed. He wasn't old. He was ancient, a truth that hid behind his youthful appearance. Such was the curse. Charles couldn't die, while those around him withered away. "I was born in 1472 or thereabouts," he said numbly. "It was a bad time."

The rabbi's eyebrows peaked in surprise. "That is amazing," he whispered. "I've experienced all sorts of monst...er, I mean..."

"It's alright," Charles said tiredly with a dismissive wave of his hand.

"Almost five hundred years!"

"Just about," Charles replied with a frown.

"I can't imagine what I would do with all that time. The things I could learn!"

"Do you want to know? I can tell you. You would watch all the people you've grown to love die. One by one, they grow old and die...if they grow old, that is. Some of them die quite young, and there isn't a pain in the world that can compare to burying your own child."

The surprised look on the Jew's face decayed into one of despair. "I am so sorry, Charles. I was insensitive."

"You are a human. Insensitivity is a natural condition."

"We should all strive to be better. I do hope you accept my sincerest apology."

Charles nodded, relieved to move onto less melancholy subjects, like the hunt for his father. "I suppose the question is, what do you know of Wallachia around the year 1470?"

"As you put it so succinctly, it was a bad time. The Ottoman Turks were on the march and the Romanian territories became Europe's battlements. Which worked, for a time, but when Vlad III died during the winter of 1476-1477 all resistance collapsed." The rabbi had grunted his way out of the chair and poked and prodded his stack of dusty books, then gave a noise of satisfaction on the discovery of one ancient tome, its leather cover cracked and stained with age. "Here we are," he said with a hint of happiness. "A History of the Voivodes of Wallachia!"

"What's a Voivode?"

"A ruler, much like a Grand Duke."

"Ah," Charles said.

"Vlad III had been the Voivode of Wallachia when you were a child."

"And Vlad III was…"

"You don't know about Vlad III?" the rabbi gasped.

"Should I?"

"You should be ashamed, that's what you should be," Bekhmoaram castigated Charles as he flipped through desiccated pages, searching for some specific entry. "He was the greatest of the Wallachian rulers. From a military standpoint, anyway. Vlad was able to stop the Ottoman invasions using a largely medieval army against an overwhelmingly large and better armed enemy! He was a strategic genius."

"I still don't know who Vlad III was."

Bekhmoaram threw his hands in the air with disgust. "He is certainly the most famous personality to ever come out of that part of Europe! Vlad inspired stories of folklore that have echoed down through the ages!"

"Give me something more…he just sounds like some old dead guy to me."

A smile flashed under Bekhmoaram's beard as he found the reference he had been searching for. "Well he should certainly be far more than just a 'dead guy' to you, Charles," the rabbi beamed with satisfaction as he pointed victoriously at a sheaf of parchment. "After all, he *is* your grandfather!"

"What? No!"

"On the maternal side. He was also the last of the line of Drăculea."

"Drăculea…as in Dracula?"

"If you've seen Bela Lugosi's Nosferatu…no, not like that. But yes, as in Dracula. He was also known as Vlad the Impaler."

Charles knew about the Impaler. Who didn't? "You could have just said that, you know."

Bekhmoaram ignored him. "From all the tales, Impaler is a well-earned moniker. Any rebellious spirits were impaled, their bodies spiked and lining roads as a warning. An effective deterrent to the more militant among the nobility, I would imagine."

Standing over the rabbi, Charles looked at where his pudgy finger traced an old family tree. It was an antiquated script, the extravagant letters faded to a brown, but Charles was able to decipher its formal Latin. "His daughter," Charles said, his mouth open with awe. "Ioana."

"This is an old family history of the rulers in that part of the world. The houses of Drăculeşti and Dăneşti were close cousins, yet incessant opponents. It is said that if they had set aside their differences, the Ottomans never would have been able to overcome Romania. Yet they didn't, and so the Ottomans did. Anyway, to my knowledge this is the only record of these lines that includes their daughters. Vlad III Drăculea married Erzsébet, who was named after her mother. One of their daughters was Ioana."

"My mother."

"Yes, your mother. But there is an error in here."

Charles saw the error to which Bekhmoaram referred. Ioana had married a Cosmin, a man who had no date of birth or death. Ioana's grandmother, the earlier Erzsébet, had also married a man named Cosmin, who himself also had neither dates for birth nor death.

And both Cosmins were of the house of Rădescu.

****

"It was a common thing to name the first-born after grandfathers, so perhaps these were cousins? Rulers married rulers after all. But wait…" Bekhmoaram trailed off, his lips pursed and eyes closed. He stood still for several seconds, deep in thought, and Charles waited quietly until the old man suddenly perked up. "Let me check something else."

He scuttled off, rambling incoherently as he poked through piles of books and clutter, before disappearing to another part of the little house. Charles let the man go as he studied the family tree. There was no telling its provenance, no way to know its accuracy or legitimacy, yet at the same time there was no reason for inaccuracy, either. His family was unimportant among the people of Western Europe. They were considered barbarians, barely civilized enough to be anything other than mountain savages, so a counterfeit lineage would lack any significance. Still, Charles's finger traced the line from Erzsébet, a name he knew to be the Romanian version of Elizabeth, and her husband Cosmin down to Ioana and her husband, a man *also* named Cosmin.

Only one descendent of Ioana and Cosmin was listed below their names, and it was a boy named Constantin.

Charles had not been called Constantin for nearly five hundred years.

"I've found it!" Bekhmoaram declared proudly, and Charles jumped at its suddenness, the rabbi's outburst shocking Charles from his reverie. He held up a heavy book, its age appearing to nearly match the tome with Charles's lineage, its name indecipherable. "An Account of Obscure Folk Tales," the rabbi smiled knowingly. "Compiled in Bavaria around the year 1600. Perhaps earlier. It is a compilation of many oral folk traditions from the south and east of that country, including the Balkan states and Romania." Bekhmoaram happily flipped through pages as Charles's head swam. All this new information threatened to overwhelm him, and he sat heavily in the seat that had been so recently occupied by the portly rabbi.

"Normally I would be indignant that someone should inhabit my favorite chair," the Jew said, his nose buried in the book. "I will let it stand on this occasion, though. I am far too consumed by your most interesting family."

"I'm grateful," Charles managed to say.

"You *are* grateful, and I have found it."

"Found what?"

"A most interesting story, and it's just as well that you are sitting. This will take a while to explain. Folktales are, by their very nature, filled with incredible stories that are founded on some hint of truth. Take what I'm about to tell you with a grain of salt."

"Of course," Charles nodded.

"There is a story of an old people who inhabited the mountains of Wallachia. They were refugees from somewhere to the south or east…or southeast…it isn't quite clear. Anyway, they are proclaimed to be a people blessed by the gods or God, and one of their number is chosen to represent them in an ongoing struggle between good and evil."

"It sounds cliché."

"All folktales have become cliché. Consider the tale of Cinderella. Anyway, the chosen one is always a girl who is verging on womanhood. She is referred to as a "vessel", which I imagine is in reference to containing some sort of power, and as she enters womanhood the power reaches its peak."

"Convenient, that."

"Not really. This godly power invites some kind of jealousy from the devil. Things awaken as the power grows. Terrible things, apparently. This says that the dead crawl from their graves, and men turn into animals, and strigoi drink the blood of their family."

"Strigoi?"

"One of the oldest monsters of Romanian folklore! They are wrongly believed to be vampires. The tradition of blood-sucking comes from the strigoi."

"Then what is a vampire?"

"I'm getting to that. The chosen one, what we refer to as the vessel, appears once every five hundred years, give or take."

"What does that mean?"

"It means that once the vessel's destiny is fulfilled, five hundred years or so are needed for the power to grow again. But not exactly five hundred years. This tale includes assumed dates for the vessel. It ranges from less than four hundred years to more than six hundred."

"Interesting."

"Five hundred years is probably a good average. So the vessel's power can be used to banish the evil things or to invite more evil things."

"Well, that makes no sense! What's the point of it, then?"

Bekhmoaram's hairy chin wrinkled. "I think what it is saying is that the vessel's power can be harnessed for both good and bad. There is some apocryphal evidence that the power is capable of opening some type of door between Earth and Hell, and so it's lusted after by the devil. This same power can be used to seal the doorway, though."

"What does this have to do with my father?"

"Ah! Straight to the crux of the matter. Another tale refers to him…right here," the rabbi said as he scrutinized the pages. "Cosmyn the Wycked, the orygynal vampyr…it's written in old English, for some reason I can't fathom…anyway, Cosmin the Wicked was the original vampire. He was a wicked man in life whose body, in death, was possessed by the devil. No, that's not right. *Consumed*, not possessed. This devilish power consumed Cosmin's body, or…or…*melded* with his corpse to create something *new and terrible.* That's so interesting!"

"Cosmin the Wicked is my father?" Charles asked, aghast.

"It does makes sense, does it not? That makes you a half-breed vampire."

Charles sat, stunned by the revelation. He had always known that he was something different, something other than all those people who surrounded him.

"I don't make these things up," Bekhmoaram continued. "It goes on to say that he had many children, who are half-vampires called *dhampir*, and they are blood-sucking, demonic beings, with a flushed complexion and whose bodies are…boneless?"

"That's not right," Charles frowned.

"No, it would appear not. You certainly have bones. But that's what it says, you're a dhampir."

"I don't suck blood, either. I've never done that."

"Can you bear the sunlight?"

"Of course I can. I came here, didn't I?"

"Okay, that lines up. I mean, it's a folktale," Bekhmoaram shrugged. "Fantastical stories with an origin in truth."

"What the hell does that mean for me?"

"I'm not done. It looks like Cosmin the Wicked is condemned to hunt for the Navă, which is the vessel, and that some of his dhampir offspring thwart him!" the rabbi laughed. "Poetic justice, that. They are stories, Charles. Don't put so much stock in them, but you should allow the stories to guide you."

"Does it say anything about a curse?"

The rabbi frowned. "No, no curses."

"There has to be."

"Nope. Not in this book, anyway."

Charles's eyes narrowed to black slits. His entire life he had felt cursed. How else could he look at his life? He was condemned to live while all those that he had loved died. "I've heard somewhere that if the vampire dies, all those he's turned into vampires will die too."

"That may be true, I don't know. But you're not a vampire, you're a dhampir."

"So if I kill him, I won't die?"

"It's impossible to say!"

"But it's not impossible, either?"

"Charles, you are consumed by this supposed curse that you've convinced yourself exists. Sometimes the easiest answer is the most truthful one. I implore you to come to terms with one thing, if nothing else: you are what you are."

"I'll kill him anyway, if for no other reason than he brought me into this God-damned world."

Bekhmoaram smiled mournfully. For some reason, he had begun to like the tortured dhampir. "That is a noble quest. If even a portion of the folktales are true, then Cosmin the Wicked is evil incarnate. Let us see what else we can learn, for knowledge is more powerful than the strongest sword. Ah, here we are...you see? This section is titled *Ways to Destroy the Evyl Vampyr, Cosmyn the Wycked*. This should be interesting."

****

"Good-bye, Bekhmoaram," Charles said, his tall, lean frame blocking light from the Jew's open door. They had spoken for many hours more and now an inkling of a plan had formed in the dhampir's mind. "Thank you for your time and the knowledge you've gifted me. You have no idea how helpful you have been for my journey."

Bekhmoaram smiled deeply underneath his trimmed beard. "It is my eternal pleasure, Charles. I hope your journey treats you well and you find what you seek."

"Inevitably," Charles said. "I will inevitably find him." He turned to leave, but something stopped him. Charles turned his head, saw the door closing, and he blurted out the Jew's name. "Bekhmoaram!"

The door opened abruptly. "What is it?" the old man asked, his eyes darting up and down the street.

Charles looked around, ensuring they were alone, then he spoke in a low voice, almost a whisper, so quiet the slight breeze made him difficult to hear.

"The Pogrom begins tomorrow. They will attack any business, any home, any building that houses Jews. Saarbrücken is not safe for you. Flee tonight, man. Go anywhere, but get out of the city."

Bekhmoaram frowned. He was tired of running, tired of violence, but Charles was right. He should leave for Alsace in the night, and with any luck he would escape the damned German nationalists. "I imagine you are correct, Charles. I had hoped to die in this house an old man. Yet we don't always get that which we desire."

Charles's lip curled at the unfairness of man. "Hardly ever do we get what we want."

Bekhmoaram's frown deepened for a moment. "I have something for you," he said after a minute's hesitation.

"You've already given me plenty!"

"It's so very important, Charles. I had always hoped to use it again, but in truth my time passed long ago."

Charles waited anxiously in the Jew's doorway. A few townsfolk wandered past, ostensibly ignoring him, yet he knew that nothing escaped observation. Bekhmoaram must hurry if he is to make it out of the city. With every passing moment, the danger from the state's secret police increased.

"Hurry up, man," Charles hissed into the darkened parlor.

"One moment, one moment," Bekhmoaram said impatiently from some corner of his apartment. Charles breathed a sigh of relief when the old man reappeared.

"This is very old," Bekhmoaram said matter-of-factly. He held a sheathed knife gingerly, his eyes inspecting it in adoration. "I'm not entirely sure of its provenance. It is said that it was wielded against monsters a long, long time ago."

Charles's brow furrowed. "It's an antique."

"Yes, it is very, very old."

"I'll break it."

The Jew chuckled, a bit of wetness glistening in the corner of his eye. "You shouldn't concern yourself with that. It is quite robust, I assure you."

"What does it do?"

Bekhmoaram pursed his lips. "Under the right circumstances, it is quite powerful. However it does have its limitations. I'm afraid the answer to your question is not a straightforward one," he said at length. "It is a special weapon. Its properties are such that it is capable of striking down the undead."

Charles whistled with a new appreciation for the knife.

"But there are constraints. This is a fragment of a once-powerful weapon, and only a whisper of its former abilities remains. Even given that, it will be an ally for you."

"How does it work?" Charles asked.

"Um, it's a knife."

"Yes, I see that. Do I have to say some magical words?"

"No. You stab things with it, Charles. Slashing works as well."

"Very good, so it's easy to use. Are you sure there are no special chants or anything?"

"I'm very sure. I can tell you from experience that it is especially useful against the brainless."

Charles took the knife from Bekhmoaram. It was surprisingly heavy, its blade quite wide, half the width of his hand, and as long as his forearm. "Will it strike down my father?"

Bekhmoaram shrugged. "I don't know. I've sent ghouls back to their graves. Changelings are also susceptible to its powers."

"It needs a new sheath," Charles noted as he fingered the cracked leather.

"Yes, probably."

"Will that affect its power?"

The Jew raised an eyebrow. "Why would it?"

"I don't know," Charles replied, "I'm just making sure. Its metal is unique." He had slid the knife back from its sheath a bit to expos the gray of its blade. Clearly the knife was made of iron, but not like any iron Charles had ever seen.

"It is not of this world, Charles."

"What does that mean?"

Bekhmoaram sighed at the man's obtuseness. "The metal cannot be found on Earth in a natural state. Its blade was forged from an object that fell from space, long before mankind discovered how to smelt iron."

"You could have just called it a meteorite. I have to go now, people are noticing us."

"There is a prophecy tied to the sword, as well."

"That's nice, hurry up, man!"

"It is in one of my manuscripts. *He Who Destroys, Shall Be Destroyed*. That's what it says."

"What the hell does that mean?"

"I don't know, Charles. I wish you good luck on your quest, and I will pray for mine. Let us hope they don't ruin the country," the Jew agreed.

"I think that is a foregone conclusion," Charles growled. "Thank you, my friend. I won't forget you."

## 2

Valea Întunecată, Romania
May, 1944, morning

Ruxana's excitement was growing, and Elena couldn't help but to feel her mother's anticipation. It was a contagious excitement. All of the village's Old Families were preparing for the coming celebration, because spring had passed into early summer and with it came another transition, but this one was for the young passing into adulthood. Elena didn't know when the boys would celebrate coming into their own. Nor did she care, truth be told, because right now the Old Families were preparing for the Vârstă de Măritat, when the girls of the village had reached the age of marriage. Outside of the religious, this was the most important festival that the people of her little village could even consider celebrating, so Ruxana hummed a gay tune as she went about preparing cakes and pastries. Similar preparations were taking place all over Valea Întunecată, as all the households pitched in to prepare for the festival. As her mother baked happily, Elena had her own preparations to make, but first came the all-important daily chores so she made herself busy.

Along with a handful of other girls, she was the focus of this year's Vârstă de Măritat. Even so, the chores wouldn't do themselves. Elena made the morning's cooking fire, swept the kitchen out, and had hurried to finish all the other tasks so she could fetch the colorful flowers from the market. Ruxana had insisted on making bouquets and garlands of carnations, which the newly confirmed young women would have woven into their hair, and that was one chore Elena was looking forward to. So she cooked and swept, and when Ruxana smiled and nodded at her daughter, Elena happily bolted to the little bedroom to change.

It wasn't much of a bedroom, but then theirs wasn't much of a house. Like the rest of Valea Întunecată, Elena's family was poor. They lived the hardscrabble life of mountain shepherds, as most of the Old Families did, in ramshackle tenements clumped together on the edge of town. None of this mattered to the girl, though. Her Vârstă de Măritat was only a few days away, and not even the increasingly common nightmares would be able to steal her happiness.

Ruxana clucked at her daughter as the girl hurried to change into proper clothing now that the chores were complete. "Don't dawdle," she said. "Hurry to the market and then hurry home. We still have a lot of work to do."

"I know, Mamă," Elena said happily. Weaving flowers was fun, not a chore. She had helped with preparations for last year's Vârstă de Măritat and that experience made her even more keen for this year's celebration. She bolted for the door, anxious to retrieve the flowers, but Ruxana was faster.

"Not so fast, Elena!" she scolded the girl, then began tutting as she fussed over Elena's braids and straightened the elaborately embroidered skirt that girdled Elena's waist. "My daughter," she said finally, with a face beaming from happiness. "So close to becoming a woman."

"Stop it, Mamă!" the girl squealed, then she wriggled free from Ruxana's embrace and bolted for the door. "I'll be back soon!"

"Hurry!" her mother called, but Elena had already disappeared into winding alleys.

Valea Întunecată's market square lay on the far side of town, a brisk walk of at least fifteen minutes, but Elena's mind drifted as she skipped from their little apartment onto a cobbled street. She had never been to any other towns, but she imagined her little village was much like all the others. It was old and filled with myriad buildings constructed in a haphazard jumble. Most of the streets were narrow, a muddled warren of constricted pathways, and only the main thoroughfares were wide enough for a pair of carts to pass each other. Automobiles were a foreign monstrosity, completely alien to this little mountain village. Most of Valea Întunecată's simple folk had never even seen a car or truck, much less owned one of those stinking vehicles that spewed noxious soot, and so the cobbled roads barely sufficed for even the little carts they used. Wayward visitors to the region were few and far between, but any of them would marvel at how the town was frozen in time, a study in medieval society and architecture. Realistically, anyone with an ounce of sense wouldn't venture into the mountains to visit their dark valley. That is where the town of Valea Întunecată got its name from: Dark Valley. Mountains soared from the fertile vale, itself long and narrow and surrounded by primeval forest, so that the days were short and everything lay in shadows. Save for the heart of day, Valea

Întunecată and its namesake valley was shrouded in near-perpetual darkness.

Elena danced her way down the street, brown hair bobbing in mid-morning shadows. Windowpanes, smeared with dust and grime, reflected the girl's happiness and she stopped to check her hair. Sun slashed across a leaded pane of glass, her face reflected in one of the cleaner windows she found, and as she reached up to fix a stray strand of hair, the face that stared back was not her own.

Black hair and bushy eyebrows returned the girl's gaze, with a haughty nose and upturned lips. Elena's breath caught in her throat, but then a cloud obscured the sun and, after an eyeblink, the strange reflection disappeared. Elena saw only her own deep brown hair, her own wide-set eyes, her own nose and lips. She brushed cold fingertips across her face, making sure it was her own, and then realized she had been holding her breath. Confusion clouded the girl's eyes. She was sure that it had been another face, the face of a strange girl that had stared back at her.

Elena stepped back, unable to tear her eyes from the window. *What was that?* she wondered. It was a strange sensation, seeing another's face in the window, but then Elena pushed it from her mind and forced her legs to move. She had an errand to run.

The market was near and its unique mix of noises drew Elena's attention. It was as heady a place as any in Valea Întunecată, with its cacophony of haggling voices and creaking carts and braying donkeys. Mere minutes before, she had been happy to buy the carnations and had been elated to weave the flowers into garlands that the ladies of the celebration would wear in their hair. It was going to be their day, the festival that welcomed girls into womanhood, but the haunting face in the window caused an icy tingle to dance up her spine.

Maybe it was an illusion or a daydream? Maybe even a forgotten girl she had seen in passing?

The face which stared back at her wore old-fashioned clothes. In a way, all the girls in town wore old-fashioned, traditional clothing, but the girl in the window wore *really* old-fashioned clothes, like something Elena had never seen. Her grandparents had once griped about the "new" clothes the women of Valea Întunecată wore. That was before Elena was born, though. Ruxana would laugh when she told the story.

They were like that. The anonymous face wore clothes that weren't just traditional, but old-fashioned.

"Hello, young lady," a voice said, the deep rumble snapping Elena from her reverie. He was Radu the flower-seller, and Elena looked around in wonderment. She had been distracted by the mystery of the girl and hadn't realized where she ended up. "Have you come for the carnations?"

"Oh, hi Mister Balan," Elena exhaled. She always laughed when she thought of Radu Balan, because Balan meant blonde, but his hair was a fiery red. The girl wasn't laughing now, though. "Yes, my mamă said you would have them today."

"When is the big day?" he asked politely, but she figured he was just being nice. Everyone knew the Vârstă de Măritat was less than a week away, especially the flower-seller. He must have been selling carnations by the bushel.

Elena didn't hear him, though. She looked past Radu Balan, past the flowers and the stalls and the people.

She saw a priest, but he wasn't the Orthodox priest who preached in the village.

He looked old, much older than her grandfather when he had died. His face was creased with age, his tonsured head liver-spotted and pale. The eyes, though, the eyes are what held Elena's attention. They were deep-set, sunken within sockets purpled over with pooling blood, with hard, gray pupils and whites shot through with red. A massive crucifix of gold and silver hung from his neck by a gold chain, glittering with colorful gems, so blinding in its glory that she didn't register his threadbare brown habit or the crook in his hand.

The priest was staring right at Elena, as if he were looking through her.

"Elena?" the flower-seller asked, his fingers snapping in front of the girl's face. She blinked once, twice, then looked at Radu, her face clouded with confusion. "Are you alright?"

"Um," she gulped, then with a glance realized the priest had vanished. "Yes, I don't...I just don't feel well."

"You don't feel well?" he asked with an air of shock. "That won't do, the Vârstă de Măritat is just around the corner! Maybe it's nerves, young lady?" he asked with a wink.

She blushed, forcing the priest's image to the furthest corner of her mind where it resided with the strange face of the girl. "Mr. Balan!" she said. "I'm not a lady yet. Not for another six days."

He returned her wan smile. "Don't grow up too fast, Elena. Give your parents my best."

Now, Elena really did hurry home, with an armful of flowers, the strange girl's haunting face, and the staring priest burned into her memory.

****

Elena woke that night, her rustic straw mattress soaked with greasy sweat, blood pulsing and chest clenched with anxiety. It had been getting worse lately, these night terrors, and this one had been the most vivid. Typically the visions were elusive, they were hideous dreams, their details fleeting in her slowly waking mind, but she knew the demon's face was always the same. He unfailingly came to consume her. Inch by inch, bit by bit, his yellow teeth and rancid breath tore agonizingly at her flesh.

Usually the memory of her dreams faded quickly, but not this time. This time she remembered the dozens of guttering candles, a distant chanting, and the demon's greedy maw. She remembered the symbols carved into the cave's stone floor, and she remembered the crone squatting in the middle of those candles, her hideous face distorted in ecstasy as she plunged the blade of black glass into her hapless victim. Elena remembered all this and more, and the tears began to flow, until Ruxana wrapped her daughter in her arms to try and comfort away the sobs that racked Elena's body.

"Elena, dear thing," her mother soothed, her arms hugging the slight girl in a loving mother's embrace. "It will be okay, Elena, it will be okay." The girl pressed her face into her mother's breast, tears soaking through the linen night shirt. Despite her mother's insistence, it would not be okay.

It was getting worse. Every night, the terrible dreams became longer, more vivid, more horrible, and after comforting the girl, Ruxana would shuffle off to her own bed. Elena would be left alone to sniffle away the tears until they had dried and the dream had faded from memory.

Not this time, though. This time, along with the chanting crone, the demon's face haunted Elena's mind's eye. It was hideous and ghastly, its face flushed a deep crimson with steel-gray teeth, sharp as razors, that protruded haphazardly from black lips and gums. Great strands of coarse black hair hung from its chin and cheeks and lumpen head, its skull crowned by a half-dozen protrusions not yet erupted into black, lancing horns.

Its face haunted the girl, the memory of it stubbornly clinging to her brain as if it had sunk its steely claws deep into her mind.

She sniffed again, the skin of her cheeks salty with dried tears. A candle guttered on her side table, its flame jumping in a slight chill breeze whose icy touch had made her shiver. Elena sighed and pulled the light blanket tight around her shoulders, tired but unwilling to go back to sleep for fear the dreams would return. She rubbed at her eyes, trying to will away the burning fatigue.

"Hello," a voice whispered, more an idea than a sound. She jumped, the familiar fear lumped in her throat to choke off a cry.

"I said hello," it whispered again, the voice an itch in her eardrums. "Don't be afraid."

Elena was seized with fear. She tried to scream out in terror, wanted to shout away the voice, but the shrieks were locked deep within her breast. She cowered in the bed's corner, hunched into a ball against the little home's rough stone wall.

A shade lay beside her, just a hint of a girl, as faint as if she were looking at a reflection in a leaded glass window. The ghost wasn't a child. Like Elena, the spirit seemed on the cusp of womanhood in her own right, with black hair and black eyebrows, a familiar haughty nose and upturned lips, but it was difficult to be sure as she was barely more than a fleeting shadow. Her mouth was moving but the words were low, quiet and indistinct, and tears rolled silently down Elena's cheeks.

The apparition leaned forward slowly, her ethereal nightshirt a soft rustle.

"My name is Adina," the whisper came again. "I won't hurt you."

Adina was a ghost, the spirit of a long-dead and restless girl, and Elena was a frightened child who cowered on a peasant's bed, but slowly her fear subsided. Adina reached out to her, cajoled her to be unafraid, and her manner was gentle, so Elena began to relax.

"Who are you?" Elena whispered.

The ghost giggled. "I'm Adina," she smiled, though Elena had to concentrate to understand the spirit's whispers. "I already said that."

"But who *are* you?"

Adina's lips moved and the spoken words were out of sync with the shade, a delay that disconcerted the girl as she strained to hear the words. "I was a girl like you, once," the spirit said. "I've been sent because you are special, the way I used to be special."

Elena shook her head. She wasn't special. She was the only daughter of a destitute family, a peasant girl born to a landless sheepherder. She would become a woman soon, and then she would marry, and her parents certainly couldn't afford a dowry, and that was just one of many things that worried her. "Why am I special?" she asked, tears again wetting her cheeks. Elena was just another poor girl in a village filled with them. There was nothing special about her.

"You are from one of the Old Families, just as I was. You are the Vessel, the one chosen to receive God's grace."

Fear and wonder clenched Elena's heart. It sounded ominous, this concept of God's grace that the ghostly girl had produced so readily. "What does that mean?" Elena gurgled. "What is the Vessel?"

"Your purpose has come," Adina said solemnly, but then her solemnity again broke down into adolescent giggles. She struggled to control the laughter and eventually prevailed, though not without great effort. "Soon you will be called to fulfill your destiny, the way I was supposed to," Adina said, her voice now stiffly formal even though those giggles were always perched just on the edge of her words. "Now is not a time for fear, but for triumph. No matter the trials which shall befall you, it has been deemed that you are blessed, that you are God's chosen one for the coming battle."

"The way you were supposed to? What trials?" Elena whispered urgently, but Adina was beginning to fade. The shade reached out with a ghostly hand, translucent fingertips brushing Elena's forehead to bestow a blessing from the spirit's beyond.

"Don't let fear take root, Elena. We will be with you."

"Who?" the girl asked urgently. Adina's spirit had begun to fade.

"Me, and the priest, and then there will be another. We will prepare you for the battle."

"Who is the priest?" Elena asked urgently, remembering the gaunt figure in the market hung with the cross who had grasped a shepherd's crook. "Who is the other one?" But then she closed her eyes, the acute sensation of fear temporarily fleeing from her body under the ghostly touch of Adina. She had been freed from the earthly chains of torment, as if her soul would soar among the birds and the clouds.

And then she opened her eyes, and Adina's spirit was gone.

*What is the battle?*

\*\*\*\*

## Near Valea Întunecată
## Night

Leathery flapping filled the night sky, a roiling cauldron of flitting bats frantically making their way across the swamp's watery morass. This was the domain of the night's witch, of things that slithered and slunk around in stinking shadows. The mass of flying things banked this way and that, screeching echoes guiding them through the black of night to find the single pinprick of light that punctuated a damp knoll in the swamp's fastness.

They flew as one, a single entity that skimmed bog water before suffocating the swampy hummock with its vast numbers. The mound of rotting vegetation and waterlogged soil barely rose above the surrounding fens. Black and screeching, they swarmed about a single shack whose only window betrayed the wan glow of lamplight, then the cacophony of shrieks and flailing wings rapidly died away as they coalesced into the form of a man. He stepped from the boil of flying rodents with a crimson frown, revolted at the necessity that brought him here.

Yet here he was, and the witch was expecting him, so he moved noiselessly across tufts of swamp grass illuminated by moonlight to approach her hovel. Its door opened noiselessly, unseen hands beckoning him into its wretched confines, and as he folded his long frame to pass through the hut's low door, a racking cough caught his attention.

"Hello, mother," he smirked, and the witch spat phlegm in greeting.

"Look what the rats dragged in. When was the last time you came to visit?" she ground away, refusing to make eye contact, the gravel of her voice rattling in her throat.

"Not long enough," Cosmin mumbled.

"What did you say? Speak up, son. I'm old and can't hear very well."

The vampire knew the lies his mother told. Unul Vechi looked like a rotting bag of pus, but her faculties were in fine repair. "You're a spring chicken, Mother!" Cosmin wheedled with a shrug. "Perhaps a bit rough around the edges. Nothing a touch of polish can't fix."

He noted with satisfaction that she ignored his false compliments. Their relationship was based on mutual revulsion, yet each had a use for the other and so he knew that she would bear his insults with a skin thickened by the callous of thousands of difficult years. How many thousands? He hadn't bothered to count. She was old, her foul body pickled in a brine of magical spells and potions. That was all that mattered. Cosmin did enjoy getting a rise out of the old bitch, so he would just have to try harder to get a reaction, and the expectation of a decent verbal sparring drew a smile on his lips. Unul Vechi was nothing if not clever, though. She was canny and cunning and would do nothing that was not of a selfish benefit. He rather enjoyed their periodic dance.

"What do you want?" she rattled on. Cosmin's smile widened when he saw her feet. Or, rather, the wrinkled flesh where her feet used to be. Now she sat in a mildewed chair, legs swinging with the puckered skin of her footless ankles. Some things never change.

"The Navă has awakened," he said, certain this would perk her up.

"Of course she has," the witch spat back, certainly not perked. "The fucking corpses are wandering all around this place, nasty things that they are."

The ghouls to which his mother referred were the remains of the recently deceased. "Now that the Navǎ has come to the valley, the rotting undead and all those other foul creatures of the swamps and mountains have risen. No thanks to you, they've become a pestilence around this place."

Cosmin smiled. They were mindless creatures, but if they heard Cosmin's thoughts, then they would do his bidding. If he didn't command them, their mindless nighttime wandering would send them to hunt the warm, succulent bodies that infested Valea Întunecatǎ. Which, on balance, would be wildly entertaining. Cosmin had other plans, though, so the night's beasts and ghouls would need to be kept out of the village for the time being.

That is why he had come to this hovel in the swamp. The creatures would be his pets, but only if Unul Vechi would deem it so, and the witch also had other knowledge and skills he would need to tap into. "I need you to work your magicks," the vampire said succinctly.

"Why would I do that?"

"Do we have to go through this every single time?" he sighed. She was a hard-headed old bag, one who enjoyed needling her son with every opportunity.

"Well, what's in it for me? I've been banished to this stinking hole for centuries. The only time you visit is when you need something! It's lonely out here."

Cosmin slapped at a mosquito. "If you're suffering in banishment, it's a self-imposed one. I never made you come here."

"Liar," she spat.

"It was a strong suggestion, not a banishment. Besides, I very generously had this home built for you."

"Humph," the witch whined. "This home is no better than a pile of rotting sticks, but at least this toilet is closer to the things I need to work my spells."

"See?" he shrugged. "It's not so bad!"

"If you'd give me a slave, I wouldn't have to live out here. It's your fault."

"*Maybe* I would give you a slave, if you would stop with your little tricks. *Perhaps* I would give you a slave, if you would stop blaming me for every little thing that's happened to you!"

She lifted her stumps in reply, showing off the creased flesh at the ends of her legs. "Like this?"

Cosmin burst out in laughter.

"I birthed an animal," Unul Vechi snarled, her mouth twisted into an angry rictus.

He wiped a happy tear away with a finger. "Ah, good memories. Seriously. I need your help."

"And *I* said: what's in it for me?"

"This time we will win, mother! I have it all planned out in impeccable detail."

"Oh, really? Pray tell, my idiot child. How will we win this time?"

"For starters, my plan is much simpler. Not like last time. That plan was far too complex, it was destined to fail."

"You don't say?" the witch drooled condescendingly.

"It's just you and me, as long as you don't double-cross me again," Cosmin said, and he began ticking off his fingers. "Vlad isn't here to thwart my plans, which is a great start, truth be told. With the village so impoverished there are no warriors to protect the Navă. I mean, really. It couldn't be better!"

"Who will lead the Cohort? Have you thought that through? I know it's a stretch because you have difficulty thinking past the end of your prick, but that really is a crucial detail, is it not?"

Cosmin smiled carnivorously. The Devil's Cohort was his army, a sleeping giant waiting to be unleashed. "My son is returning, and his hate burns deep. He will be easy to turn. As I said, my plan is simple. My son, the general. The unprotected Navă, a girl. And no Vlad to side with the peasants."

The witch cocked her head to one side, a tuneless hum causing her lips to quiver. All the better that her mouth was closed. That way Cosmin didn't have to look at her rotted teeth. "What is there to consider?" he blurted out impatiently. "The creatures have awakened and their hunger grows. Now is the time, now!"

"Instead of Vlad, one of your other sons will be your general? What if he doesn't join you?"

"Then I'll kill the miserable son of a bitch," Cosmin barked. "Believe me, his heart is as black as mine. I see this as a positive."

"I'll help you, but only if you let me play."

Cosmin rolled his eyes. Unul Vechi was conniving and untrustworthy. Through the ages she had tried any number of ways to usurp his power in this valley, though her methods were full of subtlety. That was the real reason he had sent her to the swamp. His eyes narrowed. "Very well. You'll be on a tight leash, though."

Finally, the witch gave an acquiescent nod. "Okay, I'll do it," she said. "Just don't fuck it up this time."

"I've got my eyes on you," Cosmin said through pursed lips.

"Fat lot of good that will do you," his mother spat back.

# 3

Italy
The same day

Rain pissed down on his head, little rivulets of chilled water coursing down his face to drip from his chin. Charles stared at his hands. It was a nervous tick, he knew, but he took comfort in analyzing familiar things, and what could be more familiar, more unchanging, than the creases worn into his palm, etched into the lines of his fingers? Country people insisted that these patterns told of a person's past, present, and future. They believed that the eye was the gateway to the soul, and the hands held a person's destiny. Charles wasn't so sure about all that superstition. He was much too pragmatic, but he had learned not to dismiss the beliefs of the simple folk. Regardless, he still found himself studying the familiar patterns in his hands, and then his mind wandered and he wondered what story Private Simpson's hands would tell.

Their squad, just a handful of nine hard men who formed a single detachment from a much larger platoon, had been formed to a man years before. The platoon itself was a special group tasked with a special mission, and each squad could be detached as needed to perform unique tasks.

Charles, though, was an outsider. A foreigner. Someone who didn't belong to the inner circle of blooded soldiers who had fought through hell to get to this place. His fellow soldiers weren't the welcoming sort. He didn't blame them, it was far too easy to mark someone who didn't belong, especially with an accent and look such as his. Besides, only two weeks had passed since Charles had penetrated the intimate group of soldiers, and the welcome he received wasn't a warm one. He hadn't expected it to be, of course. Six months of hard fighting could pass and he would still be a stranger to these men.

Still, he reckoned that Private Simpson was a good soldier, the type of dependable warrior who was farm-bred and who seemed to have a good head on his shoulders. At the same time, he figured that Simpson wouldn't last too much longer. *Maybe he could survive*, Charles thought to himself. *Maybe he will make it.* To where, though? Where would he make it? The end of the war? Laughable. They were fodder, no matter how much training the squad had suffered through.

In another time and another place, Charles may have felt different. He had once been a leader of men, a decorated warrior in his own right, and he could tell a tin soldier from the real thing. Private Simpson was a good soldier, as was Corporal Smalls. Hell, they were all good soldiers, which is why they had survived such punishing training. Charles smiled, cold and melancholy. Good soldiers were always willing to die. It is what made them good soldiers.

Charles had become a scout when war broke out, his language skills and knowledge of European culture of great use to the Allied war effort. Those skills allowed him ever-growing latitude in mission planning that culminated in this operation.

Tomorrow the mission would kick off. Lieutenant Morris would brief the men around mid-day, and then no later than two or three in the afternoon the plane would be airborne. By dusk, they would be winging over Bulgaria and getting ready for the jump.

Out of the plane and into the wilds of Eastern Europe, into a land of monsters, mythical and otherwise. There was a very real chance that none of them would survive the mission, which was brutally convenient for Charles. If every last one of his companions had to be buried in the Romanian mountains to keep his secrets hidden, then that is what had to happen. Smalls and Simpson and the rest may be tasked with searching for objects of the occult, but Charles's mission was far more critical. His quest could not be compromised, and if they knew his true aims?

It didn't matter. They would never discover the secret he harbored.

Charles's plan was a stroke of genius. War's outbreak meant that Charles had to flee Germany, first into France and eventually to England. His skills, though, were in high demand and critical to the war effort. As an intelligence agent, Charles's experience and knowledge had been crucial to Allied planning, but where Charles truly shined was as a guide and scout for special teams that hunted behind enemy lines. These missions elevated his status within the Special Operations Executive, and before long Charles had been given carte blanche to plan his own missions.

He was never able to travel further than southern Germany, though, while his true desire was Romania and his father, Cosmin the Wicked. Charles had an inkling of how to get to Romania, a mere whisper of a strategy, yet it wasn't until the last month that he was able to apply the flesh to his plan's skeleton.

Charles squinted, his keen eyes inspecting the lines of his palm which had become fouled with flecks of dirt. Adolf Hitler's fascination with the occult had become the lynchpin that Charles had searched for. Intelligence reports suggested the German Führer sent agents to find all manner of mythical weapons and paraphernalia, so this mission he had concocted was an easy sell to the British officers.

This mission meant suicide for the squad, and though such a notion may have been obvious to the casual observer, military planners suffered from tunnel vision. Any task, any operation that either helped the Allies or hindered Germany, no matter the risk, was considered acceptable.

That is why Charles knew the soldiers of this elite squad were no more than cannon-fodder.

Regardless, as far as the Allied planners were concerned, Charles's Romanian partisans were the mission's ticket to success. He knew differently, of course. As soon as they had crossed the border his partisans would melt into the Carpathian wilderness. It was almost as if Charles had planned it that way.

****

Twilight had fallen, the last remnants of sunlight just peeking out from behind the distant mountains that bordered the Tuscan landscape. Lieutenant Morris led the squad into an aircraft hangar whose doors were shut tight. Inside was a secret so sensitive that an entire platoon, some four dozen soldiers, was tasked with protecting it.

Some of the men gasped when they saw the aircraft. One crossed himself and kissed the crucifix he kept around his neck.

It was an old Nazi plane.

A Junkers paratrooper transport, to be exact, an obsolete workhorse whose distinctive mark was three massive engines. A German plane flying across a bevy of Axis-aligned countries would be a normal sight, and the advantage of surprise it afforded the squad would be a great tactical benefit.

"How'd we get this tub?" asked one of the Privates.

"None of your concern," Charles replied, his accent a confusing amalgam of Bavarian and French with a touch of English East Midlands. "We were lucky, though. That is all I will say."

Grumbling and nervous, the men gathered their gear and shuffled toward the plane, apprehension showing palpably on each face. These men were confident in themselves and their abilities, even eager to fight Germans. This, however, was a massive curveball and it planted fear in their hearts. There would be no chance, no chance at all, for support should things go badly. It truly was a suicide mission, and every man knew it even if they refused to utter the truth.

The flight was a tense one, with mountainous terrain below causing turbulent updrafts and every man hoped the old German Junkers wouldn't rattle itself to pieces before their jump. An eternity passed, more than enough time for each man of the squad to contemplate their questionable life choices, but then suddenly the word was sent up and down the row of soldiers.

They were approaching the jump site.

"Aright, gents, let's go. Quickly, quickly. Hurry up daggone it!" graveled the First Sergeant. "Lieutenant here ain't got all day," he said, a smile flashing his gap-toothed grin.

Clouds carpeted the land a few thousand feet below, their old plane creaking along in brilliant sunlight, and the soldiers lined up. Charles gulped involuntarily. He wasn't afraid of much, but even with a dozen such jumps under his belt, the dhampir could never quite get used to the notion.

"I'll be glad to get the hell out of this piece of shit!" another Private laughed nervously. Charles smirked back. All soldiers were the same, no matter the country they fought for or the era they fought in.

Then the door was thrown open and bodies tumbled from the sky.

****

Lieutenant Morris sat, hunched over his map. Some stroke of luck meant they had stayed together, their parachutes depositing every man of the squad within a half-mile of each other, even with the low cloud cover. He whispered to Charles, knowing they were in unfriendly territory and every sound they made brought undue risk. "We are here, in the hills south of Ruse," he muttered, a finger indicating a town on the frontier border between Bulgaria and Romania. "We'll rendezvous with partisans over here, and they're going to smuggle us across the border where we will meet up with your Romanian friends."

Charles grunted agreement.

"They have arranged for us to receive two German army trucks," the Lieutenant continued, his finger tracing a line along an unlabeled country road. "We will drive north, bypassing Bucharest, through Pitesti, until our journey ends...*here*." The Lieutenant's slim finger now rested on an unnamed point in the mountains.

First Sergeant Willey cleared his throat. "And, uh, what exactly is there, sir?" he asked.

"A castle ruin." Lieutenant Morris turned to Charles. "Captain Resseguie, what's the name of it?"

"Cetatea Orașului," Charles replied laconically.

"That is where our objective is," the Lieutenant nodded.

"What are we looking for, sir?" Willey asked. It wasn't everyday they dropped into enemy controlled territory to look for an old jumble of stones.

Morris looked at Charles, who gave a slight shake of his head.

"I'm sorry, First Sergeant. Unfortunately, that must remain a secret for now. I will say that it's a relic, and if the Germans get their hands on it then their war effort will be given a jolt. They're on the back foot, and we have to do whatever we can to keep it that way."

"Yes sir," Willey said flatly, clearly resenting the control that Charles was exerting over this strange operation.

****

They had enjoyed a promising start to the raid, but no one whispered words of good fortune for fear of tempting fate, and the Bulgarian partisans did nothing to help alleviate the squad's apprehension. A tough looking group they were, curt and secretive, though Charles wasn't intimidated by them. He had dealt with far worse in Poland and Norway. Private Crowder, Charles noticed, kept his rifle loaded and his finger on the trigger. "Just in case," he said more than once, though the dhampir knew that firearms would do none of them any good out here. Instead Charles fingered his knife, comforted by the heavy iron blade.

Their Romanian allies didn't make the soldiers feel any better, either. The unkempt men kept talking about the Făgăraş Mountains and the evils they hid, that the forests were filled with wicked creatures. When First Sergeant Willey drilled them for more information, the partisans would shrug their shoulders and say, "no good, no good," in their broken English.

Charles heard Crowder grumble to himself, his eyes darting left and right, then the last light of dusk retreated past mountain peaks and an impenetrable blackness fell. "Stay close to me," Charles whispered, and Crowder eagerly grabbed the proffered lifeline as a cold sweat beaded his forehead. They crept forward, Crowder cradling his rifle at the ready, moving slowly to keep from making noise, Charles close by to make sure the nervous Private didn't accidently shoot anyone.

He marveled that these hardened killers had regressed to unblooded "boots" once the prospect of support had evaporated. Meadow grass gave way to a forest floor littered with dry leaves and twigs and the slightest misstep would result in a racket that seemed to echo off the trees. Charles shushed Crowder more than once when the Private stumbled through fallen branches.

Charles figured the forest was deserted of any living things. Any smart Nazis would have been hunkered down in cities and villages instead of traipsing through haunted nightscapes, but he also knew other things were out there, waiting for their prey to make a bone-headed mistake. The dried leaves and twigs certainly didn't help matters. Crowder pointed his rifle at skittering in the leaves in front and he chuckled lightly at his nervousness. "Almost blew away a fucking rat," he whispered to Charles.

"Shut up," the dhampir whispered back.

"Crowder!" another voice whispered hoarsely from behind, the sudden noise causing the Private to jump.

"Jesus Christ, you scared the shit out of me," he whispered back with irritation.

"Would you two shut the fuck up?" Charles blistered.

"Sorry sir," Private Simpson offered lamely. "Willey is trying to gather everyone up."

****

First Sergeant Willey had pulled his squad into a crude circle with just an olive colored issue light to illuminate Lieutenant Morris's map. Charles knew that Willey was proud of his men, his boys, though Charles also knew they wouldn't understand his brand of tough affection. Willey was from the Old Army where men were hard. Experience had shown that a velvet hand allowed soldiers to grow soft, so instead he employed an iron fist. Charles had witnessed it first-hand in the short time he had been with them. The squad's soldiers didn't appreciate the First Sergeant's brand of leadership, but Charles knew that Willey didn't care about their feelings. He only wanted them to make it home alive.

So the First Sergeant rode them hard, he beat them into shape, his efforts forging elite soldiers from laggards. Charles had paid attention, he had heard the whispered stories amongst the Privates, but then those stories reverberated down the years. Charles had heard the same from the soldiers he had once led, the farmers he had once whipped into hard men in their own right. Willey was the hammer that drove weakness from the men, and Charles felt immense pride radiate from the First Sergeant. After all, they had been specifically selected for this mission.

"Alright, boys," Willey whispered, his finger pointed at a mountain range on the map. "We're here, where this river meets the road. The castle is here," his hand moved to indicate a spot about fifteen kilometers from their current location. "We only have about five hours until sunup. That will give us enough time to make it about halfway to the objective. I know it's obvious, but it's dark out there. Don't be idiots, and don't get lost. We'll make camp at sunup and hunker down."

Charles saw Crowder roll his eyes. *This one has an attitude*, he thought wryly. Junior soldiers were all the same, no matter the circumstances. The dhampir knew the type intimately.

**** 

They struck out for the castle, working their way slowly through the rugged terrain. Each man was paired up with another, except for Charles who insisted on traveling alone. All the better to wander between the pairs of soldiers where he could keep an eye on them. Crowder and Simpson had naturally gravitated to each other, because they were both farm boys, respectively raised in the American South and Midwest, and so each had an affinity for the other that could only come from growing up in similar circumstances. Charles had often overheard their jokes about farm life, and only the two of them could laugh about it as the other men in the rifle squad couldn't relate to a childhood on the farm.

Charles could relate. He, too, didn't belong.

"You hear that?" Crowder whispered, his hand held up to stop his friend. Charles crouched nearby, the soldiers illuminated in wan moonlight.

Simpson shook his head, but Crowder wasn't watching for the gesture. Crowder tapped him on the shoulder. "I heard you," Simpson whispered. "Stay quiet."

"The two of you prattle like old women," Charles hissed through the night's stillness.

An unseen twig had snapped somewhere in the black forest. The Privates froze at the sound, rifles held at the ready, straining to see into the night, but Charles felt his muscles relax. He balanced the ancient knife in his hand, ready to strike out at the first provocation, but this was his natural environment. He was a hunter, a killer, and had been one for the past number of years. Dark of night was a blanket that smothered him in anonymity.

The rest of the squad was nearby, unseen and unheard. Except for that single twig, the night was still and silent. Anything could have made that noise. A soldier's careless step or the soft pads of a wolf. Perhaps, even, a roving band of ravenous Nazis, however improbable. *No*, Charles thought as he heard the rasping breaths of Simpson and Crowder, shallow and quick and anxious.

*There are no Nazis out here.* If anyone knew that to be fact, it would be Charles.

Something shuffled through dry leaves to the right and Simpson shifted his rifle toward the noise, but silence poured into the void left by the sound. "Who's there?" the Private whispered, but his challenge was met by still more silence.

A blood-chilling scream split the night, punctuated by sharp reports of gunshots. The paralyzing cry, long and ululating, screeched on before being abruptly cut off. Crowder shouted, Simpson swore vehemently, and both men dropped to their stomachs. "We under attack?" Simpson cried out.

"I don't know, I don't know!" Crowder said.

"I thought you two were soldiers," Charles sneered. "Crying like a couple of ninnies."

"Christ, who was that?" Simpson moaned.

Crowder didn't reply. Shouts floated through the primeval forest, men calling to each other, pleading for leadership, but both Crowder and Simpson fell to silence, and Charles swore he could taste their fear.

****

Morris's light showed the horrible truth in the forest. The unfortunate soul was another Private, a Bostonian by the name of O'Rourke, and Charles stood emotionless over his ravaged corpse. Blood and gore had sprayed out over the needles and leaves of the unforgiving forest floor, bits of flesh mingled with the vegetation, and the rest of the squad talked of bears and wolves. Charles knew better. Any natural creatures of the night would have cowered in their safe places far from the party of men, and, at any rate, wolves hunted in packs. This attack was perpetrated by a loner, judging by the jumble of leaves.

It seemed to him that Crowder and Simpson also knew better. He knew they had grown up on farms and in forests and surely had an intimate knowledge that only came from a lifetime spent pursuing game and predators. They would understand that no mere animal would hunt a man in such a manner. No animal would maul a man in this way. Whatever stalked them, it had enjoyed a thrill kill, and Charles saw they were disturbed, the fright seared deep into their souls.

Charles knelt to whisper to the pair of soldiers. "What are you boys talking about?"

Simpson glanced at Crowder before answering him. "This is strange as hell, sir," he said. "I've never heard of such a thing. I could maybe understand if O'Rourke was alone, but I've never heard of something like this happening to a group. Even at night."

Crowder nodded assent. "Yeah, this wasn't no wolf. I'd bet my momma's life on it."

Charles glanced around to ensure nobody overheard them. "Both of you are correct," he nodded. "Don't tell anyone else. We need to complete the mission."

"What the hell do you think it was?" asked Simpson. "Uh…sir," he added hastily.

"I've no idea what creatures hunt here," Charles lied smoothly. "It does not matter. Stay close together, keep your heads up, and you'll be fine," he said with curt finality.

"Yes, sir," Simpson mumbled, but Charles had already disappeared.

\*\*\*\*

Lieutenant Morris gathered the men together, an attempt at motivation which fell flat. "It's a shame what happened to O'Rourke, but nothing changes, gents," he said flatly. "Stick close together and the animals will stay away. We still have a long way to go. Let's stay safe, be quick, and be silent."

Some of the men were whispering to each other and Willey shushed at them to be quiet. "Shut your sorry cock holsters, you miserable bastards," he hissed. "Let's get the hell out of this God-damned place."

They moved out, each man of the squad instinctively closing ranks this time, a natural reaction to feeling as if they were under assault. Morris neither motivated the men nor allayed their fears. They were blooded soldiers, used to fighting an enemy across the field of battle, but an unseen and unknown adversary thrust them into an unfamiliar phase of warfare. It unsettled them, dealing with the mysterious and invisible, and Charles could sense that their nerves were frayed as they crept slowly through the forest. He knew they were moving far too slowly, but the Lieutenant seemed to be doing his best to balance the squad's palpable fear against progress. Morris himself stayed close to Willey, never more than a few feet away from the First Sergeant. All of the soldiers had closed in together so that moonlight illuminated their meager numbers. Charles stifled a laugh at the sight of it. Traveling in such a way was a tactical mistake, but the men were fearful, afraid of the unknown that confronted them. *Tactics be damned*, Charles thought with amusement.

None of it mattered, anyway, but O'Rourke's erstwhile battle buddy had now gravitated toward the dhampir.

Charles's superhuman senses could easily discern the mustiness of the soil and decomposing leaves, the acrid bite of pine needles, and the ferrous tang of new blood. All the whispers, every delicate step the soldiers took were picked up by his ears. He didn't want them all to die, not necessarily. The men of this squad were merely a vehicle, one that carried the dhampir inexorably toward his destination. They skulked over ridges, the rush of the river to the east ever-present. Charles heard the Lieutenant quietly curse the noise of the water, a burbling rush that obscured the most subtle of forest sounds to all ears but his. Light, ever so faint, kissed the far horizon and brought a whispered promise of the coming dawn. The Lieutenant exhaled, a breath of relief that Charles noted, and with it came a trivial slackening of tension, but then Willey slowed to a stop. He turned, about to whisper something to Lieutenant Morris, when his face screwed up into horror.

Charles had turned to survey the landscape when he saw Willey's face distorted with sickening terror, the mute sounds of the forest drowned out by a terrible crunch, a cracking of bone, the welling sound of the Lieutenant's keening quickly muffled.

Morris had sunk to his knees, a pathetic mewing noise escaping his lips as hot blood flooded the ground around him. Forest soil and detritus mixed with the sticky, steaming gore to make a cloying mess.

Willey, his face pale with shock, shouted something indiscernible and lifted his carbine, but then Charles saw a figure pounce from the darkness onto the helpless First Sergeant. He rushed forward, a shout perched on his lips and an outstretched arm readying to spear the creature with the knife, but then the thing grabbed the First Sergeant's arms and bit into his neck. Charles, despite his superhuman quickness, was far too slow to help Morris and Willey, both men now suffering from mortal wounds.

The soldier who had once been O'Rourke's partner stood in shock as he watched the Lieutenant's lifeblood soak the black soil. "Come on," Charles spat, has hand grabbing the man's uniform to pull him away. "Come on!"

## 4

Wallachia, Romania
The same day

"What a mess," Charles said. The squad's remaining men had scattered during the attack, but the dhampir had rounded them up and now they stood around the bloody corpses of Lieutenant Morris and First Sergeant Willey. Their necks had been mangled, their throats torn out by ghastly teeth and half of Willey's face was chewed off, the Lieutenant's skull missing a great hunk of scalp and bone. Even their limbs had been torn from their bodies by the horrid creatures. Dirt and leaves had been churned up, the iron-tinged scent of gore mixed with the earthy smells of the forest. Corporal Smalls had witnessed the carnage while it was happening and now he was sitting against the bole of a tree, his knees drawn up, arms wrapped protectively around them. Spittle quivered from his lip and he mumbled quietly to himself.

"Sir," Crowder said to Charles, his eyes wide and face bloodless. "What the fuck happened?"

He studied the boy, carefully formulating a response. What had happened was that the men could only watch the monstrous human-like *thing* as it ripped flesh from Morris's neck and face. What had happened was it twisted Willey's arm, its graying lips smacking grotesquely, as the limb popped and cracked until the flesh finally gave way with a sickening tear. What had happened was the foul thing groaned with pleasure as it chewed on the flesh and bone of Willey's arm before it loped back into the forest carrying its grisly treat.

The thing, Charles had noted with fascination, was gray and bloated, yet it was immensely strong. He couldn't say all of that, though. Some of the soldiers had witnessed the attack but most refused to believe what they saw, and what Charles said now would determine the course they would take. The mission was all that mattered, though. He had to get to the castle, no matter how many lives fell victim to the monstrous fiends in the forest. *This one isn't a fool*, Charles finally decided, though he certainly couldn't tell the Private the truth. "No telling," he lied smoothly. "But the sun is already coming up and there is going to be daylight soon. Let's hunker down for a bit, rest up, and we will make the objective by nightfall."

Charles, though an outsider, was now the only officer and the last person of any significance left alive, so the junior soldiers wordlessly deferred to him. He saw the paralyzing fear in their faces, noted their jittery eyes and halting breaths, witnessed them jump at every sound in the shortening shadows of the forest, and so instructed them to move away from the bodies of the Lieutenant and First Sergeant. *Better to get that mess out of sight*, he decided. Charles curtly ordered the quickly diminishing group to move off to a ridgetop where they could survey the surrounding countryside.

"Crowder," Charles said with an air of authority. "Assist Corporal Smalls to the ridge, if you please."

Crowder made to help the Corporal get up, but as he touched the other man's shoulder, Smalls shrieked in pain and struck out. "Get away!" he screamed, his eyes bulging with fear. "Get away!" the Corporal shrieked again. Crowder made to scramble away from his friend's wild blows. "He'll eat me," Smalls cried out. "He'll fucking eat me!"

Crowder swore and jumped on the man, trying to keep him from fleeing into the forest, and then rolled slowly onto his side, an audible groan escaping his lips. Corporal Smalls leapt up and bolted for the murky trees, quickly disappearing from view, his screams and cries fading into the darkness of the trees.

"Fuck," Crowder said. "Awe shit, oh fuck."

"Private Simpson," Charles said abruptly, his brows stitched together as he tried to contain the situation. "Help Crowder, he's injured. The rest of you, let Smalls go. He won't go far and it's dangerous out there."

Simpson stood, staring wide-eyed at the leather discs of a knife's handle protruding from the side of his friend's chest. Crowder knelt on a thick bed of pine needles, chin lolled onto his chest, staring at the spartan handle of the knife. He gingerly touched it, winced in pain, and coughed wetly. Iron blood, metallic and sticky, leaked from his mouth and bubbled on his lips. He looked at Simpson questioningly.

Private Simpson knelt next to his friend. "Hang on, brother," he whispered, his hand rooting in his rucksack for a bandage. "You'll be alright, Crowder. You'll be alright." The men were trained in first aid, long hours in the field spent practicing for just such an event, and as Simpson fumbled with the bandage, trying as he might to put pressure on the wound, Charles saw the tears in

Simpson's eyes which betrayed a stubborn refusal to accept the inevitable.

Nothing could be done for Crowder. He held on a few short minutes longer, but the knife's blade had severed an artery and punctured a lung. He died with Simpson at his side, tears dripping from his chin to mingle with blood and dirt. The squad was down to half-strength, which did not go unnoticed by the others, and conflict pulled at Charles. He was pleased to be so near the objective, yet he hated to see these soldiers die in such an odious manner. Lip stuck out, his resolve hardened into steely determination. Nothing must compromise the mission.

Simpson was struck dumb by Crowder's death. He didn't move, he didn't make a sound, and the rest of the squad's meager number avoided his lifeless gaze. Charles felt a slight pang of pity for the boy and crouched next to him, a reassuring hand on the soldier's shoulder. "There's nothing you could have done, Private."

He nodded weakly. "What did Smalls see?"

"I am not sure," Charles lied.

"Did you hear him?"

"I didn't catch it," he lied again. "There was too much commotion."

"He said it was a man. A man chewed Willey's face off." Simpson was pale, ghostly, the blood gone from his face. "He said it was a man."

Charles considered the boy, for Simpson was closer to boyhood than manhood. *Not a day past nineteen years*, he thought with regret. "Have you heard the folk tales of these hills?" he asked.

Simpson shook his head.

Charles looked around, unsure of how to proceed through this unfamiliar situation. Comforting others was never one of his strengths. "These people believe in the undead. They believe the dead come back to life, to prey on the living."

Simpson looked directly into Charles's eyes. He didn't have the courage to speak, but the words came anyway. "Undead?" he choked out. "Like Count Dracula?"

"Dracula isn't real. Vampires are not real, obviously," he said without conviction. "War does strange things to the mind, and who knows what Crowder thought he saw? Stories can twist reality."

"He said it was a man," Simpson insisted.

Charles sighed. "The peasants of these forests believe in strigoi. Have you heard that name?"

"No," Simpson whispered absently.

Charles glanced left and right, hoping the others were out of earshot, though the circle had grown smaller and so their faces turned to him. The sun was just now kissing the high mountain ridges, its fiery radiance a promise of life amongst the dead, and though Charles knew danger was near past, the other men were ignorant to this fact. They were jumpy, but what is done is done. There was no helping that now.

"I've heard that a strigoi is demon-like. They were once men but were cursed in life, and so in death they continue to haunt the living." He stopped and looked at the few remaining survivors. They had circled together, Charles's voice baiting them in. Simpson was staring at him, his face shocked by the dhampir's unbelievable story, yet convinced by the unbelievable events of the night.

Charles returned his gaze. He almost felt pity for the boy, but the squad's sacrifice was insignificant compared to the evil he was about to confront. "Or something like that," he finished lightly. "Remember, these are folk-tales, and a forest tends to play tricks on a person's mind. I'm sure they were attacked by animals, nothing more, nothing less."

And only he had heard the faint snapping of twigs in the forest.

Four men remained, not including Charles. These four men unwittingly stood between Charles and his target, the castle on the mountain, an epicenter of evil. If they knew the real reason they were crouched in this forest, they never would have come on this mission.

Which, of course, is why they would remain in this God-forsaken land. None of them would escape to bring the truth back home with them, even if their broken minds weren't to be believed by others. Charles's secret would remain a secret, the monsters of peasant folk-tales would see to that. Every one of them would die here. Another twig snapped, another leaf rustled, the faint noises unheard by Charles's rapt audience. His right hand dropped low, fingers caressing the bone handle of the long, heavy knife that was sheathed at his side, and he raised his left hand to signal silence as his eyes shifted left and right.

Charles's acute vision picked otherwise invisible details from the dawn's dark recesses, his superhuman hearing sensing a brushing of padded feet amongst a soft carpet of pine needles. His fingers tickled the scrimshaw carved into the knife's yellowed bone handle, ready to draw the foot-long blade into action. It was old, an anachronism, a weapon issued by no military on earth, yet it would give protection that no rifle could offer here. Lead had no effect on the monsters of Wallachia, not bombs nor guns nor any other modern arm. Even ancient weapons had no effect, save for the enchanted blade that hung at his side. *Or so I've been told*, Charles thought wryly, hoping beyond hope the Jew had been correct.

One of the men, whose name Charles couldn't care to recall, began to speak, but was shushed harshly. "Quiet," Charles hissed. "Something else is out there."

The soldiers hefted their rifles with sweaty palms. "No," Charles whispered. "Rifles are worthless. Fix bayonets," he said, but the valuable words were wasted as a dark shape leapt howling from the dark. A soldier shrieked and wildly fired off rounds, the deafening crack of the rifle's bullets eliciting howls and moans from among the black trees. Charles stared at the creature in perverse interest as its clawed grip pulled the soldier's rifle from his grasp. Monstrous, vaguely humanoid, the beast was large and hairy, with the muscular body of a man but with the massive head of a wolf. It stood on hind legs and grasped at the soldier, whose last words were a pleading cry for help before the wolf-thing sank its teeth into his head, silencing him forever.

Men scattered. They were soldiers, trained for war, taught to rush into the steel teeth of an enemy's barrage. Even their worst nightmares couldn't conjure up the horror of facing these impossibly hideous monsters, these creatures from a twisted imagination.

Charles knew, though. He had learned the truth of the hill-peoples' tales, he had read through archival stories of an impossible savagery, one that had been growing more violent over the past few years. All the long centuries of preparation and study had led Charles to this place and this time, as he slid the long knife from its scabbard, the dull glint of ancient iron flashing in the first rays of the long day's sun. Dawn's lance had just pierced the sky, a midnight hue of night still holding court over the land, and the werewolf's predatory attack was only just beginning.

Down on all fours, it loped after another soldier, who had only made his escape of a dozen or so paces before being set upon by the ungodly beast. It's a dream, a nightmare, the poor man undoubtedly thought as he screamed in terror, but his protests ended with his arm violently ripped from its socket, the muscles and tendons and skin tearing reluctantly as the wolf-thing rent his body in two. Blood spewed from severed arteries, black liquid spraying through pine boughs. He didn't scream now, he just lay in the dirt with his life leaking into the black earth around him.

Simpson had collapsed to the forest's dirt and detritus, shrieking cruelly. He sat there, legs crossed like a child, hands covering his ears and eyes squeezed shut, with the wild howl of a beast screaming from his lips. *It's like the shriek of a dying horse*, Charles thought absentmindedly, a distant memory from the Great War decades ago. The boy didn't even breathe, Charles marveled. He just sat there, screaming.

One last soldier died noisily. He had tried to run, his rifle long since discarded, but an unseen ghoul pounced from the dark to seize the poor man, its hungry jaws chewing noisily on the soldier's neck and spine. He screamed briefly, but then stopped abruptly as if he were comically trying to understand why someone would want to devour him. Effortlessly, the rotting ghoul tore his head off so the headless body dropped bloodily into dirt and discarded pine needles, before disappearing into the forest with its gory prize.

Charles stood still, his long knife brandished menacingly towards the werewolf. He was calm, unemotional, sure and confident that he could easily kill the lycanthrope, and equally sure such an outcome was unavoidable if the beast came for him. It snarled monstrously, threw its head back to expel a haunting howl, then loped without warning at its prey. Relying on speed and power rather than canny tactics, the hairy brute leapt, but Charles slid nimbly to one side as his wrist flicked deftly. Their eyes locked for an instant as the fiend flew past, the wolf-thing's face twisting, human-like, into a look of surprise, and Charles returned a triumphant sneer as he shoved the knife deep into the werewolf's throat. The blade bit, its edge sawing through tendons and gristle to grind against bone as hot blood spurted over Charles's hand.

Its roaring howl was cut off in an instant as momentum carried its body clear from Charles, who rolled backwards, letting the force of the attack carry him. He bounded to his feet, ready to meet the monster's counterattack, but instead it curled into a ball, yelping in misery and snapping at the twigs that littered the forest floor. The creature convulsed, thick blood oozing from its maw, black hair quickly thinning until it disappeared completely. Its nipping muzzle rapidly shrank to a pug-nose, the creature's face reverting to a familiar humanity.

The thing was dead.

\*\*\*\*

Simpson was frantic, pale and sweaty. He had witnessed the incomprehensibly ghoulish creatures devouring his friends, his comrades. Bullets had no effect on these devils. Survival depended on fleeing, so the Private ran, plunging headlong through shallow streams and scrambling over boulders, anything to escape the horror that befell the rest of his squad.

Charles chased the Private. He ran for a long time, but time was relative to the insane, and Charles knew that Simpson's faculties had melted from the morning's monstrous onslaught. So Simpson had ran, Charles followed, and then just as he made to catch the fleeing soldier, he caught a glimpse of the parapet of a castle on top of a cliff, its crumbling walls proud and eternal through the dawn's mist. Simpson changed course to head for the promontory, desperate for any semblance of safety.

"Simpson!" Charles called out.

He stumbled briefly, caught his feet, and ran on.

"Simpson!" Charles yelled again. "You're safe!"

Simpson ignored him, though, and Charles cursed as the lone remaining soldier ran on, tearing through brambles and stumbling over rocks. He tripped once, twice, gashed his palms against sharp stones where he landed hard, but he continued the flight to dubious safety.

Charles finally caught up with the Private as Simpson stumbled over a boulder to sprawl in pine needles and old leaves. The dhampir grabbed the soldier by his collar.

"Damn it, man, stop running!" Charles spat, his ruddy face flushed with anger.

Simpson was crying hysterically.

Charles pushed him down, holding him still. "Get ahold of yourself. They're gone. The sun is coming up now, they've gone back to wherever the fuck they came from. Calm down!"

But Simpson was hysterical. Charles saw his eyes clouded with a temporary insanity, the soldier's eyes darting back and forth, seeing monsters in every bush and tree. It was understandable. Simpson had just witnessed horrific, human-like things feast on his friends, he saw their limbs twisted from their bodies with barely any effort. No doubt, their screams echoed within Simpson's skull, within his mind, the agonizing sound driving him mad. Charles understood all this, and he also understood in that moment there was only one humane action he could take.

"Why?" Timothy said, the only word he could muster.

"Why?" Charles parroted the soldier. "Because it's what they do," he said temperamentally. "Animals eat."

Tears streamed down Simpson's face. He was the only soldier left of the men who had tumbled from the old German plane.

"This was inevitable," Charles said, his cold voice tempered with a touch of regret. "There wasn't any other way."

Simpson stared at him in horror, agonizing realization painted across his face.

Charles towered over the Private, whose last shred of fragile sanity was quickly fracturing into irretrievable bits and pieces. "There is a secret in that castle, and it can't be released. It's mine to deal with," he continued irately, motioning around the quickly lightening forest, the sun's fiery corona now clearly rising over the high mountains. "What's happened in this forest must stay here. I'm sorry. I wish there were another way." Charles swore and looked at Simpson sadly, knowing what had to be done. Without hesitation, he lifted the heavy knife and slashed downward, his blow well-aimed and quick, a humane strike to end the boy's suffering. Immense power, inhuman power, drove the blade through Simpson's brow, the knife's edge cutting so deeply that the soldier's head was cleaved in two, blood and brains spilling onto his uniform and splashing audibly across the leaves and detritus of the forest's floor.

"I liked you, too," Charles spat angrily.

****

The castle, or what was left of it, was called Cetatea Orașului, the Citadel of the City. Its few remaining walls were ancient, thick, and gray, and most of the fortress had decayed from a fine chateau into a jumble of stone. *As ramshackle and tumbledown as the rest of Europe had become*, Charles thought. What once was great had been reduced to a pile of rubble during some long-ago battle, with green weeds and woody trees sprouting between bits of rock and immense boulders.

But that wasn't quite right, was it? A portion of the castle still stood, the remaining citadel just a fraction of what had been an immense building, and within the harsh stones to Charles's front, a door hung improbably on greased hinges within its decaying stonework. Masonry, finely worked and close-fitting, rose three stories from the clifftop, with intact glass panes glinting with the earliest of the sun's rays. The door was sumptuous and ornate, a hand-carved relic that stood in stark contrast to the rest of the decrepit fortress. It was also slightly ajar, as if the old castle's occupant was waiting eagerly for Charles to enter. He took a deep breath, one hand laid hesitatingly against the door and the other gripping his blood-crusted knife, then finally obliged its summons. Charles pushed the door open and immediately froze, the sight of a pale, gaunt figure shocking the dhampir into inaction. The creature before him was, somehow, both what he feared to meet and precisely what he expected to see.

"Hello, Costache," the vampire hissed in the darkened vestibule, the only artificial illumination an oil lamp. "You look exceptional for being, what? Five hundred years old?"

Charles clenched his jaw, afraid to say anything. It was monstrous, it was hideous. A skinny, sickly looking freak with sharp yellow teeth edged in brown filth. Lank ivory-colored hair hung over pointy ears and a grotesquely hooked nose protruded from above blood-red lips. It was not a human, did not exude even a shred of humanity. It was an atrocity.

Instinctively flexing his muscles into tense knots, Charles's jaw grew taut with loathing.

This thing was the reason for Charles's curse, and he leapt at it with a howl, the knife's blade flashing in oily lamplight.

****

The knife slid through parchment skin and desiccated flesh, the iron bite driving mercilessly to embed itself deep in the vampire's chest. It stood still, the creature, a droll look pasted on the sardonic face that stared back at Charles. He expected the creature to crumble into dust or burst into flame from the blade's magic. Something, anything to signify his knife's power.

Instead the creature sneered, its face full of amused mirth. "Really?" it questioned, before a howling laugh burst from his mouth. "How long were you planning that, Costache?" He guffawed through dirty yellow-brown teeth. "You must be so disappointed! Here, try again," the creature offered, its sunken chest extended towards the dhampir. "No? Fine, then shut the door, you slack-jawed twit," it cackled.

Charles stood still, dumbfounded and at a loss of words. In his mind it had been so clear. Strike hard and fast, before his father could mount a defense. He had never even considered if the knife would fail.

"Quickly, before you let all of the heat out!" it rasped. "You weren't raised in a sty, were you?" The creature looked around the room in exasperation. "Who knew a moron could have slithered from my loins?"

Charles's eye twitched, his mouth opening and closing like a dying fish. He hadn't known what to expect, but surely not this?

"Oh, for the love of the nailed God," the vampire hissed, reaching past his trembling son to slam the castle's door shut. "I'll make this quick, you witless turd. The sun is rising, which means I must retire *very* soon." He snatched the knife from his chest to let it dangle between pinched fingers. "Take your disgusting pigsticker. Good, thank you. I will show you to your room, and when the sun sets tonight we will meet in the study. I know, this isn't the welcome you were expecting. It's your own fault, you know that? If you hadn't dawdled then we could have warmed ourselves next to the fire. As it is, I need to sleep and you…you must wash yourself. You are disgusting. At any rate, you must be getting tired," Cosmin said plainly.

Charles mind had sunk into a numbing pit of failure. "I could stand to rest for a bit," he managed to bite off.

"Very good, I will show you to your room and we'll continue tomorrow? Most of this old castle is in disrepair…"

"An understatement," Charles whispered angrily under his breath. Cosmin ignored him.

"…however you should be comfortable. Only fifteen rooms remain habitable. Sixteen, if you count the latrine, but don't worry, I haven't crapped in ages. It's clean."

Cosmin glided from the castle's vestibule and into a hall, and Charles followed his father dumbly. The creature was clearly not afraid of his son or the enchanted blade. *Why had it failed?* the dhampir thought again, but any answer eluded him as he shuffled along behind Cosmin, his mind smothered with defeat. A thin layer of dust coated the floor and sparse decorations, while ancient, tattered tapestries hung on stone walls. Yet the space was atmospheric and impressed with a shabby elegance. Wood trim, rich and deeply polished with bee's wax, framed newly plastered walls. "Replastered within the past fifty years, at any rate," Cosmin remarked lightly. Charles walked in brooding silence, following Cosmin's light and soundless steps, as if he drifted across the carpeted floor with mere toe-taps moving him along. Dawn's wan light peeked through gaps in drawn curtains, the only real illumination cast from flickering oil lamps that lined the passageway. Before long Cosmin stopped abruptly in front of a door, its ancient oak panels carved with scenes of knights battling snarling dragons.

Cosmin smirked apologetically. "Absurd scenes, these. It was fashionable at the time."

He pushed gently and the door swung open on freshly greased hinges. Cosmin motioned for Charles to enter the room, his arms sweeping around with a flourish.

"This was intended to be the bedroom for a prince! He didn't live to see it, though. He had been staked through the ass, which seemed to be rather painful."

It was indeed a princely space, and unlike the hall there wasn't a speck of dust to be seen. A bed, framed by ornately carved posters, sat in the center of the room, a thick Persian rug muffling Charles's footfalls. Tall windows stretched from the oak floors to the thick joists above, their lead-glass panes covered with woolen curtains dyed a scarlet hue.

Charles, not easily impressed by material things, merely sat on his bed to remove his boots. Cosmin sniffed indignantly and covered his nose. "Savage," he said haughtily. "If you remember your Stoker, Nathanial was instructed not to leave his quarters. I am not Stoker. However, I would suggest you remain on this floor for reasons of safety."

"There's a village nearby, isn't there?" Charles grumbled moodily. "Can I go there?"

"That's no concern of mine, but you may not find the warmest of receptions. The yokels don't welcome outsiders. I really have to go, Costache. The sun isn't good for my complexion."

Charles shrugged. "What if I get hungry?" he asked the quickly retreating vampire's back.

"There is a butlery at the end of the hall, it is stocked with bread and meat. You may stuff the meat within the bread, as is the custom these days," Cosmin called back to him.

"It's called a sandwich."

"I know what it's called! I refuse to lend respect to such a boorish meal. Anyway, the sun is rising and so I must sleep. Until tonight…" Cosmin turned silently, then looked back at Charles with a jaundiced eye. "…Son."

5

Valea Întunecată
Morning

"Hello," the girl said, her familiar black hair bobbing as she talked. She was young, on the cusp of womanhood, just like Elena was. "Do you remember me? I'm Adina."

She had been afraid to go to sleep. Every night the terrors had come to her, nightmares of sacrifice and witches and demons. Even Elena's will wasn't strong enough to force away the eventuality of night, though, and so she had succumbed to the terrible expectation of the night's horrible dreams. Only on this night, the demon and witches and all the other horrors stayed away. Instead, the black-haired girl began to giggle. "Hi Adina, I remember you. I'm Elena. Are you dead?" she asked, her flat voice asking the question as if it were a simple matter of fact.

The other girl frowned, her giggles melting away. "Yes," she replied, a slight tinge of sadness in her eyes. "But that was a long time ago. I've been waiting for you."

Elena looked around. The world had become gray, a slate-stone hue washing all the color from the trees and houses and even the sun's warm rays. It was a dreamworld, and it chewed at Elena's happiness. "Why am I here?"

Adina's frown deepened. "Because the demon's son needs you."

"Demon's son?" Elena thought it sounded ominous. She didn't want anything to do with any evil thing, especially a demon or his son.

"Yes. The blacksmith."

"I don't know any demon-son blacksmith."

"His name is Costache, and he will restart the ancient forge."

"You have a funny way of talking for a little girl."

"I am not a little girl," Adina huffed, her dark eyes flashing annoyance. "You're a little girl."

"Nonsense!" Elena said through lips twisted into a haughty frown. "I'm nearly sixteen, and you are definitely a little girl."

Adina was a slight thing, small and petite and dark to Elena's eye. "I was sixteen once too," she said sadly. "My age doesn't matter now. All that matters is Costache restarting the ancient forge."

"I don't know who Costache is, and I don't know where the forge is."

"The forge is within him. He is tied to it, through blood and God's will, and when he assembles the sword's shattered pieces, he will become the forge."

"Why are you telling me this?" Elena felt hot frustration grow in her stomach. All she wanted was to make it to the festival, to be showered with the gifts of womanhood. "It doesn't make any sense. I don't even know who Costache is! I don't know of any sword."

"It is the ancient Sword of Kizağan. You will meet Costache, it has been decreed, because only Costache wields the strength to withstand the forge. God has chosen him to fulfill this duty. It won't be easy, but you and he are tied together, Elena. Forever. Your destinies are intertwined. One without the other is destined to fail, so you must ensure he gathers the fragments and restarts the forge."

"I don't know hi-" Elena began to shout before checking herself. "Adina, who *were* you?" she asked.

"Cosmin the Wicked touched me long ago. He wanted to make me do unspeakable things, and I wasn't strong enough to deny him."

"Why are you here?" Elena asked, afraid to hear the answer.

A cloud descended across the ghostly girl's eyes. "I was once the Navă, but I was forsaken," she said. "And now I will walk the land for eternity. You are the Navă now, every day your power will grow and grow, and now you must go. Go and find Costache and help him, because you are intertwined, and if one of you fails, everyone will die."

She woke with a start, sweat cascading down her brow and soaking through her nightclothes. Morning's light tried to illuminate the little bedroom but it was a wan light, as if clouds fought with the sun to control the world. Today would be gray and oppressive.

Elena laid in bed, feeling the beads of sweat roll down her temples to settle in strands of her brown hair. Dreams were fleeting things, often forgotten upon waking, but this was no dream. Elena remembered every detail on the girl's face, every word spoken, the import of Adina's urgent message not lost upon her. She must find this blacksmith Costache, whoever he was, and implore him to restart the forge.

Whatever that meant.

\*\*\*\*

Valea Întunecată's old town had been fashioned from rough-cut sandstone blocks held together with home-mixed mortar. The people of this village had learned over centuries to be completely self-sufficient, with only the occasional merchant coming from surrounding towns and cities like Braşov and Pitesti. As far as their neighbors were concerned, nothing of value was manufactured here. The town's people were focused on subsistence living.

Different clans of the Old Families had learned to specialize in trades and thus had inadvertently made their own limited economy. Many of them were shepherds and farmers, while others had learned to make and repair shoes, or sew and embroider their traditional clothing. Bakers and butchers and others had handed down their knowledge through generations.

Over the ensuing centuries, new families had come to the valley as well. Many of them were refugees, be it from conflict or persecution, and those people had built their homes from logs in the post and beam method, but by and large, the town was populated with the Old Families. Local lore spoke of ancient conflicts between good and evil, that the Old Families were God's chosen, and so they had stayed here, in this valley, because it was their place.

After all, a tree's roots ran deep.

It was here, in one of the stone buildings that sat off a twisting alley, that the blacksmith's shop had been built, and Covaci toiled away, sweating at his forge. Bellows were being worked by an ingenious, water-driven contraption, and as the bellows roared air into the furnace, knotty lumps of coal glowed in reds and whites and yellows.

Just like the coals, Covaci glowed yellow, and Elena stared as the giant man let his massive iron hammer drop on a metal rod, itself glowing yellow and hot.

She didn't know Covaci well. On occasion, her father would need tools made or bits repaired, and so Elena would accompany him to Covaci's forge. He was a hideous looking beast, scarred by hot sparks and embers, his face crisscrossed with healed wounds from a lifetime of difficult labor.

Covaci was also one of the nicest people one could ever wish to meet. He always had a kind word and helpful hand, but it was the yellow glow that seemed to radiate from his very being that had caused Elena to stare, open-mouthed.

He dropped the hammer with a bang and stretched, his hands knuckled into the small of his back. "I'm wondering if you're going to just stand there and stare," he said, a friendly wink taking the some of the sting from his words. "Or if the young lady is looking for help?"

Elena forced her eyes to the ground, acutely embarrassed at the rudeness of her staring. "Hi Mister Covaci, I…um…"

"Come here. You're Gavriel's daughter, are you not?"

"Yes," she nodded. "I'm sorry to bother you."

"A pretty young lady such as yourself is no bother at all."

"I'm not a lady, not yet. Not for another five days."

"Is that all?" the blacksmith laughed. "Still a lady in my book. I haven't finished the repairs Gavriel asked for. Give him my apologies, I just need another day or two."

"It's not that," Elena smiled. "I'm looking for someone. A blacksmith or something."

Covaci threw his arms wide. "Well, you've found him! What else could a lady want?"

She giggled. "His name is Costache," she said.

Lips pursed, the blacksmith tapped a finger on his chin as if he were deep in thought. "Costache, Costache. I can't say that I've ever heard of a Costache. If you need a blacksmith, though, you can't find a better one than myself."

Elena frowned. "Are you sure? I was told there is a blacksmith named Costache and I had to tell him something." Her face flushed, sudden realization causing her embarrassment to come flooding back. "I'm so sorry! What a rude thing to do, asking a blacksmith about another blacksmith."

"I have to admit, it is a strange thing to do."

"A girl told me to give him a message, that's all!"

Covaci leaned down to look Elena in her eyes. "If I was worried about another blacksmith in town, then I wouldn't be a very good craftsman, would I?" Another wink, then a smile split his scarred face to reveal gapped teeth. "I haven't heard of any Costache...blacksmith or otherwise."

\*\*\*\*

Elena stood in the market square. Embarrassment still burned her cheeks, even though Covaci the blacksmith was kind and gracious in the face of her mild disrespect, but then that shame was quickly forgotten.

All the people in the market, from the hawkers to the townsfolk, from peasants to merchants, they all had a glow about them. It was a luminosity, as if they radiated colorful hues. She looked around in awe, dumbfounded. Here, a man whose radiance was a light blue. There, a woman yelled at her children, her body illuminated in deep purples and greens. Elena couldn't necessarily see the colors, the glow wasn't something that registered in her sight. The light was more of a feeling than anything else, a sensory experience inherent in her mind. She simply *knew* the colors. A man skulked about, eyes shifting left and right, his glow almost a predatory black. He was a killer, she realized, a man who would slide a knife into his mark's back just as easily as one would wring a chicken's neck.

She ducked into an alleyway to avoid that man. He scared her.

A marvelous power, this, and Elena quickly turned it into a game to see how many colorful lights she could sense. There were yellows and oranges, which seemed to be the happy ones, and the vibrant greens and purples and blues which seemed to be brooding, a malevolent range of colors. Some of the glows were like rainbows, colors shimmering and swirling, a conflict within a person's soul. Elena wandered through the market square, in awe of the sights before her. She recalled the ghostly Adina blessing her from beyond and wondered if seeing these colors were an effect of that blessing.

But there was more.

Beyond sensing a stranger's luminescence, if she passed close enough to a person, she would sense their thoughts and hopes and intentions and once, when jostling against a young mother, a lightning bolt of experiences lanced into her consciousness. The excruciating pain of giving birth coupled with intense joy and satisfaction, even the acute sadness of new motherhood. Elena had stumbled that time, her legs nearly giving out under the onslaught of the woman's most treasured memory.

And then she saw him.

He was a stranger, tall and lean, his handsome face flushed red and blemished with the bristly hairs of a forgotten shave. He was strange, eminently strange and alien in this small town, as if he were a visitor from a nearby valley wandering through the village's outskirts. Then the man stopped to converse with a mici vendor, the woman's wobbly cart sizzling with the little street sausages.

Elena couldn't put her finger on why he felt different. The man was dressed as any other of the townsfolk, and even from this distance he seemed to speak Romanian fluently with a hint of the local inflection, but there was something out of place about him. She stood at a market stall, her little basket filling with the morning's fruit and vegetables, and regarded him as his conversation with the mici seller turned heated. The woman had yelled at him then, she gestured violently to shoo him off, and he backed away with hands held out defensively. The townsfolk, her friends and neighbors, all had uniquely colorful glows, but this man...this man's aura itself was different. He looked like a normal person, he talked and interacted with those around him, but then Elena realized he had no glow, no colorful radiance belying his emotions. It was as if he existed separately from all the others. Her hand trembled slightly at the realization, her fingers absentmindedly feeling an apple for minute bruises. Though Elena's body went numbly through the motions of the morning routine, her full concentration was on the strange man backing away from the mici stand.

Though she was still getting used to this newfound power, his complete absence of any sort of colorful aura caused fear to creep up her spine, but in spite her misgivings something made the girl move closer, to look at him.

To sense him.

He took another step back from the mici vendor, turned to flee, and locked eyes with Elena. Self-consciousness flashed over her as their eyes met, and in his black pupils she saw nothing. No soul lurked in the depths of his eyes and Elena struggled against the strength of their pull.

An explosion reverberated in her mind, louder than the loudest shell of war, a violence deep within her consciousness, and she recoiled backwards with the force of his gaze.

****

They stood apart from each other, separated by a chasm of distance and time, and Elena could see that the man was reeling. In a fleeting instant the market around them had disappeared to be replaced by a landscape of toneless morass. There was no heat in this place, nor was there cold. No sadness or fear, just skies of stark gray over an expanse of black water. This was a realm of nothing, a place of profound emptiness in which nothing existed, not even the basest senses of touch or smell or sound. Liquid lapped at their heels, yet they couldn't feel its wetness. This had become their entire world. They had looked into each other's eyes for the barest moment and then a thunderclap had struck, it had brought them here, to this place, and he stood reflecting her terror.

Elena had felt his probing consciousness seizing on the terror that threatened to overwhelm her, then she felt that terror pulled inexorably into his mind. She felt it gobbling up his own waning courage, the greedy grip of her terror icy and cold, the only sensations in this otherwise numb world. He stood still, rooted and immovable, and she was unable to tear her eyes from his. They were joined across the chasm, entwined, and he absorbed her fear as she cried in silence. He pulled it deep within, so that as her terror began to ebb, a new courage grew within the girl, and that too she shared with the man so that her fear wouldn't consume him.

"Who are you?" he tried to ask, but no sound escaped his lips though she understood the words in his mind. "Who are you?" the man screamed mutely.

There was no sound or air or even *being* in this realm, only a consciousness that pervaded everything, and in that terrible reality, her voice broke through.

She wasn't scared any longer, her fear having been devoured by the man's courage, and now her bravery was a beckoning lighthouse that pierced the thick fog of dread that had begun to eat at him. Their shared strength and courage flowed between them as a stream, just as the fear and horror had. His subconscious had reached out to her, and she spoke to him through their bond, her voice comforting and strong, the lifeline he now desperately needed.

"I am Elena," she said in his mind. "And you are Charles, aren't you?" The name had just come to her, a label that seemed to appear as if from ether. "I don't know where we are." She looked around the vast gray-black expanse of this realm, wondering at the purpose of this place.

"How do you know my name?" Charles demanded.

"I don't know," she admitted. "I just do. Am I right?"

He glared through squinting eyes, then shook his head. "Yes, I'm Charles. I don't know where we are either, I just don't know. I was in the market, and now…" His voice trailed off. She could sense that there was nothing he could say, that there was nothing *to* say. Like Elena, he simply did not know where this place was. They had been whisked out of Valea Întunecată and landed…who knows where?

A new voice spoke, a disembodied sound forcing its way into their shared consciousness. It rumbled, timeless, an interruption of their thoughts from somewhere above and below and all around them. "I brought you here," it said. "You are my guests in this place." Elena recoiled, looked all around, confused yet unafraid, though she felt a new fear growing from deep within Charles. "You two are unique in all the world," it continued.

Charles began to shake and Elena felt him try to force the growing fear down, felt him probing for her courage to steady himself. She took a deep breath, willing him to be brave. "Why did you bring us here?" he managed to think, the words floating in their minds.

"An evil is rising, Costache. Left unchecked, it will consume all. You two are the best weapon to contest it."

*Costache,* Elena tried to say, her thought a jab into Charles's subconscious. She was calm, accepting of this strange voice, and sensed that he needed her, this Charles or Costache or whatever his name was. She had implicitly known that the strange ghost of Adina had imbued her with a great ability and, though she knew she had been uniquely blessed, she also realized this astonishing power she had been given would extract a terrible cost.

Now she would learn the scale of that cost. "Best weapon," she noted, her silent voice reverberating in the other man's head. "Not weapons?"

The voice floated in its void. "You two are intertwined, you are inseparable. Since Costache's birth, Elena, your future was written. The time had to be right to bring you back into the world and now that time has come. It has come, and through sacrifice, you both will be unleashed."

Elena felt a tingling in her palm, the first sensation since being transported to this ghostly plane. The tingling slowly morphed as the voice spoke; it grew, needling, the pain stabbing deep within her hand, and finally erupted into a fiery agony. Elena gasped and grabbed at her wrist. Blisters had formed on the palm of her hand, bubbling and bursting, pus leaking from the sores. She looked at Charles or Costache or whatever he called himself, and he too had gripped at his wrist, the man's face twisted in pain.

"Remember that you are not alone in this war," the voice spoke again. "Remember that through the trials which will come, you do not stand alone. You have each other, and only with each other will you be victorious. Separately, however, your defeat will be inevitable, and many millions would suffer from your failure."

Noise, the great roaring noise, came again. An astonishing pressure built in her head until the thunderclap burst, and Elena involuntarily jerked back, stumbling against the immense surge of sound.

****

The town's folk milled about the market, oblivious to the incredible realm that had just released Charles and Elena. The people of Valea Întunecată picked through fruits and vegetables as if nothing had occurred. Charles stood still, his arms raised in defense against the unseen explosion of light and sound as he looked about at the market's stalls. Elena was gone, the only evidence of her presence a basket on the cobbled street, its contents strewn haphazardly. He looked at his hand, the painful blisters fresh in his memory.

No scars creased his hand, no boils or blisters. It was just as he remembered, every line and furrow familiar.

Every line, that is, except for one.

Charles hurried to find the girl. Her importance to his quest was now laid bare by the strange encounter, even though vast unknowns rattled about in his head. Charles hurried deeper into the village, searching for Elena. Cobbled tracks twisted between houses while alleys snaked off to either side through a narrow maze of crumbling buildings. Charles was lost, turning left and right, letting serendipity be his guide.

"Why do you flee?" a voice asked. It was a sultry voice, silky and gruff. Experienced. Charles spun to face an open door, the room beyond dark and gloomy and hidden by beads that hung from the door's jamb. Its only illumination was an ancient oil lamp spewing noxious soot. The building was white-washed and nondescript, with no sign over the doorway whose sill was painted a sumptuous purple. Beads hung down haphazardly, and the silhouette of a veiled figure beyond, seated at a small table, was womanly and alluring.

"Flee?" Charles croaked. He cleared his throat. "I flee from no one," he declared with false bravado.

He saw the face smiling, though she was obscured by deep shadows. "If you don't flee, then you are in search of something. Come closer," she said huskily through slightly parted lips. "Come in, and find that for which you search."

"I have no money," Charles answered. "And even if I did, I have no interest…"

"Come in," she interrupted him. "Your father wills it."

Charles was taken aback. "What do you know of him?" he demanded urgently against her rising laugh. "How do you know who he is?"

Her laughter grew gentler, softer. "I know things, Costache. They are like whispers in the night, the things I know. Mere suggestions, you see? Fleeting as they are, these dreams give me knowledge. I've seen him, and I see him in you now. So come in, and maybe I will help you to find what you seek." She motioned to him gently, temptingly. Charles gave a last glance up the cobbled roadway, pushed through the beaded doorway to enter, and then he very nearly retched.

Sunken eyes stared at Charles from deep in their sockets, pupils black as night surrounded jaundiced whites. Her face was crisscrossed by weeping scars, deep gashes leaking a rancid milky fluid. Hair, greasy and thin, hung lank over gray and rotting skin. She didn't look ancient, nor was she young. Instead she had the appearance of a corpse who refused to die. Charles staggered backwards and turned to run.

"Stop!" she commanded angrily. "You dare not run, Costache!" Her voice held a command over Charles that he couldn't resist. Cowed, choking down bile, he refused to look her in the face. Instead he slunk across the floor, contorting his body to avoid her gaze.

"Sit," she said simply while indicating a chair. The table was ancient and round, covered in a dark cloth ringed in archaic silver symbols. The only objects he could see were the lamp with its weakly jumping flame, a deck of tarot cards, and a human skull painted in ochre, its dull red finish haunting and ghostly. Ghastly fangs hooked from the skull's maxilla, long and thin, mutated canines with needle-sharp points.

Charles shuddered, his head shaking in denial. "No…I can't."

"Sit, you petulant boy."

"What are you?" he pleaded.

She cackled, her voice no longer sultry and pleasant. "I have been called a wise woman, I've even been called a seer. A witch. I practice the old arts, the oldest religion that our people believed long before the nailed God conquered our land, even from long before the older gods were worshipped. Now sit down, as your father desires."

Charles swallowed again, choking back his fears, his eyes darting this way and that, hoping for an escape. The room was small and cramped, plaster cracked and flaking from stone walls, tendrils of mold crawling inexorably towards the ceiling's oak planks. The sole escape seemed to be the way he had come in, but he worried that his only hope for salvation lay in complying with her demand. He sat gingerly.

"Very good, Costache. It is Costache, is it not?"

"Charles," he replied. "My name is Charles."

"If you desire," she said as she sat across from him. "One name is as good as the next. There is no special magic in a name, no matter what the country folk think. Give me your hand."

He refused her request, unwilling to touch her putrid, deathly flesh, but she seized it anyway. Charles instinctively tried to pull away, but her grasp was hard as iron, her strength belying the dying body. She silently dared him to struggle, her gaze steely and galvanizing.

Reluctantly, he gave in, and she tutted and stroked his palm gently with her right hand, tracing the lines on his palm, before fondling his fingers.

"Has anyone read your palm before? No? It is a very ancient knowledge. The Greeks called it Cheiromancy. Each line, each finger, even each nail imparts hints to your past, your present, your future. How the lines start, how they end, how they intersect…they tell the story of your life, while the fingers illuminate who you are presently."

She cooed gently as she probed and cajoled the secrets from his palm before letting his hand slip from her grasp. She sat back and released a long, breathy gasp.

"What is it?" Charles asked.

She didn't answer immediately. She clucked and chuckled and shook her head slightly. "You are a very interesting boy," the crone said. "Very interesting indeed."

"I'm not a boy! What did you see?" he demanded urgently.

"Everyone is a child to one as old as me," the crone said dismissively. "What, indeed, did I see? A very interesting future. Short, perhaps, a short future, but very interesting and eventful. You see, you have a fire hand, which indicates strength and anger...a temper which flares easily. Your life line intersects with your heart line and ends abruptly, while your head line is very robust. There are other things as well, that are uninteresting. But there is one more curious thing…"

"What curious thing? What do you mean I have a short future?"

"Another life line. Two, on a single hand. And where they cross, one ends abruptly and the other grows more vigorous. Quite unique, Charles. Quite unique, indeed."

"What does that mean? Does it mean I'm going to die?"

She waved her hand at him, lightly dismissing his fear though her face betrayed a hint of confusion. "These things aren't to be trifled with! Knowledge is powerful, perhaps too powerful. Maybe I've said too much already."

"God damn it, tell me!" Charles became angry with the old witch, his previous queasiness gone.

"Ah, that is the fire hand talking! As I said, a short temper," the hag smiled.

"You hideous thing…"

"Calm down, boy, before I give you a reason for anger," she scolded him. "All will be revealed. But first, I have questions for you. Questions about the quest you are on."

He threw his hands in the air in frustration. "You can't do that!" he said.

"What? Can't do what?" the crone said defensively.

Charles's face flushed in anger. "You can't tell me I have a short future and then change the subject. You can't tell me my fucking palm is…is…unique, and then, what? Start asking questions about something else? It isn't right!" he said.

"This is my house," she insisted, her voice rising in anger. "My rules, child, and I'll tell you in my time."

He stood abruptly to send the chair tumbling backwards, its frame clattering across the floor. "This is idiotic. That's what this is. You're a charlatan. I don't know what game you're playing or why Cosmin put you…"

She cackled. "Cosmin, Cosmin! It's not even his real name! He has another one that is far more ancient than that."

"Another name?" he shouted in exasperation. Why would his father lie about his name? Of course his name was Cosmin, it was written all over Bekhmoaram's old documents.

"Oh, yes, another name! It is a name that shall not be spoken!" she said, her voice full of joyful mirth as tiny flecks of spittle quivered on her lips. "It is the name of evil!"

Charles spat on the floor to avert the foulness of her words, then spun on his foot and pushed the doorway's beads to the side, stabbing sunlight temporarily blinding him. Ignoring the jarring pain of light, he stepped through the doorway.

The crone sat at the round table, her deathly hands folded neatly on the tablecloth, Charles's chair neatly upright and inviting. "What the…" he murmured, then looked back at the doorway where the beads swung gently, a rectangle of sunlight flashing through the opening.

"Back so soon? Your seat awaits," she cajoled.

"I…I had walked out…" he mumbled, thumbing behind him, indicating the swaying beads.

"And I'm not done with you, petulant little boy. Now sit!" the hag commanded, a new iron edge to her voice.

"Who the…*what* the fuck *are* you?" Charles demanded, a sudden fear welling from the depth of his stomach.

"Who am I? You're a stupid boy, just like your father. I am the ancient one, the one who knows all, the one who sees all. Knowledge and time began with me, they flow through me, and they will end with me. What am I? I am the one who cursed your father!"

Charles stumbled backwards, his mind a confusing jumble of thoughts and fears. *It can't be*, he thought, *that witch had to have died centuries ago!* He tried to keep from falling, an unfamiliar vertigo making him clumsy and disoriented, and try as he might the floor's flagstones crashed into him. Charles was vaguely aware of the old witch giggling gleefully. She was dancing in her seat, the puckered flesh of her ankles beating against the chair's legs as she cackled.

The stubs of her ankles where her feet used to be.

Charles scrambled to the door, crab-walking backwards, his palms bloodied on the floor's sharp flagstones, then bolted from the dark room. He fled the tormenting cackle of the evil sorceress and stole a quick glance backward as his feet pounded across ancient cobbles. The beads had disappeared, replaced by a rotten wooden door, shut tight and with its rusty deadbolt shot securely home.

# 6

## Valea Întunecată
## Mid-morning

Elena was trembling. The courage she had felt in the strange gray-black realm was a fleeting mettle. She was still a girl, still not quite a woman, and so she was largely unexposed to the evils that the world had wrought. Now she sat huddled in the corner of an abandoned farmhouse, her knees drawn up tight to her chin and trying her best not to cry. Elena's family were simple people from the hills, they were sheepherders who traded bundles of raw wool for meager coins with which they bought meager food. They attended church regularly, took care of those they could, and tried their best to live a good life.

What had she done to deserve this fate?

Sniffling, she drew a dirty sleeve across her nose, a filthy and snotty streak marking her cheek. Her hand no longer hurt, the blisters that had burst in the other realm miraculously healed. Tracing a finger along the lines in her hand, she wondered what they meant, if they really foretold her future as some believed.

"Stupid," she sniffed, swallowing down a wry chuckle. But what if it wasn't stupid? Could a palm reader really tease out fate from the lines in her palm? Elena clenched her hand into a fist. She didn't want the responsibility that these miraculous abilities demanded, whether destiny decreed it or not. When she had first realized she could feel a person's glow, the feeling was a novelty. The vibrant, swirling colors were some kind of aura, a reflection of their souls. Elena had been let in on the person's deepest secrets, she had been given a glimpse of their wild emotions. She couldn't see the colors, which was an absurd notion that made her chuckle nervously. No, the colors weren't like the bursts of reds and yellows and purples that dotted the fields of mountain wildflowers where her father's sheep grazed. They were hints and inferences, whispered suggestions, but still so powerful. She felt when a person had bad intentions, she could feel when a person was sad or happy or angry. Then there were the more primal things, as if she knew when a person was just...evil. Of more fascination for the girl was sensing a person's experiences, such as when the new mother brushed against her in the market. Elena knew, she simply knew, that the intensity of emotion is what let her absorb those memories.

Charles was different. He had no glow, he had no aura. It was as if he didn't really exist, as if he was an empty, soulless husk who was relentlessly driven. To what, though? She instinctively knew that he was driven to an end, a final goal, a mission that would end in destruction.

But then something changed in the strange man. When the two of them were sucked into the gray-black void of the other world, he had burst out into intense brightness, his radiance overwhelming, as if only in that weird, gray place could he realize his full potential. His radiant aura was stark white, a blinding light that would consume everything, and for the briefest moment, when she had looked at Charles and his explosion of radiance, she knew no fear or anger or sadness. That is, until their consciousnesses had melded together. Power flowed between them then. Her courage became his, and his fear became hers.

Elena realized something else, too. His white radiance was a fleeting thing, gone as soon as it had appeared. The void's voice had changed Charles yet again. When it spoke, the man's blinding white glow had turned rapidly to the deepest black. The white and the black, two sides of the same coin.

White and black, the hues that enabled the gray of the void to exist. The hues that enabled all colors to exist, and she realized those same hues fought over Charles, and, she was sure, they were the same colors that fought over her. An evil blackness had risen, the white a holy barrier against that wickedness, and now she knew the cross that she bore in the coming battle. Steeling herself, Elena rose with new determination. *I won't be cowed,* she thought, her jaw set. *I won't be driven to fear.* She would be a woman soon, which meant she wasn't a weak girl who would be bullied by dead girls and strange men.

First, though, she had to fetch the produce from the market. Elena had no desire to face the very real wrath of her mother.

****

Hot mushroom soup waited for Elena, its fragrant steam carrying the scent of tomatoes and garlic and onion to make the girl's mouth water. Most of the fruits and vegetables she had scattered in the market had been saved by the kind merchants, but even so, she had felt an acute embarrassment for her harried flight.

No matter, she had made it home with the mostly-full basket and without even a glance of strange dead girls, old priests, or even that Charles fellow.

Still, an uneasiness had crept into Elena. She already had been subconsciously brooding over Adina's revelations, and then that bizarre encounter in the market pushed Elena deeper into confusion. She was certain that Charles's battling auras also battled over her, that he was this mysterious blacksmith that Adina the Dead Girl was talking about, and that whatever her future held, it was tied to his. Equally, she was certain that belonging to one of the town's Old Families had sealed her fate, whatever that fate would be.

"Mamă?" she asked, the hot soup burning the tip of her tongue deliciously. "What are the Old Families?"

Ruxana was preparing dumplings for the evening supper. "The Old Families were the first ones to settle in this valley, a long time ago."

"I know that, but what *are* the Old Families?"

The woman looked at her daughter with furrowed eyebrows. "What do you mean?" she asked, a hint of concern flavoring the question.

Elena gulped, suddenly afraid to admit the truth of her dreams. "Nothing, Mamă. I've just been having weird dreams, that's all."

Ruxana slowly wiped flour from her hands, concern plastered across her face. "What dreams, Elena? The night terrors?"

"Uh-huh," she nodded, her mouth full of another spoonful of mushroom soup.

"Tell me about them," the woman whispered with a stern edge.

Elena gulped again, her eyes darting down so as to avoid her mother's gaze. "I don't remember," she said. "Not everything."

Ruxana grunted, her eyes narrowed. "You are a poor liar, Elena. It's one of the things I love about you. Tell me about the dreams that have been plaguing you."

With a racing heart and the anxious tang of iron in her mouth, Elena mumbled what she could recall from her haunted memories. There was the monster, and the crone, then the dead girl who had talked to her.

She saw the concern in her mother's eyes, though, and couldn't bear to tell Ruxana about the priest and Charles and all the strange events of the past day.

That would have to wait for another time.

\*\*\*\*

Valea Întunecată
Late morning

Valea Întunecată was a small town tucked into a narrow valley and inhabited subsistence farmers at best. Isolation meant travelers were few, that understandably resulted in a lack of accommodations. If one is a traveler, he must know where to look and who to talk to, and it was that knowledge which brought the Cossack to the town's only tavern. He was used to hard living. It was the lot of the hunter. Spartan quarters, scarce food, and discomfort were really the only consistent things about this life, but that consistency was in itself a morbid comfort. Stepan Ivanovic knew the only thing he could rely on was himself, and he had learned through experience to find a quiet tavern, because every barkeeper knew where to find accommodations.

Creating friendships, some called it, but Stepan the Cossack was a loner and creating friendships came unnaturally hard to the man. In his line of work, though, he had to learn the particular and uncomfortable art of creating friendships. It was how he survived.

"Vodka, please," he grunted in pidgin Romanian. He had never learned the local language, which was absurd in a way, because the very reason for his life's work had slithered its way from this poxed place, but he knew enough to croak his way through simple conversation. Russian, his mother tongue, was not spoken in this part of the country. Some people in Romania knew German, which was fortunate as Stepan was fluent in that tongue. French also, to an extent.

"No breakfast?" the barkeeper drawled back. "We don't have vodka. We have țuică and ale."

Most of it the Cossack understood, or at least he thought he understood. It was hard to tell. In this town, they only spoke Romanian, and in an odd dialect at that. He assumed it was a consequence of the isolation they endured. One road led in, if you could even call it a road, and one led out. It was really more of a wide trail, if one was to be honest with themselves. Sheer mountains exploded from the valley floor with thick forest creeping its way nearly to the village's edge, and a river worked its way lazily to bisect the length of the place.

If not for the creatures that stalked the night, Valea Întunecată would be a wonderful place to settle down. Of course, the very existence of these monsters is what brought the Cossack to this valley. He was a hunter of the dead, of the undead, and of the damned. His quest had led from Russia to France, and from there to the unhappy country of Germany, then to Italy and finally here.

Romania.

He should have known it would be Romania. The place has a reputation to uphold, after all.

"I no eat breakfast. Vodka fires the belly," the Cossack smiled, a meaty hand patting his stomach. "Swee-kuh?" It was a new word to the Russian, but he wasn't partial to ale.

"No, you make a *T* sound. Țuică."

"Tuh-swee-ka," the Cossack tried. He was a butcher to the unfamiliar.

"Tswee, tswee. You make a hard *SW* sound, you see? Țuică."

"Tswee…kuh."

"Very close. Tswee-kuh. Say it all at once."

"Tsweekuh."

"Yes! Very good."

"Swee-kah."

"No, not swee-kah. Țuică."

"Tsweekuh. Tsweekuh. Țuică."

"You are getting better. Țuică is what we drink in my country, it's a specialty."

Specialties, as the Cossack knew, were a dangerous thing. Much like delicacies. "Fine, I will try it," he frowned.

"Good choice!" the barkeeper beamed, but Stepan knew that had yet to be determined.

Gunshots had rang out some time before, the rapid *tat-tat-tat* issuing from somewhere in the mountain forests. The reports weren't loud though. Distance and thick trees had dulled the gunshots' sharpest notes, but the Cossack recognized them for what they were. He heard them just as the first light of day breached night's fastness, just as he had entered the town and seen the tavern's sign. Sleeping off the road wasn't the most intelligent thing Stepan had ever done, given his knowledge of the damned creatures that prowled these lands, but he had taken precautions. Tonight, though, he would tuck himself safely into a warm bed.

Stepan grimaced slightly. Charles Resseguie was out there, somewhere, and the rapid-fire gunshots couldn't have been a coincidence. "Ah," he smiled as a glass of liquor plunked down in front of him. "What name you?" he asked the barkeeper in broken Romanian.

Hesitation and confusion creeped across the barkeeper's face before he barked a reply. "Tomas," he said.

"I am Cossack," Stepan introduced himself proudly. "My terrible, Romanian. My Romanian terrible? Tell me, this țuică."

"What are you saying?" the barkeeper asked, his face pinched in confusion.

"I don't talk Romanian. You understand?"

"Speak slower," Tomas offered, as if that would help Stepan communicate in the village tongue.

"You not talk German, no? Or French?"

Tomas shook his head.

"Shame. What...is...ţuică?"

The barkeeper smiled at this minor breakthrough. "Yes, ţuică. I make it myself, the best in the valley. It's a liquor made from plum..."

"Slow, slow! I no understand."

Tomas sighed and started over, slower this time.

"Ah, plum. Very good," Stepan smiled when the barkeeper finished. He took a sip and grimaced, the liquor burning like a firebrand.

"The best ţuică in the valley," Tomas chuckled knowingly. "The very best."

Stepan coughed to clear his burning throat. "Do you room? I can rent?"

"No," Tomas said regretfully. "Once, long ago. But I know a widow, she may have room. What work brings you here?" he asked.

The barkeeper's question was a common one. Everywhere Stepan traveled, every hunt he had prosecuted, people wondered at the strange man with his strange accent. Lies had come easy, but Stepan hated to lie. To lie is to bear false witness, and bearing false witness is a grave sin. The Cossack did not disregard God's laws. To do so would be to invite terrible consequences, and the life he led was fraught with enough danger. He feared alienating the comfort of his religion.

Half-truths, though...they weren't so bad. Anyway, he could blame any misunderstandings on his poor grasp of Romanian.

"I hunt on contract."

Tomas raised an eyebrow. "Hunt? You hunt what? Big things, small things? There are many things here, some very dangerous things."

"Yes! I hunt things. All things, more dangerous…more better."

"Ah, you're a bounty hunter. There aren't many wolves or bears around here, but if you want to hunt dangerous game, you've come to the right place. Valea Întunecată is the most dangerous place in the world," Tomas said cheerily.

Stepan knew this to be true. To an extent, at least. There used to be wolves and bears in these mountains and forests, and the further one traveled from this valley, the more wolves could be seen. There was a curse on the world, and its epicenter was this valley.

At least, that is what Bekhmoaram the Jew had told him.

****

The widow did, indeed, have a spare room, accessed by a door set in a stone wall off a nondescript alley. Stepan nodded in satisfaction and paid her in hard currency, a full week's worth of rent.

If he had to stay longer than a week, then it was because he was dead.

The apartment was a single small room that smelled of dust and stone, the only furnishings a writing desk and its creaky old chair, one narrow bed with a straw-stuffed mattress, and a ratty rug.

"You can piss in the bucket at night," the widow gummed. "And shit out back."

Tomas assumed there was vaulted latrine "out back," probably of the community variety. Not exactly the definition of luxury, but he was used to it. All these rural villages were similar, no matter the country or language.

He thanked the woman, who shuffled out wordlessly, then set to work putting out his things. Stepan lived a life of chaos, of moving from one crisis to the next, and so he subconsciously craved order, even going so far as having built a daily regimen. The Cossack withdrew a sheaf of paper and nibbed pens from his rucksack, then placed them carefully on the writing desk.

His nightly ritual, so important to maintaining order and sanity in Stepan's little world, was to write down all the events of the day, no matter how mundane. Stepan had learned that the smallest detail could contain critical information, even if that information wasn't obvious at the time. Once complete, he would study the words, reading and rereading his cramped, neat handwriting, committing it all to memory. Once satisfied, Stepan Ivanovic would neatly roll a cigarette and strike a match, drawing in sweet tobacco smoke to feel the delicious burn deep in his lungs, all the while eyeing his match as it burned down slowly. He would exhale smoothly, savoring the rush of energy the cigarette provided. Finally, after the match had burned down, he would file away his notes into a journal he kept. The day's events would be committed to his memory, and his knowledge would be passed on to another generation of hunters. This was the legacy that Stepan Ivanovic the Cossack would leave behind.

"Ah," Stepan smiled, his hand hefting a bottle of clear liquid. The barkeeper had sold him a bottle of the plum brandy. It was a surprisingly tasteless drink, yet warmed the belly just as well as the Cossack's beloved vodka. He would modify his ritual by enjoying a glass or two, or even three, as the case may be, while documenting his daily adventure.

That would come later, though. The sun still burned, and he was a hunter who had caught the scent.

****

## Valea Întunecată
## Afternoon

Gavriel balanced the steaming cup of black coffee on one knee, his eyes tracking Ruxana as she moved stiffly about the kitchen. Something was plainly bothering the woman. She was strong, both in mettle and in constitution, which meant his wife felt like all problems were hers to solve. Gavriel did appreciate that about her, because he had less to worry about when tending his flock. The long days would soon begin, when he would spend stretches of time in the high pastures with the sheep. Up there, the ewes would birth lambs, and it was the menfolk's responsibility to keep them safe and healthy until summer's warmth began to give way to fall's biting chill.

Meanwhile, the town's womenfolk tended to their homes and families. They were a hardy breed, but even that knowledge didn't ease Gavriel's mind. Something was bothering Ruxana, something that sat heavy on her shoulders and made her brow wrinkle with concern. He had asked his wife what bothered her, but the only reply he received was a stiffly clenched jaw, that in turn brought a silent reproof.

"Elena," she said, a bit too firmly. Their daughter was dicing vegetables for their supper. "We're out of cream. Please fetch some from Missus Munteanu."

"Yes, Mamă." Elena's face was flat and numbed, Gavriel noted, and he watched as she slipped out the front door.

"She is having bad dreams," Ruxana whispered once Elena had gone. She would be back in just a short handful of minutes, so they would need to talk quickly.

"So?" Gavriel grunted. "We all have bad dreams."

"No, Husband. Her dreams are terrible. Every night I have to comfort her."

He shrugged. "The Vârstă de Măritat is only a few days away, I'm sure it's just excitement and pressure that she feels."

"Listen to me!" Ruxana seethed. "Her dreams aren't childish. They are dreams of the devil, sometimes she is even having *visions* when she's *awake*. It's not some childish nightmare of falling or being chased by dogs." Tears had burst to quiver at the corner of her eye. "Our baby is tormented, Husband!"

"No, no, Wife," Gavriel frowned, his head shaking with denial. "Listen to what you're saying. Listen to what you're saying!"

"It's a madness, Gavriel."

"What would you have me do? Take her to the priest?"

Ruxana blanched at the thought of it. Elena was their only daughter. If the village's Orthodox priest knew about Elena's visions, he would no doubt demand an exorcism. Failing that, their poor daughter would be committed to some hellish institution and they would never see her again. If that were the case, their only daughter would be better off dead, and the thought of it shattered her heart. "No!" she whispered urgently. "Father Eugen must not find out! This is Romania," she croaked, her voice full of fear. "Who knows what they would do to my baby?"

"What would you have me do, then?" he said again, his voice a pained whisper. "If her affliction is a spirit then we must go to the church. If she is mad, then I don't know what to do. No! She is simply excited and nervous about the Vârstă de Măritat, that is all. I'm certain of it."

"She asked about the Old Families," Ruxana continued, as if Gavriel hadn't even spoken. "She asked where they came from, what they believed, why they settled in this valley."

"It's meaningless," Gavriel said with assurance. "She is only curious."

"Elena asked me what the Navă is. She asked me about the Navă! We've never told her about those terrible old stories. We must talk to the Mayor, he will know what to do."

Gavriel leaned back in the chair and chewed on his lip for a moment. Some of the old tales were nearly forgotten. Certainly, the old tales weren't common knowledge, not anymore, and the myths and legends surrounding the Old Families were some of the oldest of all. She was right, Gavriel realized. He must talk to the town Mayor, and his coffee would turn cold by the time Gavriel returned. "Tell me what she told you," he said, resigned as to the path he would need to travel. "But be quick about it."

****

"Come in, come in, Gavriel!" the man beamed from his chair, faint afternoon sun peeking through the single window of his office. "To what do I owe the pleasure? The Vârstă de Măritat is coming, am I right in assuming that your daughter's excitement grows?" Lazăr was Valea Intunecata's Mayor. He was an influential man of middling stature, whose power stemmed from the prestige he enjoyed among the Old Families. More than just the town Mayor, Lazăr's ancestry included men who had safeguarded the secrets and the stories of the valley from time immemorial.

Those secrets were still safely guarded by Lazăr and his family, and that was why Gavriel had come. He smiled sadly. "Elena is why I'm here."

"Oh?" Lazăr asked as he leaned forward, his elbows propped on his knees. "What's wrong with her?"

Gavriel nervously licked his dry lips. He had taken a risk coming here. If Lazăr wished, he could have Elena taken away, where she would be subject to the awful healing that the church always demanded. Gavriel hoped it wouldn't come to that, but he had nowhere else to turn. The Mayor was the only one who would have reliable answers. "She has been having disturbing night terrors. Ruxana is worried, but I told her it's just the excitement of the Vârstă de Măritat."

The Mayor smiled gently. "Of course it is! Yet…yet you don't think so?"

"I don't know what to think. Every night, the terrors grow worse."

"Maybe the doctor can give the girl something?" Lazăr offered matter-of-factly. "Before long, the festival will be over and she will be better."

"Elena asked her mother about the Navă," Gavriel whispered, low and hurried and urgent. "The Navă, Lazăr!"

The Mayor sucked in a breath. Gavriel knew that the Navă was God's Vessel, and that it wasn't a common folk-tale. The story of the Navă was among the most ancient of all their legends and was nearly forgotten. He was certain they had never spoken of it to Elena. Why would they?

"How did she hear of the Navă?" Lazăr demanded softly.

"A dead girl from one of her dreams."

Another sharp intake of breath. "No!" the Mayor whispered, his face twisted with concern. "Was the girl named Adina?"

"How did you know that?" Gavriel started. Ruxana had only just pulled that name from his reluctant daughter.

Lazăr leaned forward even more, so far that Gavriel was sure the Mayor would tumble from his seat. "Adina was a Dăneşti. She was the last Navă, and she died nearly five hundred years ago. As the stories go, that is the cycle. Every five hundred years, a new Navă is born and the undead wake up. But it's just a story! It's not real. She is just having bad dreams. At some point she heard the story of Adina from someone, maybe her grandmother."

Gavriel's breath caught in his throat, his heart thrumming madly. *What will happen to my baby?* He cried silently, though his face turned cold as he nodded at the Mayor.

# 7

Valea Întunecată
Late afternoon

The bar was empty again. Stepan wasn't used to a town as bustling as this one, and yet the little village's only tavern was as devoid of life as a midnight graveyard. How could Tomas the Barkeeper stay so busy with nothing to do?

"I'll be right with you," Tomas nodded across the oak bar top as he wiped down glasses with an old towel. "Was the room sufficient?"

"Very," the Cossack said with a nod and a cocked eyebrow. "That suhwee-koo, I have one."

"Țuică," Tomas corrected him.

"Yes, that one. Tsweekuh."

"Close enough," the tavernkeeper shrugged a smile. "It's good, isn't it?"

The plum brandy wasn't Stepan's beloved vodka, but it would certainly suffice. "Yes, the best I've had."

"You've never had țuică before today," Tomas pointed out.

"That is good," Stepan admitted in his butchered Romanian. "A good point. I enjoy tsweekuh."

Tomas smiled. "I knew you would. Țuică, coming up."

"Have you seen any strangers in this town?" Stepan managed to say, the words strung together hesitantly.

"You're getting better! Yes, only one. A man, with dirty black hair and a filthy beard. He looks like a rough sleeper. Smells like one too. He just walked in here."

Stepan's eyes narrowed into annoyed slits. "Your joke is not funny." He looked as if he lived a hard life for a reason, but his look was born out of necessity. A man who appeared destitute didn't invite attention, such a man wouldn't be remembered by the people who ignored him. At any rate, this appearance was just one costume among many in the Cossack's arsenal. He once had masqueraded as a nobleman to finagle his way into another dhampir's inner circle before striking the killing blow. Stepan certainly didn't like being filthy and unkempt, but his work demanded it, so yet another hardship was endured until his ultimate task could be completed.

Now, Stepan was so close. Bekhmoaram had told the Cossack of the dhampir's plan, and from that knowledge, the Jew had deduced the probable location of Cosmin the Wicked. Stepan traveled halfway across Europe to find this valley and hunt down the mysterious Charles Resseguie.

Yet Tomas hadn't yet seen Charles in town. Was Bekhmoaram wrong? Had the dhampir gone somewhere else? "Are you sure?" he asked, intensity etched into the lines of his face. "No other strangers?"

Tomas frowned slightly. "No, no. Not that I know of. Another țuică? Ah, good man. I don't do much, though. I come here, I go home. If someone doesn't come into my tavern then I probably won't see them."

"You have not heard from...your customers?" Stepan asked, a quick glance confirming the tavern's emptiness. His stomach burned from the strong brandy.

"Come in later, once the market clears out and the men have time for a little țuică."

"Please, look for this man. He is tall and thin, with short brown hair. Always angry."

Tomas laughed. "If you are looking for an angry sort, then stick around. Many angry sorts come and go. They are angry at everything. At the Mayor, at the country, at the Spaimă…"

"Spaimă? What is this? I do not know this word."

"It is the horror. The terror."

Stepan perked up, the strange word a line for him to grasp. "Tell me, please."

Tomas smirked as he tipped the jar of ţuică to refill Stepan's glass. "There is a monster in these mountains. It is an ancient creature."

"You allow it to live?"

The barkeeper burst into laughter. "It doesn't live! It is Spaimă. It is strigoi. You know this word?"

Stepan had heard of strigoi. Within the wild mountains and valleys of this cursed country they are known to have spectacular powers. Shapeshifting, reading thoughts, controlling animals, even. All driven by the power of the blood they drank, of the souls which the strigoi devoured.

Outside of Romania, they are known as vampires. Stepan knew the strigoi and vampire as the same creature, the same evil thing that hunted people in the night. "This strigoi. Why has it not been destroyed?" he whispered through tensed lips.

Tomas sat down. "Now, *I* will drink ţuică. The Spaimă has not been destroyed because we can't destroy it."

"Nonsense. They walk, they can die."

"We have learned to live with the Spaimă. There is a truce between us and it."

"Why would you do such a thing?" Stepan demanded, revulsion clear on his face.

"Because it keeps the other horrors under control. If not for the Spaimă, then the ghouls and the werewolves and all the other things would be unleashed. He leaves us alone, and we leave him alone."

"Does this…this thing, does it have a name?"

"Cosmin," Tomas nodded gravely. "Cosmin the Wicked."

Stepan sat, bolt-upright. "Where does Cosmin haunt?" the Cossack asked breathlessly, scarce believing his luck. Through all the years spent hunting the undead, the Cossack had dreamed of this moment. Yet here he was, and Cosmin was not far away.

"The old castle above the town. I must warn you, though. Others have come for the Spaimă, and none have left this valley. It's a stone best left unturned."

Stepan stood, a handful of coins rattling on the table to pay for the țuică. His brow and jaw had tensed with a newfound determination. "Thank you," he rumbled. "I will be back."

"Be careful, hunter," Tomas said. "The horrors of this land are unforgiving."

"It's to be expected!" Stepan said, suddenly cheerful, his straggly black beard splitting into brilliant white teeth.

****

Cetatea Orașului
At the same time

Dejection, that's the word Charles was looking for as he stared at the ceiling in his private chamber. Elena, the girl, had disappeared as if she had been plucked off the Earth to be transported back to that terrible gray world in which they had connected. What did it all mean? *You two are intertwined, you are inseparable*, the voice in his mind had said. *Through sacrifice, you both will be unleashed.* That last bit sounded ominous. Whose sacrifice? How will they be unleashed? Charles had come here to destroy his father, but then everything had become complicated. He was still no closer to understanding how to destroy his father, and something strange was going on in this strange town nestled deep within its strange valley *I'll have to find the girl*, he realized. *Maybe she will know what I have to do?*

So Charles lay on his sumptuous and ornate bed wallowing in dejection, wondering where the girl had disappeared to, while his keen eyes inspected the bed's tall posters carved with myriad mythical beasts. Gryphons, dragons, gargoyles, all manner of horrible creatures had been expertly chiseled into the bed's hardwood. The beasts' eyes were hollow, as if they once held precious stones, and minute flakes of gold leaf clung to the bed's crevices and crannies.

Perhaps the bed wasn't as sumptuous as it first appeared. While solid and expertly crafted, it was old and had plainly seen better days. *Much like the castle*, Charles thought. Its citadel, once massive and imposing, was reduced to just a comparative handful of rooms, including the spotless latrine. A handful of rooms of the most ordinary and unremarkable kind, yet something nagged at the edge of his consciousness. He was missing a detail of some sort, overlooking the obvious. Cosmin disappeared somewhere every day, only to magically appear again every night. If Charles was going to strike his father down, he would need to find where the bastard slept away the day.

He was hiding somewhere, Charles was sure. Cosmin was hiding, and his son would find out where.

First, though, the girl. He resolutely decided to find her in the small, ancient, deteriorating village nestled below the castle itself, and if he was lucky he would get to taste his beloved mici, those greasy and garlicky little sausages revered by all true Romanians.

****

Long shadows stretched across the landscape as Charles crossed from mountain forest onto the cobbled town boundary, and the air began to chill slightly. Noon had long since slipped away, but there were still a few hours of sullen daylight left. Enough time for Charles to slip into the village and search out where Elena had secreted herself away.

*Mici*. Its scent floated on a slight breeze, and though Charles brooded at the prospect of being accosted by the objectionable mici vendor again, his mouth watered incessantly. The delicious little sausages must wait. Unless, of course, the mici cart was conveniently close by? Charles strode confidently down one of the village's little side roads towards the main square, determined to find Elena, the girl whose life was twisted into his own.

He turned left at the square, the greasy smell of mici thick in the air, the scent of spices and garlic mingling with searing beef fat making his stomach grumble delightfully, but then his appetite quickly vanished as he entered the town square.

The piazza was empty. Not a soul to be seen, not even a crow to pick at the sizzling beef sausages. Charles looked around, trying to locate anyone who may be hiding. Baffled, he looked inside market stalls, through open doors, behind crates and carts.

The market square was abandoned.

He walked slower now, furtively glancing left and right, his confidence long since evaporated. White knuckles on his right hand gripped the handle of his knife, determined to fight off anyone, or anything, that was waiting to pounce on him.

Nothing pounced. Nothing creaked or squeaked or made even the slightest noise, save for the sound of a nearly imperceptible wind through the market's stalls. Charles stopped in the middle of the square and spun in a circle.

"Helloooooo…hello? Is anyone here?" he called out. Slight echoes were his only answer, punctuated by silence and the incessantly feeble breeze. "God damn it," he cursed, and glanced around once more. "Damn it all to hell."

"Be careful with blasphemy," a voice cackled from behind. Charles spun, his knife whipped out instantly, a curse frozen on his lips. *She* was there. The witch. Seated in a chair that hadn't existed just a moment before.

"Where are they?" Charles rasped through gritted teeth.

"The townsfolk are here, there, everywhere," she replied with an air of nonchalance. "I see you've returned to finish our discussion?" It was a question, but she didn't expect an answer, so Charles stood still, his lips clamped shut over clenched teeth as he gripped the knife tightly. He couldn't move, though. He was frozen in anger and fear, terrified what she would do if he leapt at her, yet furious enough to consider the attempt.

*Do it*, a voice whispered inside his head. A grating, ancient voice. Her voice. *Do it, you cowardly little boy. Drive your blade between my breasts, cut through my ribs and pierce my heart, let my life blood flow onto the cobbles. But you can't, can you? You can't bring yourself to destroy the very thing that has the answers you seek.*

Charles was shaking in furious anger, twitching involuntarily, his knife's blade wagging perceptibly. The hag sat in her chair, puckered ankle-stumps swinging gayly, satisfaction plain on her face.

It was a battle of wills, a battle she had plainly won. Charles gave in and sheathed his knife, his hand still clamped onto its handle. "Fine," he said acidly. "Ask me your questions, you wrinkled old bitch. But then it will be my turn, and I expect answers."

"Fair enough," she smiled through toothless gums. Very nearly toothless, that is, save for a small handful of blackened, rotted stumps. She ran her tongue across cracked, ghastly blue-black lips.

"How old are you?" she asked, an eager fire dancing in her eyes. She plainly was enjoying herself.

"I don't see…" Charles started.

"Of course you don't see, you turd. I asked how old you are."

"Four hundred and…"

"I don't care. Where were you born? Where did you live? In Germany?"

"Does that matter?"

"I'm asking the questions," the crone spat. "Are you homosexual?"

Charles grew irritated, his lip curled into a snarl. "No! Not that it matters, what kinds of questions are these?"

"Humph," she grunted. "That's what they all say. Who told you about the castle? Who told you about your father?"

Charles frowned, unwilling to divulge such answers.

"Oh, *fine*. You don't want to answer my questions. How about this one: why do you want to kill your father?"

Charles's irritated sneer disappeared. Cosmin had sired Charles, had brought the dhampir into this cruel world which had given him nothing but misery. "He's a piece of shit who doesn't deserve mercy. I'll cut off his head and burn his heart."

The crone laughed. "Peasant magic, that. It won't work on Cosmin. Really, the Jew should have told you this. I want to know the real reason why you are here. Why did you come?"

Charles blanched at the mention of Bekhmoaram. *How did she know about that meeting?* He loomed threateningly over the hag, his face flush in anger at her incessant questions.

"Will you kill me?" she asked without concern. "Will you run that knife into my chest?"

"I will, you rancid old bitch," Charles swore. "I swear that I will if you don't shut your rotting mouth."

"You petulant bastard, calling me names! You said I could ask questions." She sneered at him, frothy dribble caked at the corner of her mouth, bloodless lips screwed into a grotesque smile. Her skin was papery and thin, blue veiny tendrils snaking down her arms. She had appeared hideous before, but even more so in the sunlight.

"Your questions are stupid!" he spat accusingly. "Only an idiot would ask such things."

"Well, these are the things I'm curious about," she said, voice dripping in sarcasm. "If you have a better idea, go ahead and share it with the other children in class."

"Three questions," Charles seethed. "Ask three questions, that's it. And then it will be my turn to ask three questions."

She nodded assent, the hideous smirk stretched across her face. "Why do you want to kill Cosmin?"

Charles nodded. "That's better," he said, brow still angrily furrowed. "His evil infected my life, it infected me. I'm cursed by his foul touch and my soul will be damned to hell unless I destroy him. It's my penance."

"Very well," she said. "That would be reasonable…to a simpleton. Why do you think destroying your father will lift some obscure, foolish curse?"

"Because that's how it's done."

"I should have known. Last question: who told you that piece of drivel?"

"What?" Charles spat incredulously.

"Who told you that killing Cosmin will lift the curse? Who fed you that line of dung?"

"It's well known! He is the source of the curse! It only makes sense that he has to die."

"If you really want to believe Cosmin is the source of your pain, then it's your prerogative. Truthfully, you're just too much of a coward to realize that your life belongs to you. Besides, if a dog bites you, and you kill its parent, will it stop biting you?"

Charles sneered back at the old hag and wagged a finger. "Ah, ah, ah! No! Three questions, that's all. That was the agreement."

She rolled her eyes at the dhampir. "Fine, very well. Ask your questions."

Charles smiled victoriously and cracked his knuckles. Now he would get some answers! To destroy your enemy, you must first know your enemy, and he was sure that this hag was not his friend. "What do you know about Cosmin?"

"We've a business arrangement," she answered flatly.

The hag's answer piqued Charles's interest. She was certainly powerful, given the way she bent reality. It wasn't stretching the bounds of reason to think his evil father and this witch were in league together. If this horrid creature was working with his father, then the simple fact that she knew about Bekhmoaram meant that his arrival wasn't the secret he had assumed it to be. *But then*, Charles thought, *Cosmin was waiting for me at the castle. He knew I was coming.* His head began to hurt. "How did you know about Bekhmoaram?"

"Simpleton!" she laughed. "The Jew is our enemy. We keep our enemies close, very close, indeed."

"Who *are* you?" he asked, his skin prickling with ire. He had underestimated the dangers on this entire adventure, foolishly thinking the task was an easy one.

"What an unexpectedly atrocious question. Just as relevant as me asking if you've ever buggered a boy."

Charles frowned. "Will you just answer me?"

"Very well. You've already asked three questions, but I'll give you this answer for free. My name is Unul Vechi, though I've gone by other names before and since."

"Unul Vechi? That's not a name!" Unul Vechi translates simply as Old One in the local dialect.

"It is my name, I don't care what you say."

"It is not a name! Maybe that's what the locals would call you. Where does my father sleep during the day?" he demanded.

Unul Vechi sat and looked at Charles, her blue lips clamped tightly shut over stumps of rotting teeth. "You are idiotic and absurd," she said with more than a hint of malice. "Precisely what I would expect from the seed of Cosmin. Now I will ask three more…"

"I'm done answering your questions! Tell me where Cosmin is or I'll cut your black heart from your foul body!"

"I would love to see you try," Unul Vechi dribbled happily, and then the witch and her chair vanished, replaced by the hustle and bustle of people and mules and dogs, the sudden noise jarring Charles out of his furious anger. He looked around, thoroughly startled, and felt as if he were going insane.

\*\*\*\*

Valea Întunecată
Evening

Ruxana ladled vegetable stew into Elena's bowl, clucking at the girl as she did so. Her daughter had a drawn look about her. "Don't let your dreams trouble you, my dear child," the woman said gently, a hint of sadness hidden in her eyes. "Such a beautiful girl who will be celebrating the Vârstă de Măritat shouldn't be so sad!"

What could Elena say? That she had been pulled into a gray world that rumbled with the voice of some god? Maybe even God Himself? That she was haunted by a dead girl and a priest?

Gavriel patted his daughter's hand. "You can talk to us," he said softly. "Whatever bothers you, we are your family. I will help with anything."

Ruxana waved a hand at Gavriel. "Maybe her flow is beginning."

"I can't help with that," the girl's father said succinctly as he snatched his hand back. "It's your mother's responsibility."

Elena loved her parents deeply. They were rooted in the customs and traditions of this valley. The Old Families of Valea Întunecată weren't just their neighbors, they were Elena's cousins as well. Hundreds of years had seen them grow close to the land and the families had intermarried and developed into an extended kinship. They all looked out for each other, but then the New Families began arriving some years back, and their arrival meant that much of the knowledge and unique culture of the valley's oldest people had been suppressed.

Not all of it, though. Many of the ceremonies were still observed, such as the festival of the Vârstă de Măritat and the bloody ritual that accompanied the movement of the sheep to the summer grazing grounds.

"Soon I will move the sheep," Gavriel said, happy to change the subject from female afflictions. "So you ladies will be alone for a few days. I will be back for the Vârstă de Măritat, though."

Elena's haggard look turned to sourness. She knew what the flock's move to the summer grazing grounds meant. "You're going to sacrifice the lambs?" the girl asked sadly.

Her father tentatively patted her hand again. "Yes, it's necessary. You know that."

"To keep the wolves at bay," she affirmed woefully. Elena loved the lambs and every year was horrified at what happened to them.

"It's only a few, dear girl. Their death means life for all the rest."

"And life for us," Ruxana reminded her husband.

"Yes," Gavriel nodded. "The lambs also mean life for us."

Because wolves weren't the only things that stalked the forests and meadows.

**\*\*\*\***

Sleep came fitfully to the girl. Elena was troubled by her night terrors, by the visions in the market, by meeting Charles or Costache or whatever he was called, and by the fate of the poor lambs who were to be killed. Moonlight shown around the single window's curtain, a ragged thing little better than a dishrag, and Elena wondered how far her newfound power extended. Sensing a person's glow was a fun distraction, while delving into their thoughts an exhilarating feeling. Could she do more? *How much power have I been given?* the girl wondered. *What is its extent?*

Elena closed her eyes to shut out the faint moonlight and pictured his face, the craggy visage of the man in the market who had the look of someone twice her age. His hair formed in her mind, unruly and brown, and then the flushed red of his face, his deep black pupils and wiry frame. This man, who had been called Charles or Costache, had been decreed by the voice as Elena's *other.* Their fates had been intertwined, and as she thought about this Charles, a notion lanced from her mind into the dark of her bedroom. It flew, this thought, straight as an arrow to God knew where. *Are you out there?* the girl asked the sky. *Am I alone?*

*No,* the reply came back instantaneously. *I am here.*

Elena started, forcing her eyes to stay closed. *Who are you?* she thought.

*Charles,* he said.

The girl gasped, a slight interruption that forced his form to vanish from her mind. *Are you still there?* she begged the æther .

Silence.

Again, she focused on the sharp definition of his jaw and cheeks and eyes, the brown of his hair and the depth of his pupils, the two-day-old scruff of his beard. *Are you still there?* Elena asked again.

"I'm here," he said, only this time his voice was clear as an ewe's frantic bleating.

"Where?" the girl asked the void.

"In the castle," Charles replied, and now the lips of her mind's image began to move, began to talk. He sat, as well, his long fingers cradling a glass of burgundy-red wine. "Waiting for my father to join me, wherever he may be."

"Is your name Costache?" Elena asked, an uncertain demand of a girl only now discovering her power.

He hesitated, the wine glass perched at his lip. "That was my name," he finally said. "One time. Long ago."

"You are the blacksmith," she said, a statement, yet also a question.

"No, I'm not a blacksmith," Charles said flatly. "I'm a monster, just like my father."

"Adina said you're the blacksmith who will start the forge."

"I don't know what you're talking about."

"With the forge, you'll reassemble the sword."

"What sword? What are you talking about?"

"The Sword of Kizağan, Adina said. She wanted me to tell you that you are the blacksmith, and the forge is inside you, and that you will have to reassemble the fragments of the Sword of Kizağan."

"She said that?"

"I think so, yes," Elena said, a sudden doubt clouding her conviction.

"Who is Adina?"

"A dead girl. She was the Navă, but now I'm the Navă."

*Navă* was simply a vessel to hold something. "I don't understand what you are saying," he said.

"I don't know, either," Elena said, frustration flushing her cheeks. "She told me to tell you that. Costache? Costache!"

The man was gone.

****

Valea Întunecată
At the same time

The Cossack's room was bare. It was all he had and all he could afford, being a man of limited means. All his life he had relied on the goodwill of others. Not charity, as he refused handouts from those most fortunate. No, Stepan worked his debts off, either through manual labor, because widows were quick to take in a strong back, or through patrons who valued a man with his skills. Men with his experience. Not every patron had a plague of monsters Stepan could deal with though, and so from time to time he would resort to a more mundane application of his talents. Spying, for example. He was quite good at spying, given his ability to sneak unseen and unremembered through towns and camps. Once or twice he accepted assassination contracts, though such machinations were distasteful, even if they were necessary. Those jobs he tried to avoid, but a man needs to eat.

A groan escaped his lips as he sat on his little cot and tugged at his boots. They were old, these boots, and once Cosmin and his son were dealt with, perhaps he would indulge in a new pair. For now they were all he had. Those he set neatly to one side, as was his habit. Everything had its place, its reason for being. Consider his knives. They were arranged neatly in the desk's lone drawer, from smallest to largest, from his paring knife, which was perfect for peeling apples, to his hunting knife, which was well suited to carving the heart from a recent kill. His paper, which he used to keep meticulous notes of each days' events, was arranged neatly on the desk's worn top, and his pens, positioned meticulously to the right of the paper. Candles, though…he hated them. A candle's wick gave off weak light, and the melting, dripping wax created an inevitable mess that impacted his ability to take his meticulous notes. Every night, prior to scribing the day's learnings, he would take the candle in one hand and his paring knife in the other and slice off the cooled dribbles of wax from its shaft. Once that task was complete, he would carve back a bit of wax from the candle's top, to prevent guttering from the already weak candlelight, and trim the wick to the proper length. It was a predictable ritual, one that gave him comfort in an inescapably chaotic life. Reflection complete, Stepan flashed a weak, sad smile and set to work on his nightly routine.

He hadn't done much today, short of arranging his lodging and drinking țuică with the bartender. Yet even though his day hadn't been physically productive, Stepan extracted valuable information from Tomas the tavernkeeper. Most importantly, Cosmin the Wicked inhabited the castle's ruins, that brooding heap of stones that sat on its forlorn cliffs, keeping watch over the dark valley and its town below. Stepan resisted the urge to scribble away madly. Instead, he carefully marked down his notes that would later be compiled into a great volume of secrets. Future generations of hunters would need to stalk the undead through their haunts and ruins and deep, dark forests, and Stepan's accumulated knowledge would be invaluable to their efforts.

"Oh, hello little friend," the Cossack crooned. A tiny brown house mouse was perched at the edge of the desk, its little paws nestled together as if it were a little old cringing lady. He chuckled at its twitching nose and little black blinking eyes. "You look hungry," he whispered knowingly. "Would you like a cracker?"

Fishing around in a pocket, Stepan produced a crumb of wheat biscuit that the mouse snatched up greedily. It nibbled at the biscuit's edge, those black eyes taking in all it could see. The Cossack's life was filled with violence and death, so the tiny mouse's presence was itself an entertainment. "When did you learn how to read?" he asked, amused by the mouse's intensity. It had messily devoured the biscuit, and now sniffed about his day's notes. "Such a little wonder," he mused. "You are always welcome in my home."

After all, Stepan enjoyed furry little rodents.

# 8

## Cetatea Oraşului
## Night

"I see that you went to town," Cosmin said knowingly to the silently brooding Charles, who sat in one of the study's embroidered chairs, sipping at a glass of red wine. "Mici, I assume? You don't feel like talking. Very well, silence is the best conversation, I always say." Cosmin stared at his son, who shot back a burning look of surliness. "Anyway, it's wonderful to catch up," the vampire continued. "You look well, all things considered."

"No thanks to you," Charles grumbled. He was still angry at the magical knife's failure. Bekhmoaram had said it was enchanted, that it held a special power, and the fact his father hadn't melted into a gory pool of filth and muck soured his mood.

"Technically, it is *all* thanks to me. What are you, five hundred years old? Look at you, a veritable Adonis! I bet you must beat the women away with a stick. You get it from me, you know that?"

"What are you rambling on about?" Charles sneered at his father. "You're a fool."

Cosmin's face twisted into shock. "The manners! Really, Costache, I must have a word with your mother. Surely, you weren't raised to treat beloved family this way, but I must admit that I've been surprised by less. Still, you look exceptionally foolish for a five-hundred-year-old idiot. Is that better?"

Charles shuddered and coughed before finding his voice. "Four hundred and sixty-four years old...Father," he spat in anger. "And three months. My name is Charles now."

Cosmin flashed his son a yellowed, toothy grin. "How fortunate for you!" he said gleefully. "Your age is quite the gift, you should be happy. Terrible decision on the name, though. Costache is noble, being derived from Constantin, while Charles...well, it's a boast that only slaves can appreciate, but you probably knew that," Cosmin added.

Charles grunted, his mouth flexed into an irate frown. Some called his father Cosmin the Wicked, a moniker fraught with meaning, and the hatred ran so deep within Charles that it sat in the pit of his stomach like a sulfurous lump, its reeking stench a constant reminder of his lineage. The dhampir spoke through gritted teeth, choking back a welling anger. "My age is the only damned gift, you son of a bitch, if you want to call it that. The only one, but many curses."

"What curses? I mean, really. What curses? If you're like my other children then you don't age, you don't get sick, it is exceptionally difficult to die...I see only benefits."

"Other children?"

"Oh yes, I'm not a one-trick pony. And it's all true, what I said about your siblings. Well, except for Antoniu, I don't know what his problem was. Sickly or something."

Charles *had* aged well, a testament to his father's undead blood. The dhampir stood tall and straight, at least a head taller than most men, his wiry frame belying an immense strength. An unruly mop of brown hair stood proudly on his scalp, while the skin of his face was taut and tanned and deeply flushed. He didn't have a single wrinkle, not even at the corners of his eyes. A slight scruff of beard had begun to show as Charles hadn't seen a razor for several days, the only blemish on his otherwise perfect face.

"Why did you come here?" Cosmin asked with indifference.

"You know why," Charles whispered, his eyes locked like a viper onto the vampire's every move.

"If you are referencing that odious display of anger when I greeted you at my door? Yes, I suppose I do," Cosmin sighed. "Nevertheless, indulge me. I am curious why you would attempt to murder your loving father."

What could Charles say? Yet the words poured out before he could slap his mouth shut. "You are evil, a pestilence on Earth. Your presence infects the land, every last scrap of your being is dark and terrible and when you are dead, the damnation you've spread will end! I've been infected with it, that's the root of your curse. I'm destined for Hell unless I kill you, and I will. I will kill you. When you die, the curse on my soul will die with you."

"Ah," Cosmin giggled at his son's blooming fury. "You've bought in to the whole *soul* lie too, eh?"

"You deny it, then? It's been written. You're the original vampire, and if I kill you, then…"

"What, you'll get into Heaven?" Cosmin interrupted with a boisterous laugh. "If you believe that, I've got a bridge to sell you."

Charles bolted out of the seat, his muscles flexed and hands clenched tightly. "You are evil, you son of a bitch! You've ruined my life!"

Cosmin rose to his full height, his eyes glowing brightly. "Who are you to judge me?" he hissed. "You, a petulant little prick who was coddled and spoiled his entire existence? I brought you into this world, you bawling little baby, and I'll take you out of it!"

Charles was unmoved by Cosmin's threatening outburst. "Coddled? Spoiled?" he spat, his father's words like a poison in his mouth. "My mother died when I was still a child, and where were you? Skulking in a pile of rocks in some shit-hole backwater. I was shuttled from house to house, at best ignored by my own family. At worst?" He shuddered, remembering the horrendous beatings he had endured at the hands of his cousins. Charles had always been unwanted, even by his own kin, and when the full force of his inhuman strength blossomed his desire for revenge had grown into an insatiable thirst.

Charles didn't pursue that vengeance against his cousins, though. Even though the dhampir hadn't realized it all those years ago, Cosmin had become the target for his wrath. "Among all your other crimes, you steal children in the night. You eat them," he spat accusingly. "Who would do such a thing? It shows the level of your depravity, it reflects the stain that my own soul suffers."

"Oh, sweet baby Jesus, that's rich!" Cosmin doubled over at the waist, hands gripping his desiccated stomach as he broke out in guffaws. "I eat them? Who fed you that lie?"

Charles was taken aback by his father's sudden swings of mood and his incessant denials. "It doesn't matter," he backtracked quickly. Of course, it mattered. It mattered very much. His partisans had whispered the castle's evil amongst themselves, and though the American soldiers didn't understand the foreign tongue, Charles was fluent and had marked every word in his unfailing memory. "What matters is that I'm here. I will kill you, father, and the children and the families will be the beneficiaries of that sacrifice!"

Cosmin plopped back into the ancient chair, fine dust jumping from its embellished silk upholstery while humor danced in his dead eyes. "Stop being so dramatic, you're not going to kill me. I can't fathom why you would want to, anyway. The country people told you about the children, didn't they? Those fools are always bringing their brats up here. I've told them I don't want the little bastards. They whine and knock my things over." The vampire hesitated slightly before continuing. "I sell them to the Roma," he reluctantly admitted.

"What?" Charles blurted, his deep-rooted anger temporarily forgotten.

"The Roma pay a good deal for children. I don't know what they do to them. They say I eat their kids? I should rip out their livers for spreading that rumor," Cosmin grumbled.

"What?" Charles blurted again.

"That word…the yokels use it. Are you going to keep repeating it? Repetition hurts my head."

Charles's mouth snapped shut, temporarily speechless.

"How is your mother?" Cosmin asked.

"Wh…"

"Don't say 'what'!" the vampire interrupted crossly, index finger raised in a rigid warning. "Don't you say it! I hate that word."

"My mother?" Charles asked, failing to disguise his blatant disgust.

"Are you a dimwit?" Cosmin shot back. "Sorry, stupid question. You are obviously a gargantuan dimwit. Yes, your mother. You have one, don't you? I didn't hump a tree, you know."

"Jesus," Charles blasphemed. "I just told you that she died. She's been dead for, what? Over four hundred and fifty years."

"Oh, yes. You did say that, didn't you? I was distracted by your onerous bleating," Cosmin hissed lamely. "I'm not used to having people around here. Idle chit-chat is so brainless, but I suppose it's necessary at times, especially when…you know…you're trying to have fair company."

Charles shuddered.

"What, you think I don't like a little bit of strange from time to time?" Cosmin giggled. "I'm undead, you know, not…dead," he trailed off.

"Knock it off," Charles grumbled.

Cosmin had formed a circle with one left hand while poking his forefinger through the hole. He was leering.

"That's disgusting."

"Oh, come on!" said Cosmin. "Wait, you're not a virgin, are you?"

"After four hundred and sixty years or so? I would hope not," Charles said.

"You are! You are a virgin!" Cosmin clapped happily, taunting his son.

"For the love of God, I'm not a virgin! You didn't exactly raise an altar boy, you know. Not that you raised me at all."

"Who was she? Let me guess, I wouldn't know her. She went to a different school?"

"Oh, grow the fuck up, you shriveled prick."

"Such bitterness! What's your problem with me? First you try to kill me, then you toss about baseless accusations before hurling insults."

"I'm cursed by God because of you!" Charles snapped angrily.

"Yes, you said that, as if it's a good reason for your criminal activity. By the way, no, you're not cursed. You'll be just fine. I should know, I've been on this cursed lump of rock for millennia and not once have I seen God. Or any gods, for that matter. There is no sacred curse. I mean, really, I had never even heard of that fool Jesus Christ until he'd been dead for centuries. Doesn't that seem odd to you?"

"Don't change the subject."

"You aren't cursed, and killing me won't rid yourself of this stupid notion you have about your soul. Let's be honest, you can't kill me anyway. I'm already dead, you see?"

"I'd expect you to say such a thing. There's only one way to find out."

"I've given you a great gift!" Cosmin said defensively as he ticked off all the benefits of being a half-breed. "You are human, more or less, and you can walk around in the sun, maybe enjoy a nice steak...oh, what I wouldn't give for a well marbled, medium-rare ribeye. Not that I can't eat one, but I would probably just shit out a bunch of chewed meat. The body works differently once you've gone through The Change. And I'm not talking about menopause."

"A gift?" Charles spat venomously. "You've given me a gift? Oh yes, immortality, what a generous piece of shit you are. I can never allow myself to love again because everyone around me always dies. It's not worth it!"

"Hum. I guess immortality is a recessive gene?" Cosmin mumbled evasively.

"You're a real son of a bitch," Charles groused.

"Lighten up," Cosmin replied. "What a killjoy. You're not actually immortal. Give it a thousand years or so. You just age very slowly. You'll be blessed to feel the joyous release of death! Even if you destroy me, I wouldn't really die, per se. I don't actually know what would happen, truth be told, but I don't think that I would actually die."

"Because you're already dead," Charles said matter-of-factly.

"Bravo! He was listening. I am dead, more or less. Kind of dead, but not really. I'm undead."

Charles rolled his eyes.

"If you keep doing that, you'll go blind," Cosmin scolded his son.

"That's not what makes you go blind," Charles answered flatly.

"Oh yeah, mister know-it-all? Then what will make you go blind?" Cosmin shot back, his fist pumping back and forth.

"For someone undead for millennia, you are hopelessly immature," Charles said.

"Am not! Remember what I told you when you go blind," Cosmin squealed.

Charles sat back down in the ancient chair. More dust rose from its cushion, tickling his nose so that he erupted in a series of violent sneezes.

"Cover your nose, you barbarian," Cosmin said crossly.

"Afraid you'll get sick?"

"No, I can't get sick. Another gift you've inherited, I'm sure. It's just gross. I don't like snot. The little bastards I sell to the Roma always have streaks of slimy dirt on their faces. I saw one of them lick it off his lip." Cosmin shuddered at the memory. "Tell me again why you came here?" he said, eager to change the subject.

"I already told you."

"Yes, I know, but it was so funny I want to hear it again."

Charles didn't know what to say. He had a mission he believed in, one enshrined in ancient lore, in which his soul would be saved by casting his father's evil from the land. Eradication of undead wickedness? A significant side benefit, for certain. Cosmin, the father he had barely known, this scourge of humanity, sat before him. Charles dreamed about striking out, driving the vampire into his grave, and sealing it forever. It had seemed so easy in the lamplight of the Italian village. If only it were so easy.

Now? He shook his head sadly at the failure of Bekhmoaram's magical knife. "What does a dog do, once it catches the cat?" he asked rhetorically.

Cosmin frowned. "Hump it? I don't know, I don't have a dog. They're disgusting, always licking their filthy butts."

Charles shot an acid look at his father. "No, of course not. It's a metaphor for futility."

"I like metaphors," Cosmin replied happily. "They make a wonderfully destructive impact! Such light, such sound!" He waved his hands in the air, mimicking an explosion.

Charles's lip twisted into a sneer. "Not a meteor! Not a meteor, you damned moron! A metaphor!"

"Eh, whatever," Cosmin shrugged. "Does the dog hump the cat or not?"

Charles frowned at his father. He had spent the past hundred years, almost a quarter of his life, searching for this…this *thing*…and now that he had failed to destroy his father with Bekhmoaram's enchanted blade, how could he see the task through? "I came here to destroy you," he said, a tinge of sadness in his words. "I wanted to see you die, or whatever you want to call it."

"'Whatever I want to call it,' very well put," Cosmin said flippantly. "I would prefer that we get to know each other, perhaps enjoy a Chianti, but then you'd have to watch me piss red wine because the old guts don't work like they used to. Anyway, good luck on your quest. Maybe you'll find a way to strike me down, and that way I can finally sleep. But remember, there are many cats, and just the one dog, and I don't get humped easily. Besides, I have a job for you if you'll take it, although I'm not really certain that you'll be up to the task."

*A job?* Charles thought, his head snapping up in surprise. *What job could this dried-out piece of gristle have for me?* His father, the evil vampire Cosmin, was the task at hand. To Charles, there were no other tasks and he, a half-human dhampir bastard, had dreamt of this moment. He had fantasized about it, had actually felt his hand driving the knife through his father's gristly heart, but now?

Now that he was here, he didn't know what to do. "What job?" Charles asked, immediately regretting the words.

"Never mind, you wouldn't want it anyway," Cosmin said flippantly, and Charles let out a breath of relief.

They sat in silence for a moment, each man taking the measure of the other. Cosmin certainly had the appearance of a vampire, or at least what Charles assumed a vampire would look like. Until lately, and in stark contrast to his father, Charles had been sharply dressed, even after sneaking through the Romanian countryside, avoiding Nazi patrols and various night-time ghouls. His knife was strapped at his waist, a constant reminder of the morning's failure. "I could never join you," he seethed.

Cosmin shrugged, unconcerned. "That's what I figured. So, I assume you'll try to find another way to destroy me now?" he asked politely.

"Does that make you angry?" Charles replied.

Cosmin laughed. "No. No, it doesn't. Why would it?"

"Were you ever human?" Charles asked. "*Really* human?"

"Of course I was! I didn't just crawl out of a swamp, you know. I had parents, just as you have them. Well, I suppose you still have one, anyway. It's another story for another night."

"Do you even remember her?" Charles growled tersely.

Cosmin sneered, his dirty brown teeth flashing between those thin lips. "I forget nothing, son. Yet another gift that I've given you, no doubt." The vampire's pointed ears perked up. "Ah, she was a beauty. So lovely! Raven hair and dark eyes, full lips, and two lovely kittens nestled in her bodice!" Cosmin was cupping his hands over his chest. Charles gave an angry grunt. "And what a derrière she had! Like two fawns snuggling."

"Cosmin," Charles said crossly.

"Sorry. I do wish you'd call me 'Father'. Anyway, she was really quite a sweet woman. And she was very taken with me."

Charles squinted in disbelief at the vampire.

"You think I'm lying?" Cosmin demanded. "Many of the rules of the natural world don't apply to me. Surely, you should know that by now?"

He changed in an eyeblink, so quickly that even Charles's couldn't register the speed of it. Cosmin, a pale and sickly monster just a moment before, was now a young and handsome man who was dressed in a custom-fitted suit instead of rags. His grotesquely hooked nose was now narrow, aquiline, straight and well-formed, his eyes and mouth in perfect proportion to his tanned face. He was very nearly the spitting image of his son. "I can be a cad," the vampire admitted with a shrug.

"No kidding," Charles said irritably.

Cosmin ignored his son. "Do you know who your grandfather is?"

Though his heart began to race, Charles sat stoically. Before meeting Bekhmoaram, he had no real idea about his lineage beyond the ghastly monster who sat across from him, and even Cosmin had been a blank spot on his life's map. His mother had died when he was just a boy, the victim of some plague that had swept through the countryside. Even before her premature death, the woman refused to talk about family. Bekhmoaram's old documents shed some light on that distant past, yet even so Charles wasn't sure what the truth was.

Now the truth sat here, in front of him.

"Your mother's father was none other than…wait for it…wait for it…" Cosmin said tantalizingly. His hands were spread wide with wriggling fingers, his eyes glancing furtively around the room.

"Spit it out, you primitive cretin."

The vampire's grin grew wider. "He was none other than that great and terrible scourge of Turks, Vlad Tepes! He was a wonderful man, truly warm and caring, unless you had the unfortunate luck of being a Turk or a boyar. Or most peasants, I must admit."

Charles stared at his father. *Bekhmoaram was right.*

"Yes, that's right, I can see the elation on your face!" Cosmin continued. "Vladislaus III Drăculea himself!"

Charles involuntarily sucked in a breath at the abrupt confirmation. Vlad Tepes, the feared murderer of innocents and enemies alike and the scourge of Romania's nobles, was truly his grandfather. "They say he was a vampire," Charles said breathlessly.

Cosmin laughed. "Oh, no, not him. I've heard that lie. These country rubes will believe anything. I admit, old Vlad could get carried away at times, but he really wasn't a bad guy. He was truly generous when he wasn't stripping the skin from his enemies' backs."

"Who were your parents?" Charles urged.

"Mine, you ask?" Cosmin grinned widely. "It's a complicated story, but I'll make it simple so your pea-sized brain isn't taxed too much. My father, your grandfather…Gepid royalty, he was! My mother was Attila's cousin. Of Hun fame, that is. I killed them, along with everyone else in the village. That's one reason why I'm like this, although not necessarily in that order. Same old story, you see? A curse was placed upon my head by a witch after my own friends and family betrayed me. Then the old bitch ended up eating her own feet," Cosmin said in satisfaction. "Whoever survived…well, I flayed them," he added simply.

Charles looked as if he would be sick. A footless witch, like the ancient crone in the village. But she said they were in league, she said they had a business arrangement! Why would they work together?

"Let's change the subject, so that you don't spoil my rugs with your vomit," Cosmin offered. "I've told you all about myself. Now it's your turn. Let's start with why you are here, I'm positively dying to learn how you found this place! And leave out that part about destroying me. I just can't see it happening!" he giggled.

"Very well, Father," Charles said after choking back the bile, a touch of sarcasm in his voice. "As if you didn't know I was coming for you…there is a war going on that has engulfed the entire world, and…"

"I am not a moron, son," Cosmin interjected. "I am very aware of what is happening on this cursed planet."

Charles glared at his father.

"Hurry up. You look like one of those slack-jawed yokels in the village, and I don't have all day. Or night, as the case may be."

"That's right, you don't have all day, but rather an eternity. Please don't interrupt me. It's rude."

Cosmin rolled his eyes in mock exasperation at being reprimanded by his son, but he let Charles continue.

"Anyway, the Germans are trying to collect all manner of relics and religious artifacts. Hitler seems to think…knock it off!"

Cosmin had a finger over his upper lip and his right arm stuck rigidly in the air. He dropped both hands sheepishly.

"Hitler…"

"Sieg Heil!" Cosmin shouted as he clicked his heels noisily, dust leaping from the ancient floor's planks.

"Hitlerthinkstherelicswillhelphimwinthewar!" Charles shouted quickly.

Cosmin smiled like an idiot.

"You're a pain in the ass," Charles said.

"Your mother thought so as well. Those legs, though. Addictive, especially when spread."

"Can I tell you my story?" Charles said in frustration.

"Fine," Cosmin replied petulantly. "Apparently you didn't inherit my boundless sense of fun. Make it quick. I have a date."

Charles glared hatefully at his father for a time, but eventually he began again. Though, in truth, he had no desire to talk further. He mulled thoughts around in his head, wondering where to begin. There must be a way to destroy this thing that masqueraded as a human, but what could it be? The knife had failed and Cosmin seemed to enjoy the utmost confidence in his supposed invincibility. "Humans are, I think, generally good," Charles opined.

"Where the hell did that come from?" Cosmin sneered derisively. "Here I am, curious about your adventures, and you pontificate on the redeemability of humanity? Oh, very well," the vampire sighed. "I'll play your game. Humans are foolish. They care more about fornicating and war than anything else. They are also selfish, greedy, and scheming, but despite all of those liberating qualities, they are generally a parasite that infects the planet."

Charles pursed his lips. His father's outbursts were quickly forming a hard callous on the dhampir's psyche. "All of that may be true, but they can also be tender and loving and generous. I have seen a man sacrifice his life to save another."

Cosmin guffawed loudly. "Then he was doubly a fool! I bet you the man he saved ended up being some type of lout, like a drunkard or a layabout or something."

Staring at the floor, Charles had one hand laying lightly in the other, his eyes inspecting the familiar lines in his palm and the comforting shape of his fingers. When he spoke, it was with a quiet solemnity. "I was the one he saved," Charles said distantly. "Even if the bullet wouldn't have killed me, he could not have known. I didn't deserve his sacrifice. Don't you understand? Even after all that, even after his sacrifice, I still would have cut his heart out, if that got me to this place sooner. If his death allowed me to kill you…than that is what I would have done."

"My son, the humanist!" Cosmin said, a smile dancing on his lips.

Charles shrugged. "There are times when I feel more human than I deserve."

Cosmin barked out another laugh. "That's not a humanist, you dolt! Do you even know what humanism is?"

Charles bristled. "Apparently not, oh wisest one," he said, voice thick with sarcasm. "Please, enlighten me."

The vampire sprung from his seat to browse the library's shelves, before he pulled down a book bound in some type of linen. "I have so much time to read, and despite humanity's failings, they do write some decent material."

"Is your vaunted memory failing you? Getting old is a bitch."

"You wound me, son!" Cosmin thumbed through dusty pages. "Philosophy is terribly boring, though. Not humanity's best. I didn't bother reading all the way through. It's so droll it would surely cause me a premature death. Here it is! Humanists believe the inherent goodness and value of human beings, and desire to solve the problems of humankind. Does that sound like you?"

Charles rolled his eyes. "Ask the men who are dead because of me."

"Perhaps stacking bodies by the bushel is one way to solve humanity's problems? It does seem to be the go-to method. Anyway, murder is a minor thing, isn't it? Take, for instance, your stated desire to cause my destruction as a means of ridding the land of...what did you call it? A pestilence of evil? So you were willing to sacrifice your compatriots if it meant bringing about goodness, yes?"

Cosmin's argument made sense to a point, but Charles would not admit it. When he was younger, before the calloused caused by a jaded world built up, maybe he could have been considered a humanist. Not now, though. Now, humans were simply a means to an end. If the vampire's death meant that Charles's soul was lifted into Heaven, then it was worthwhile. "I was willing to sacrifice them to save my soul. The rest of it is a happy accident."

"Well, maybe we can get you back to being a humanist. About that job," Cosmin said. "This world is a mess. What it needs is a strong leader."

"I'm afraid to hear what you're going to say."

The vampire smiled, his sharp teeth framed by red lips. "I'm putting a team together, son. While I would love to be at their head, unfortunately even I suffer from some limitations. Limitations *you* aren't subject to."

Charles squinted at his father. "Go on," he said tentatively. "Though I can't imagine what good can come from your shriveled heart."

"Hold that thought!" Cosmin said with a grin, his finger jabbing the air in Charles's direction. "It is an army, and it needs a general. Someone with the strength to lead, someone who can roam farther than a small handful of miles. Someone who isn't limited to the dark of night. What my army needs is you."

"Fuck you," Charles said simply.

"Don't be so hasty!" his father said before collapsing back into the chair. "The world is filled with war, it positively teems with needless death. We can bring *order* to the world. No more war! You, me, and the Devil's Cohort. That's what we call it. My army, I mean. Kind of a snappy name, don't you think?"

The dhampir snarled at his father. "I'd rather die with a hot poker rammed into my ass, you conniving piece of shit."

Cosmin patted his lap loudly before rising with a sigh. "That was fun, but now I have a date. Be a good son and ensure the fire doesn't burn itself out? Watch the poker, though. That's a lad."

Charles shot his father a hateful squint. "Where are you off to?"

"A gentleman does not kiss and tell," the vampire winked, but Charles noticed something sinister behind his innocent gesture. Cosmin had moved to a window, the heavy felt curtain pulled back. "Out there is a whole world, ripe for the picking. Mankind has lost their way and they need us to guide them. Think about that, Costache. Humanity has become a lost cause, no matter their potential Now they are simply waiting for something better to stand at their head."

Charles frowned. Though he'd been called Costache multiple times since creeping into the valley, the name felt foreign to him. It was yet another sacrifice that had distanced him from his pained childhood. "I haven't been called Costache in years."

"More's the pity. The night grows short and my date waits for me. In the meantime, I suggest you research one Saint Vasile. I am certain he will pique your interest."

"Why would that be?" the dhampir spat at his father. He had no interest in some obscure man venerated by a perpetually corrupt religion, especially if that man came at the recommendation of his evil father.

"Because I have his relic here, and it would be immensely interesting to you, no doubt. Regretfully it was the only piece of the old bastard I could save. Rather embarrassing, really."

"Why would his relic be embarrassing?" Charles demanded, again afraid of what answer the vampire would vomit out.

"Because nobody wanted it! I can understand why, of course. Nobody would want to keep someone's shriveled-up prick on their mantle."

Charles furrowed his brow. He was uncertain if Cosmin had again slipped back into his vulgar jokes. "What did you say?"

"His pecker! The blessed member of the holy Saint Vasile," Cosmin laughed dryly. "I'm sorry," he added. "It's not funny. I know that."

"Surely, you're joking," Charles said disapprovingly.

"I am certainly not! I would never joke about such a solemn subject," Cosmin remarked haughtily, his face having slipped into a serious slate. "Although, truth be told, it was ever an unimpressive thing. Poor Vasile. Perhaps being a priest was an appropriate calling for him, that way he would never have to show any woman his embarrassment."

"You're a horrible creature."

"Don't judge. Now, begone," Cosmin snapped, his hand waving dismissively. "My date awaits and you are a perpetual distraction!"

Creatures were about that night, padding silently through the forest just as Charles slunk from the study with an offended grunt.

Cosmin the Wicked looked out of the study's window, the dark of night no obstacle to his acute vision. A wolf stood still, its face turned up at the castle, and Cosmin saw the beast, their connection instantaneous. He had a message to send, and the bitch wolf would ensure its delivery. The vampire bobbed his head slightly, so it turned and loped off into the forest, a primal servant doing its master's bidding.

And the vampire smiled.

## 9

Valea Întunecată
Night

Her dream had started pleasant enough. Elena was sitting in the grass of the high pasture, her parents working the sheep as a warm summer sun bathed the green expanse in gauzy light. The swaying trees and green grass and blue sky were vivid, and wildflowers dotted the field in impossibly colorful and bright hues of white and pink and purple. She remembered this particular day. Two summers before, a child had died from eating wolf's bane on a dare. The weed would make children sick, yet they still egged each other on, children's dares that carried real dangers of the permanent sort.

Elena enjoyed chewing the bitter ends of wolf's bane. She did it often, and though the stem would numb her lips, she never fell ill. The sun was high, her parents' sheep bleated in the long grass of the high pasture, and a brooding mass of heaped cotton clouds began to crowd the summer sky.

Black shadows fell across bright green grass, a mass of darkness blotting the sheep from Elena's vision. Something shuffled through the forest's trees, a black shadow slinking among black shadows, long and raking fingers guiding its way. She knew it was out there, she wanted to scream in warning and leap from of the grass to run to her parents, but this was a dream and her limbs were leaden. The fear that rose within Elena was real, even if this was a dream, and she tried again to scream a warning to her parents. Gavriel and Ruxana were oblivious to her shrieking pleas, they were ignorant of the ominously roiling clouds, and even though the sheep had disappeared in the growing inkblot of shadow, still they worked the field with hand signals and calls, trying to guide their flock to the pasture's pens.

That slinking figure caught her eye again. It moved silently between tree boles, a whisper of wind promising evil things to come. Elena's cries burst out again, frantic shouts of warning, but still Gavriel and Ruxana continued their task with dogged determination.

Finally, Elena pushed herself up, a supreme effort to move her heavy, lazy limbs. "Mamă, Papă," she cried out tearfully. "Run!" the girl screamed, but then the great inkblot shadow grew to encompass even her parents and the black figure in the trees gave a creaking, guttural laugh. "Cry out," it taunted from across the high pasture, though it was a whispered noise that scorched within her ears. "Cry out, cry out, scream with all your might."

Elena did scream. She screamed in loathing and anger and fear, but her parents were nowhere to be seen. They had disappeared, they had been consumed by the growing evil darkness.

"You are too late, Elena," that slinking figure spoke from across the pasture. "They are mine, now. They are all mine. Soon, you'll be mine too."

"No!" the girl screeched in terror. "Let them go!"

"Why would I do that?" the malevolent whisper floated on the summer breeze. Dark shadows now encompassed the whole of the pasture, each side of its fearsome mass touching the dark boles of the trees. "Why would I let them go? They are my breakfast, my lunch, and my dinner," it cackled.

Terrible warmth was sparked deep within Elena's stomach, a lump of burning bitumen that smoldered with anger. Elena's parents were everything to her. They were her world, her foundation, because she had no siblings, and even though the small town was positively riddled with cousins, Elena had always been treated differently. Children wouldn't play with her when they were young, and in adolescence Elena was often ignored. The Old Families of Valea Întunecată had seemed to sense something strange about the girl, and her whole life was often a lonely affair.

She also sensed that imposed isolation was tinged with reverence. The girl hadn't understood why, but now she knew. Now Elena knew why she had been treated different by everyone. Everyone, that is, except her parents. Gavriel and Ruxana lavished her with love, the only gift they could afford to give. She would not let them be stolen from her so easily. "Let them go," Elena growled, the smoldering heat in her belly flashing into life.

"Come and get them," the skulking silhouette whispered from its black confines. "Come and get them, come and get them, come and get them."

Elena steeled herself as she embraced the anger that fed the fire within. Those heavy leaden legs carried her methodically down the meadow into the heart of dark malevolence, while the greedy clouds swallowed all the light to smother the land from one horizon to the other. It gobbled up the sun so that her world was plunged into the dark of a starless night, and the flames in her stomach grew even hotter, a budding inferno that pushed back against the evil darkness which threatened to consume the Earth.

Screams cut through the black to urge her legs into a run. "Let them go!" the girl screamed, her demands parried by the cackling foil of the prowling thing.

"You're too late!" it cried gleefully. "You're too late, you're too late, *you're too late.*"

Her parents' anguish steeled Elena against the blackness, then the inferno within her screamed out into a thousand stabbing rays of light, the blackness recoiling from her shrieking onslaught. It cowered from the torrent of power coursing from the girl, her light threatening to burn all of existence away, yet the silhouette itself stood against her, exposed from the depths of the fleeing darkness yet still full of evil defiance. It was a massive thing of shadowy malice, tall and skinny with twiggy and raking limbs. Yellow eyes pierced through the glare of her burning power, long fangs salivating gleefully. "You're too late," its said, the taunting voice turned to a hateful snarl.

Gavriel and Ruxana hung from its claws, their bodies torn and bloodied, unrecognizable from the violence.

Elena cried out in anguish, a lifetime of loneliness and torment flaring into a massive explosion of scorching light. The creature laughed as it burst into flames, a howling cackle of victory. Light streamed from the girl, scorching fingers that burned the nightmarish thing into a cinder of nothingness, then the light slowly died as Elena began to cry.

Gray, wan light had replaced the bright sun and black clouds, and Elena kneeled in the blackened remains of the scorched meadow, her body heaving with sobs.

"Why are you sad?" a dry-rattle voice asked. "Why does the dear girl cry?"

She wiped miserable tears from her eyes. "My parents are dead," Elena sobbed at the invisible voice.

It spoke again, the sound of desiccated leaves blowing across an autumnal ground. "Of course they are," it clattered.

"What?" Elena demanded, new tears flowing.

"Of course they are, of course they are! Your parents are dead and they don't even know it yet!" the voice cackled again, and the black form rose from its own ashes, its ember-yellow eyes glowing spitefully from the blackness of cinders. "Of course your parents are dead! You are the reason the world is dying, Elena! Nothing you can do can save them now!"

****

Elena screamed herself awake, her nightshirt soiled with rancid sweat and salty tears. Ruxana was there, soothing her sobbing, disconsolate daughter. The thing's eyes were burned into Elena's memories, they were burned into her very soul.

Gavriel and Ruxana were dead, they just didn't know it yet.

****

Near Valea Întunecată
Night

Hot embers, orange and yellow and red, floated lazily on the rising heat, with new logs beginning to crackle as fire licked at them. Unul Vechi sat in her hovel deep in the swampy fastness, far from the town and the castle. The blade she held in her hand was sharp, sharper than a surgeon's scalpel, its black edge glinting an ominous sheen in the fire's glow.

The crone turned the blade over in her hands, inspecting every faint trace of etching in the obsidian. She was old, incredibly old, this wrinkled sorceress, yet her blade was even older, a relic from a time before even the Grecian gods had come to this land. This blade had been used by things far older than her. Its history stretched back through the mists of time, back to when magic ruled. Real magic, earth magic, not some absent deity of dubious origin and His son, the prophet.

She traced its razor edge with a wrinkled finger, cackling silently, her face stretched grotesquely to reveal purple gums and black stumps, hands turning the blade over and over as she waited for the messenger. She sighed, her smile disappearing under the weight of the moment, and exchanged the archaic blade for a bundle of herbs and swamp grass that she waved through the fire's flames, their scorched tips releasing a fragrant herbal scent. She smiled again and began a low chant, an ancient verse from an ancient time.

It wasn't long before she heard the quiet whine of Cosmin's messenger. She knew it was coming to her, a feeling that passed between the crone and her son, and so she paused her chant to swing the hut's door outward.

The bitch slunk back from her, but Unul Vechi stretched her hand out in a gentle invitation. "Come here, little dear," she said soothingly. "Come to me. What did your father send? Come, little dear, tell me his secrets!"

The wolf, timid and afraid, stepped gingerly forward, unwilling to cross the hut's threshold but equally unwilling to disobey her master. Closing silently, the door latched shut behind the bitch, its lock secured by unseen hands.

"Come, dear, come sit by me," Unul Vechi crooned toothlessly. She must take care not to scare the poor thing. Even though the wolf was under Cosmin's spell, such magicks were fragile as gossamer. Even the slightest misstep would fracture its hold irreparably, so the old one mustered her most soothing tone, petted the beast gently and scratched under its chin. "Come sit by me," she said, shuffling awkwardly on the stumps of her ankles, her feet long since torn from the bottom-most joints of her legs. It was Cosmin's way of reprimanding her, and though a resulting anger burned deep inside of her, such was the cost of gaining so much wisdom! Odin of the Norse had given his eye for second sight, and so Unul Vechi had given her feet for wisdom. The wisdom of the ages, knowledge of eons, and so she bore that cross with good humor, because in taking her feet, he gave her a much larger gift, and for that she was grateful.

"Ah, here we are," Unul Vechi mumbled, sitting heavily in her old, creaking chair. The fire burned brightly now, its bundle of herbs and swamp grass flaring to give off great gouts of smoke, the flames illuminating the stinking hut's meager furnishings. She reached out and whispered to the wolf. "Come closer, my dear. Whisper your master's wishes into my ear."

The bitch whined again and stepped meekly forward. She could practically taste the creature's fear. Unul Vechi leaned forward and caressed the wolf, scratched its furry chin lightly, before moving her hands behind the ears. She murmured again, told the big wolf how good she was, that it was a good servant to the master. She scratched its neck gently, rubbing her ancient, wrinkled hands across its head and ears, and finally the bitch began to wag her tail gently.

"Tell me, my dear, tell me your father's message. Oh, that is nice. He tried to recruit his son, but of course Costache denied him. Oh! He wants to play with a woman. Of course, he does. Can't go a week without his prick making decisions. He will turn her into a vampire? That could be useful…"

And Unul Vechi still talked sweetly, telling the wolf how good she was, that she was a wonderful girl and a loyal servant, even as she drew the obsidian blade across the bitch's neck. She whispered soothingly as the wolf laid down, lifeblood pooling on the floor, its consciousness fleeing painlessly.

Now Unul Vechi had to act quickly, as the divination only worked on the still-living, so she used the same blade to slice open the wolf's stomach cavity, freeing the entrails to slap wetly against the hovel's dirt-packed floor, its coils of viscera snaking in particular patterns and leaving unique trails in the bloody pool. The old one stared coldly, her lips no longer a soothing whisper, but clamped shut tightly, her eyes capturing every detail in the dying wolf's guts.

"What's this?" the hag mumbled, spittle drying to a thin white crust on her lip. Cosmin had sent the messenger, but he was ignorant of the *real* message the bitch-wolf brought to her hovel in the swamp. She didn't care one whit if Costache helped his father. There was another game at play, one that Cosmin was ignorant of. "My grandson and the vessel. Who is the vessel, though? Why won't it tell me who the vessel is?" Her gums worked furiously as she considered the message in the wolf's entrails. The divination was an ancient one, magic that predated the Romans and even the Greeks, one that dated to the time of the Thracians and perhaps even before.

This was the ancient magic, of gods and imps and wood sprites. Just as the knife came from earth magic, so this grisly divination was of that ilk. Unul Vechi had been a goddess once, long ago, and such spells were how she spoke to those she had left behind. Her brothers and sisters would whisper things, and those whispers would be interpreted in the bloody patterns the wolf's viscera left, gory streaks in the dirt. After all, the wolf was the chosen messenger of the gods. Nothing less would do.

"Wait," the crone whispered, her eye stopping on a whorl of blood. Something else, another message from the beyond. She leaned forward to stare at the details in the coagulating gore, how it had looped and splattered. Every pattern, every droplet, held a message.

The pattern is what mattered.

Finally, after a very long time, she sat back in thought. The wolf's entrails told two stories, held two messages, and Unul Vechi was confused. A divination that foretold of life, and one that foretold of death.

She sat still for a long time, the wolf's body growing cold, and considered the prophecies held in the pile of intestines coagulating on her floor, unsure what exactly she had read. It was curious, so it was. Two messages, a life and a death, but who would live, and who would die?

****

Cetatea Orașului
Dawn

Yesterday's high clouds had dropped, thick and full of sullen rain. Charles, who had fallen into deep thought, barely noticed night had retreated from the sun's relentless onslaught. Heavy clouds hung low over the valley, their heavy gray bulk brooding over the mountaintops to gobble up the worst of the day's glaring light.

Violence. That was what Charles had expected when he first stared at the ornately carved door in the ancient keep's wall. A struggle, an encounter reduced to bloody viciousness in which he'd either emerge victorious or die valiantly. He didn't expect the knife to prove impotent, and he certainly did not expect to engage the desiccated bastard in conversation. Cosmin still breathed and the enormity of the task at hand was a great weight that threatened to crush Charles's soul.

The task, though, could not be held at bay. Charles was certain that Cosmin's destruction was the surest way to his own salvation.

*What if I'm beyond saving?* the dhampir thought miserably. *What if my crimes are too much to overcome? What if I'm too much like my father?*

This last thought caused despair to rise in his gorge. Centuries of walking the Earth had led Charles to this point, but what if it was all for naught?

Lip curled into a snarl, Charles shook his head. *At least I would have revenge for the hell he's put me through.*

A hell Cosmin had put him through, simply by breeding his son into existence. No matter what violence and mayhem the vampire had thrust onto an unsuspecting world, in Charles's eyes, siring his son was his father's greatest crime.

How would he do it, though? The knife had failed, but there must be a way. Through all the long years of his life, Charles had sought out the clues that would lead him to Cosmin.

He had also sought out those obscure clues that would lead to the vampire's destruction.

Much of it he had immediately discarded as bullshit. Holy water? *Laughable,* Charles thought. *If God really was all-powerful, then He would have struck down Cosmin long ago.* Never mind that holy water was the leftovers from baptizing bawling, snotty children. Even if the water held some mystical ability, how could it possibly be enough to cause the vampire to wither away to nothingness?

He'd read about wooden stakes, which had suddenly burst into lore only a few hundred years before. Not exactly ancient wisdom, that. As a concept, the wooden stake may help. Oak and holly were considered to have some type of godly power, at least among the ancient Celts.

*Maybe if I combined the holy bathwater and a stick of holly?* Charles rubbed his chin. *It may just work. Worth a try, anyway.*

All he needed was the holy water, a bit of wood, and his father's body.

Where *did* that bastard slink off to during the day, anyway?

*That son of a bitch said there were fifteen rooms in the castle*, Charles thought. *Not including the shitter.* His face pinched with thought. "Or was it sixteen? I've only seen a handful of them," he grumbled audibly. He had nothing better to do than investigate the decaying pile of stones. All the lore Charles had been privy to claimed vampires returned to their graves as the sun rose, but where would Cosmin have been buried? It could be anywhere.

"The crypt," Charles realized, his eyes narrowed into a suspicious squint. He looked up at the study's ornately carved ceiling panels. "You can't stop me now! You hear me, Cosmin? You can't stop me, you rotten old fucker!"

Cosmin had only shown Charles a handful of rooms, but he knew there was an entire floor above to explore, and there were certainly rooms beneath his feet. Charles had a sneaking suspicion that his father was holding out on the castle's secrets. From the outside, the ruined fortress had seemed immense, even if only a tiny portion of it had been left habitable. Charles had a lifetime of military experience, though, starting when he was legitimately a young man. These fortresses were riddled with catacombs, full of hidden chambers and bricked-off accesses, and the dhampir began his exploration by studying the main floor. "No doubt there are twice as many rooms as he admits," Charles groused silently. "Even if I have to explore all of them, I will find Cosmin."

Doors studded the hallway, a half dozen of them, all hand-carved with the same dragons and demons and imps. They hid myriad private chambers, mostly, save for the kitchen and butlery, neither of which seemed to be used save for a small stock of food. A thin film of dust, the same dust that coated every other surface in the castle, had covered the workplaces of the kitchen. Charles noticed that the floors had been swept recently, that everything was tidily kept even with the incessant dust. Irritatingly tidy, even.

Charles returned to the hallway and found a circular stairwell set into the castle's stone wall. It was a cramped stair, the narrow treads treacherous to the inside of the twisting left-hand rise, and Charles had to pick his way up carefully to avoid the dangers of a missed step. Centuries of hobnailed boots had worn the sandstone treads until a treacherous depression had formed, and Charles wondered what evil things these stairs and walls had witnessed over their long lives. Up he went, even though the stair also descended the other way into the blackness of a lower level that had no doubt been carved directly into the promontory's bedrock.

Much like the main floor, the second level was a long hallway whose walls bristled with a half-dozen doors. It was peculiar in its construction, though, as the passage was not flat. The floor wasn't even close to flat, it dipped and rose as the hall stretched off into a somber darkness kept at bay by flickering sconces. Here, as on the main floor of the castle, the doors hid bedrooms and sitting rooms and a library. No secrets seemed to be hiding here. Nothing insidious or terrible, not even a vampire.

Descending on the narrow stairwell, Charles passed the main floor into the heavy darkness below. Breathing became noticeably more difficult. The air here was heavy with moisture and it was more chilly than the living areas above, so that the walls and floor were slick and clammy. He had absconded with an oil lamp to light the way, its flame giving off greasy, sooty smoke, and as the underworld's darkness receded, Charles saw the walls had rectangular holes carved into the living stone, rock-cut tombs filled with ancient bones.

He had found the castle's crypt.

It made sense, in a sick way. What better place to hide his father's grave than some obscure crypt? He could slink off into a dark place ridden with bones and ghosts and all manner of insects, the perfect complement to Cosmin's foul soul.

Not all the graves were open holes. Many had been blocked off with stone veneers, their faces carved with armorials and initials, some even with dates. Charles shivered, though from temperature or anticipation or even nervousness, he couldn't tell. *Quivering like a damn baby*, he chastised himself. Holding the lamp close to each wall in turn, he ran his fingers between the stone blocks, feeling for cracks and crevices. He worked down the hall, slowly moving along the crypt's length, paying attention to the tiniest detail but finding nothing out of place. Frowning, he next inspected the individual tombs, inspecting the carvings that denoted the last resting places of their eternal occupants. He dismissed those that had been left open to be gawked at, whose rude recesses exposed mortal remains. Instead Charles focused on those that had been sealed, hoping that one would have obvious marking betraying his father's tomb. Most of them contained knights and dames and nobles of various rank whose names mostly unfamiliar to Charles.

*This one is curious*, Charles thought, *it's different from the others.* And it was indeed different, vastly different. The sealing block was larger, at least twice as big as the others, and there was an intricately detailed coat of arms etched into the face of the stone. The arms consisted of a shield, with three fish in the first and third quadrants, an axe in the second and fourth quadrants. A double-headed eagle crowned the shield, its clawed feet grasping a sheaf of arrows and a sword. Underneath the arms were the letters *V D*, and underneath those, the roman numeral *III*. Crucifixes, some new, some old, but one ancient, were hung about the tomb's sealing block.

Charles laid his palm against the coat of arms only to recoil quickly from the freezing cold stone. "Shit!" he spat, his hand aching from the cold. Creeping fear gripped Charles's mind, a dreadful feeling of trespass, and then he backed away from the tomb, turned and ran, his discarded oil lamp shattering on the stone floor. Light flared from the spilled oil to illuminate the chamber as Charles fled, but then darkness abruptly set in as the spreading fire was extinguished by unseen hands.

## 10

Valea Intunecata
Morning

Elena's eyes were dark and puffy with pooling blood, the night terror so vivid and terrible that any more sleep had mercifully stayed away, and she could hear mumbling from the kitchen where Gavriel and Ruxana worried about their daughter. She was mired in despair. The image of her parents dangling from the creature's limbs had shocked the girl into the depths of a hideous grief. And then there was the dead girl and the mysterious priest, what purpose did they serve other than to torment Elena with dubious gifts of power?

And Charles, or Costache, or whatever his name was. He was supposed to fix some sword and together they would destroy evil. They were intertwined, according to some twisted logic, like their souls had been joined or something. *Only with each other will you be victorious,* the mysterious voice in the gray-black place had said. *Separately, your defeat will be inevitable, and many millions would suffer from your failure.* Millions of lives were at stake, and Elena didn't even know what she was supposed to be doing.

Adina said that Elena was God's chosen one, but instead she felt madness stalking her.

She had reached out to Charles before, though, their thoughts connecting from far away. She had seen him, sitting in a chair and holding a glass of wine. They had talked, even. Maybe she could do it again?

Elena closed her aching eyes, willing the debilitating terror away from her mind. She pictured his brown hair and black eyes and flushed face, she imagined his square chin and bristly, unshaven cheeks. "Charles, are you there?" she asked quietly. "Charles, it's Elena. I need you," the girl said, her voice catching in the raggedness of her throat. "Help me."

Nothing.

A sigh slid from her lips, her concentration on her features sharpening. Squeezing her eyes shut, forcing all of her thoughts on the strange man, she called out to him again. "Charles!" she seethed. "Where are you?"

"Stop yelling," his voice said, clear as rain-cleansed air.

She sighed in relief. "Where are you?"

"Where I always am. At the castle, trying to find that dried-up piece of gristle who calls me 'son'."

"We need to destroy him!" she said urgently.

"What do you think I'm doing?"

Elena ignored his gruffness. "My night terrors are getting worse. I think that means the evil is growing stronger! Whatever you are doing, the voice said we have to do it together."

"Yeah, I was there. The voice wasn't too helpful, though, was it? How exactly are we supposed to destroy Cosmin?"

"You have to mend the sword in the forge! Assemble the pieces of the Sword of Kizağan and restart the forge that is within you!"

"I'll get right on that. Oh, right, where is the sword again? That's right, we don't know. Even if we did have the pieces, what exactly does 'restart the forge mean'?

Meanwhile I nearly froze my hand off on some tomb and now I'm getting rained on."

Elena swallowed back anger. She didn't know where the sword's pieces were hidden, she didn't know what it meant to restart the forge. How could she? Adina was the one who had said it. "Maybe Adina knows," Elena said.

"Who?"

"Adina, the dead girl."

"Oh, that's right. Jesus Christ, this just keeps getting weirder."

"I have to go find Adina. She will tell me more!" Elena opened her eyes, the image of Charles dissolving from her mind. Could she do the same trick to summon the dead girl?

Elena didn't know, but she had to try.

****

Cetatea Orașului<br>The same day

Rain was falling in great wet gobs, the sullen gray light washing out all the color of the trees and grasses and weeds that pockmarked the grounds about the castle. Charles's palm still burned with the cold that had radiated from the tomb's frigid stone, and unsure if that had been a trick of Cosmin's, the dhampir had retreated outside to let the cleansing rain rid him of the keep's ghosts, and then Elena had invaded his mind to annoy him further. How the hell would he find out where this alleged sword is?

Charles's brown hair was plastered to his scalp as he surveyed the face of Cetatea Oraşului. Windows dotted the wall's stone façade. Judging by interruptions to the stone courses, the window openings had been cut in long after the castle had been built, a concession of convenience inflicted on the ancient fortress. They hadn't been constructed with uniformity, either, at least not above the main floor. The higher windows seemed to be peppered across the fortress' face as if they had been haphazardly punched through stone so that it appeared there may be a third level.

Inside, though, Charles hadn't been able to find any sort of stairwell that would climb that high. Hidden rooms at the highest level of the castle would be the perfect resting place for Cosmin, and if there was a third level to the citadel he would have to find a way in. How could he gain access, though? The keep's stone façade was smooth, the blocks fit so tightly that even those cracks where mortar had fallen away were too tight for the thinnest finger to grip. It was a fortress, after all, a citadel designed to withstand assault from its earliest days, and absent a siege engine, Charles would have to be cunning to find a way into the topmost level if it even existed.

Hair stood up on Charles' neck, tiny fibers tingling in warning. Someone was out there, watching him from the forest's edge. He had been preoccupied with inspecting the castle's construction, and he had been stalked so that his sixth sense raised an internal alarm. Standing still, loose and relaxed, Charles surreptitiously focused on his peripheral vision to pick out any detail in the forest that wasn't natural. He wasn't necessarily afraid. Up until the last two days, very few things had scared him in his long lifetime, but he had learned to be prudent and heed these tingling sensations. Charles knew that he was mortal, he knew that he was decidedly *not* indestructible, and he was determined to destroy his father before succumbing to death himself.

Charles wasn't immortal, but he *was* formidable, and so he was not afraid.

Yet something was out there, watching him. And waiting.

Wandering back and forth in front of the fortress, the dhampir ran his fingers along old stonework as he stole clandestine glances towards the darkest undergrowth. The forest teemed with life, from the lowest insect to the greatest predators, and Charles knew they all served his father. Whatever was watching him, it wasn't one of Cosmin's servants. He was certain of that. Cosmin's servants were survivors, they slunk around nearly invisible, but he felt this thing's eyes burning into the back of his head. It wasn't as cunning as the forest creatures, so it lay there, somewhere in the forest, watching him. His hand dropped down to his knife, secure in its leather sheath. Slowly, so slowly as to be nearly imperceptible, he began to slide the knife up, freeing it from leather. Turning slightly to shield the knife from his pursuer's view, he pretended to inspect some new detail in the citadel's wall, the final few inches of the knife freed.

Then Charles spun and drew back his arm, reflexes quicker than a wildcat, and whipped his hand forward to send the knife hurtling through the air in a single, smooth motion.

Stalking silently through the fallen leaves and twigs and other detritus of the forest floor, the lynx picked its way unseen and unheard towards her hidden prey. It lay among ferns and low pine boughs, expertly hidden but still apparent to the keenest of her senses. Even as the master slept in his grave, he had given the big cat direction, had guided her to this place. The master's son was lurking around the big stone monstrosity that scarred her forest, but the lynx knew better than to defy the master. So she slunk and crept and padded silently towards her prey, because that is what the master demanded.

She caught his scent. Rain was falling to wash away most odors, the soft patter of drops on leaves and branches obscuring all but the most obvious of sounds, but her prey had a distinctive scent that guided the lynx. The cat stopped suddenly, one foot cocked in mid-step. She tensed, the tip of her tail flicking with anticipation, then exploded silently from the forest floor.

Hurtling through the air with teeth bared, the big cat's prey was nestled among the ferns at the forest's edge, invisible and oblivious to the danger. She couldn't see him, but she could smell him and anticipated the tang of his blood, her claws and teeth ready to strike the killing blow. His would be a quick death, and so the master would reward her, but he flinched slightly and then her world exploded in pain and darkness.

Cold iron struck, biting deep into her eye socket, to puncture and tear through muscle and fat and bone, its tip penetrating far into her brain.

She collided with her prey, a lifeless mass thumping heavily into the man as he yelped in shock. A split second, just an eyeblink, and he recovered, jumped from his hiding spot to sprint through the forest's underbrush, tree limbs tearing at his clothing, and Charles saw a mass of black hair and a scraggle of black beard framing a hard, scarred face.

Charles spat angrily at the fleeing figure. Obviously, he wasn't the only one interested in the castle, and now he would have to find out who his stalker was, and what he wanted. If he was going to destroy Cosmin, then he would have to be more careful.

****

The tavern was nearly empty save for the barman, which suited Charles fine as he did not want to strike up meaningless conversation with hostile locals. Whoever was stalking him wasn't a native of this valley, the man's foreign clothes were indication enough of that fact. If the man wasn't a local, then he would probably end up at the only tavern in this little village. Even if his arrival took hours, Charles had time to waste. It's not like his father was going anywhere.

He took a seat at a small table in a dark corner and brooded. Like most of the buildings in town, the tavern was old, with floor cobbles worn smooth, rafters darkened from centuries of sooty hearth-fires, and walls layered in yellowing whitewash. It was nondescript and quiet and, most importantly, a refuge Charles could use to gather his thoughts as he waited. Just a few days prior, he was confident and poised, excited even, at the prospect of facing his vampiric father. Cosmin was the reason for

Charles's misery. He was also a scourge of humanity, and all the dhampir had wanted was to carve the vampire's wretched heart from his body.

Now? Now he didn't know what to do. The knife had failed, he couldn't even find Cosmin's resting place, he was haunted by a seemingly long-dead witch of the dark arts, and now someone had been stalking him. If the stranger didn't frequent the tavern, then the only hope Charles had left was that the hidden chambers of Cetatea Orașului held secrets that would allow him to complete his mission.

Even so, his own arrogance and failure had led him to the tavern to grasp at straws, and he burned with shame.

"You're new here," the tavernkeeper's gruff voice pointed out, pulling Charles from his thoughts. "Are you from the castle?"

He nodded silently.

"Țuică? Or beer?"

It had been centuries since Charles had țuică, the ubiquitous Romanian plum brandy. It had burned the last time he had it, burned all the way down his throat and deep into the pit of his stomach. Burned like the sulfur and brimstone he was certain awaited him should he fail in his quest to destroy the curse of his father, the curse that fate had laid upon his soul, the witch's remonstrations notwithstanding.

"I have no money."

The barman shrugged. "You can pay later."

"Țuică then, please," Charles said, his head dipping in thanks. "And a beer."

"Your knife," the barman said, a tilt of the head indicating Charles's sheathed blade. "It's old, I like it. Big and heavy, like a proper knife should be." He nodded approval and wandered off, returning before long. "Mind yourself. We make the țuică strong, but the beer is weak as piss."

"Are you sure it isn't piss?" Charles joked.

"What did you say?" the barkeeper asked gruffly.

"Nothing…thank you," Charles responded sheepishly. He wasn't afraid of the barman. Indeed, his lanky frame was stronger than three of these stocky barmen, but prudence took precedence. Bar fights would attract the sullen wrath of angry locals and, besides, he still had a mission to fulfill.

The slow burn of țuică slid down Charles's throat, its fire causing long-ignored memories from his younger days to come flooding back. Charles was born in Romania, yet he mostly grew up in Bavaria before returning to his homeland when war with the Ottoman Turks had flared again.

Charles pondered the players in this terrible game. The witch, or whatever she was, was tied in to it all somehow. Then there was the girl in the market, Elena, and now the strangely wild man with unkempt black hair who was stalking him at his father's castle. Cosmin himself was at the center of the spider's web of characters. *What is the connection?*

Ungreased creaking hinges from the tavern's door made Charles look up involuntarily, and a grimace twisted his face as the wild man from the woods stepped into the dark room. He looked even wilder now, with bits of brown leaves clinging to his black hair and his patched trousers soiled with dirt and debris. For a moment Charles thought he would flee back through the door, but then his flat, scarred face hardened and he approached the table cautiously.

With a foot, Charles kicked a chair from the table so that it slid wide, a curt invitation to the strange man, who hesitated slightly, gave a terse nod, then sat tensely as a cautious predator would. "I am Stepan," he said in poor Romanian, though his thick and guttural voice had an accent so dense and alien that it took a long moment to decipher its butchery of the native dialect. He appeared to be a Slav, with his flat, meaty face and blocky features.

Charles furrowed his brow. This was a large man, with thick arms and a broad chest. His face reminded Charles of a slab of pork, pasty and meaty with a squat, flattened nose and a large, bristly mustache and beard. His eyebrows, like his hair and beard, were black and wild, unkempt and dirty, and yet he moved with a graceful agility.

This man was dangerous.

Charles leaned back in his chair and sipped again at the glass, its liquid fire settling deep into his stomach. "Why were you following me?" he demanded, his voice as sharp as flint.

"Hunter," the man replied, a meaty paw patting his chest. "A dead thing of hunt. Apologize, I am not good at Romanian language too much," he said sheepishly.

"Français?" Charles asked in French.

"No," the Russian answered in Romanian.

"Deutsch?" Charles asked in German.

"Ja!" The Russian answered happily, so Charles switched seamlessly to German.

"I am Charles," he said flatly. "Why were you watching me at the castle?"

"I am looking for something, but apparently I am not that good at looking," Stepan answered in feigned humility.

"Your accent," Charles observed. "You are Russian, but you're not from Moscow or Kyiv, are you? The inflection sounds more…more southern."

"Cossack," Stepan answered proudly, his German a vast improvement over his basic Romanian. "My family is very well known. I should say, *was* very well known. We served the Czar with distinction for many, many years, until the Bolsheviks murdered them." He spat at the mention of the Russian Marxists. "Savages," Stepan added as an after-thought.

"That must have been terrible," Charles remarked with disinterest.

"We had to flee," Stepan answered, his hands held wide. "I was just a young boy. We went to Germany. Very peculiar. We met a man there who taught us to hunt."

"Oh? Was there a bounty on Jews at the time?"

Stepan frowned at the veiled insult. "No. The man who taught us was Jewish. He was a very good man. What is happening in Germany…it is a bad thing."

Charles nodded. "You are putting that mildly. I know a Jewish man in Germany. At least, I knew him. We met briefly, but I liked him. If he is still alive, I pray he left that God-forsaken country before the fucking Nazis got hold of him."

"Yes," Stepan said. "Bekhmoaram was able to leave Germany, but his heart stopped and now he is dead."

"Wait, what did you say?" Charles demanded, his brow furrowed and teeth clenched. "You know Bekhmoaram?"

"Of course I know the Rabbi. How do you think I found you?" Stepan's gaze narrowed, his muscles tense as a predator's. "The community of hunters is very small. It is an intimate circle and Bekhmoaram was at the center of it all. Unfortunately, he has passed on to a better place, but without the Rabbi's knowledge we would be losing the war. He taught many hunters the necessary skills."

"Why would he have told you about me?" Charles's hands were knuckled into fists. However briefly they had known each other, Charles had counted Bekhmoaram as an honorable man, one that could even have become a friend under the right circumstances. The Rabbi had given him valuable knowledge, and Charles wondered why he would have betrayed the dhampir.

"He was afraid you would fail in your quest," Stepan said flatly.

"Bekhmoaram told me how to kill Cosmin!"

"Cosmin the Wicked cannot be killed. He is already dead."

"You know what I mean," Charles grumbled.

Stepan leaned back. "Bekhmoaram was a wise man who was a forward-thinker. If you fail, then there would need to be another to take your place."

"If I can't destroy Cosmin then nobody can."

"I think you mistake my meaning," Stepan said airily. "Don't you see the bigger game? Your father...and yes, I know who you are...your father needs you. Failure takes many forms. In your case, failure could be in not destroying Cosmin, yet it could also be joining him at his side." The Cossack tapped the tabletop with a thick finger. "I know who your father is. He is evil, he is undead, and my family has been sworn to his destruction." He leaned back, his eyes locked on Charles to hold the dhampir in a steely gaze. "We have been sworn to the destruction of every damned creature he has brought to this world. Nothing can stop me. It is a holy quest, and I will not fail."

Charles growled at the Cossack, animalistic and guttural, and Stepan answered in kind. The dhampir immediately disliked this man. Charles was an alpha dog, and so was this Cossack, and just as two alphas would inevitably fight, these men were destined to clash, he could feel it.

Ignorant of the tension, the barkeeper interrupted them with loudly clinking glasses held in his hands. "Did you see his knife?" he asked in country Romanian.

The Cossack shook his head, the tension broken by the barman's voice. "His knife? His knife, nobody cares," he said in crude Romanian.

"It's a fantastic knife," the barkeeper insisted. "It's large, huge. Have you seen it?"

"Mind your own," Charles snapped irritably.

"But it's a fine knife!"

"I have many knives," the Cossack said. "Many. Who asks me about them? No one. A knife it is, who cares?"

The barkeeper screwed his lip into an ugly smile, his thick sausage-lips framed by the black mustache draped like a monstrous caterpillar across his animated face.

"Such a fine knife, though! It's large. Huge, almost a sword."

Stepan shrugged, thick fingers deftly rolling tobacco into a cigarette. "It's just a knife," he said, tongue swiping wetly across his lips as he sealed the paper's edge. "I have many."

"It's not a sword," Charles groused. "It's just a knife."

"I like humility," the barkeeper replied with satisfaction. "But please, don't be so humble. It's a beautiful knife, majestic even."

"Shut up," the Cossack said curtly. "That's not a knife, not if it's that big."

"It's just a knife!" Charles insisted.

"No!" the barkeeper said. "It is not! I know knives, and this one is big and unique." He held his hands apart, demonstrating the size of Charles's knife. "This big! Like, like…"

"Like what?" the Cossack said with growing annoyance.

"Like a knife," Charles said matter-of-factly.

"Like a horse's pulă!" the barkeeper said proudly.

"A what?" Stepan gawped.

"A cock," Charles said with disgust.

"Not just a cock, the massive cock of a stallion! Have you ever seen such a horse's pulă? They are immense and long, grotesque even," the barkeeper insisted.

"The people in this town…are worrying to me," the Cossack said.

"What's your name?" Charles asked the barkeeper.

"He is Tomas," Stepan said. "I used to like him. Now? Eh, maybe not so much."

"I am called Tomas, after my father, and my father's father," the man replied, his words glowing with absurd pride. "Show him your knife!"

Charles shook his head. Plainly the man would not go away until Charles pulled out the blade. "I do hope you're talking about the massive knife at my side, and not the one in my pants."

"What?" the barkeeper asked with a hint of confusion. "You have another one in your pants?"

"Why all of this talk about cocks?" the Cossack said with distaste.

"Nothing," Charles sighed, his eyes switching to Stepan. "All this over a knife," he said as he slid the blade from its sheath and laid it on the table. "You never thanked me, by the way. For killing the lynx."

"You saved him from a lynx?" Tomas asked with a hint of concern, then he abruptly beamed. "Look! I didn't lie!" the barkeeper said proudly. "Massive, like a horse's pulă!"

"I am uncomfortable talking about this," Stepan said, though his eyes switched abruptly to the knife in front of them.

Charles sighed. "Listen, Tomas, I was talking to my new friend here when you started to run off about horse cocks. Meanwhile, my glass is empty. So why don't you get some țuică, refill my glass, and fuck off with your horse cocks?"

The barkeeper stamped off, huffing furiously, Charles watching his retreat in smug satisfaction, then turned to the man next to him.

Still as a statue, fingers gripping the table's edge, Stepan's eyes were fixed rigidly on the blade. He studied its every curve, the intricate filigree and scrimshawed ivory handle and its perfectly fitted brasses. It was beautiful, a true work of deadly art, but that isn't what drew his attention. "Where did you get that blade?" the Cossack asked in German.

"A friend," Charles answered evasively. Bekhmoaram told Charles that the knife held a special power, though he still was unsure of its extent. Stepan's interest made him pause, though.

"Please, I must hold it."

"No," Charles said stiffly.

"Please!" Stepan insisted, his face twisting into an anguished rictus. "This is very important to me."

"Why?" Charles quizzed him.

"Because it just is." The Cossack's eyes had become heavy with tears, the man clearly overwhelmed by whatever this knife represented.

Charles frowned. Stepan was closer to the door than himself. If Charles handed over the blade and the Cossack tried to run, it would be difficult to stop him from fleeing the tavern. Not that Charles was terribly worried, because he was strong and fast and would surely chase down Stepan, but it would cause a scene within the village, which would be horribly unacceptable. "Maybe," he said cautiously. "How do I know you won't run?"

"I give you my word."

"Easily broken."

Stepan bristled, his eyes brimming with tears. "You affront my honor!"

A brief smile curled Charles's lip. "I don't know you. Your honor is foreign to me."

"How can I prove my faithfulness?"

Charles didn't want the Cossack to abscond with his knife. Even if it hadn't struck down Cosmin, the blade still held an undeniable power. The rotting things in the forest attested to that fact.

"Please," Stepan urged. "I need to hold it!"

Charles shrugged with an unconcerned air, though his chest was taut with tension. "I will let you briefly touch the knife, but it will be on my terms." He hesitated for a second, then slid the knife across the tavern's table. Stepan held his breath as he began to handle the knife, his finger sliding up the thick pale-yellow bone handle. It was distinctive and ornate, with the tail of the handle curving back on itself and fanciful scrimshaw of demons dancing along its length. Charles's hand instinctively shot out to grasp hold of it. "That's enough, Stepan. The Jew gave it to me. It's mine."

Stepan's jaw hung low, his face incredulous as he stood. "Bekhmoaram? That's impossible, he would never give you such a powerful relic. That knife was supposed to be a legend, a folktale."

Charles stood as well, his hand gripping the knife's handle, ready to wield the blade if Stepan attacked, vowing that this mad Russian would not catch him unawares. "Bekhmoaram was a good man. He gave me this knife because he knew it would help me."

Stepan looked at him warily, showing his hands in a gesture of goodwill. "You don't understand its power," he said. "All the other relics are toys, but the knife? The knife! It's a lost fragment of Kizağan's sword, the one that slew the monsters!"

Charles stopped, his face warped into a questioning glare. "What the hell are you talking about?" This was the third time in the past two days that he'd heard the strange name.

"Kizağan! The Turk before there were Turks! He was a myth, a god, his sword wasn't real, but you have a piece of it! That knife has the power of the gods living within it. Please, Charles, sit! Look, more țuică." He had picked up a bottle of plum liquor and gestured with Charles's empty glass, the tears brimming anew. "Just please sit and talk with me," he begged again.

Charles glanced around the room, any shred of trust long since evaporated. The barman looked down, ignoring his two patrons. He probably didn't speak German, but Charles couldn't be sure.

"Why should I?" he growled, his hand holding the knife, tensed arm outstretched defensively.

Stepan scowled. "Because it may be the only way to save us all," he said with slumped shoulder. "Has your father told you his secret?"

"That depends. Which secret are you referring to?"

"The only one that matters!" Stepan snapped. "All of his evil acts stem from what he is, what he has become."

"How he became…" Charles squinted.

"A strigoi," Stepan said to Charles. "The same. He is a plague upon the land, but that is no secret. What he was and what he has become, it may be the very key to his downfall. And he holds that secret close."

"He's not a strigoi," Charles shook his head. "He's a vampire. You know how he became a vampire? He hasn't told me. The bastard won't shut up about everyone else, but he refuses to talk about...that."

"Strigoi and vampires are the same thing!" Stepan insisted.

"No, they aren't. That is one thing I'm sure of."

"I shall tell you what I know," Stepan sniffled through purple eyelids.

"I know there was something about a girl, and he was sentenced to death, that a witch did something to him."

"Did he say that she ate her own feet?"

"Cosmin said he fed her own feet to her."

Stepan shuddered. "I had heard that. Despicable. There is a reason for everything he does."

"What do you know?" Charles asked after a slight hesitation.

Stepan sat back in his chair, face shaded in deep thought, eyes staring stiffly at the iron blade still gripped in Charles's hand. The tumbler of țuică rolled between his fingers absentmindedly. Charles nearly repeated his question, he had opened his mouth to speak again, but Stepan began to talk.

"What I know are stories that had been handed down through the generations. I don't know what is real, I don't know what is not. Cosmin's origins lay far back in the mists of time. He may have been born sometime after Rome burned, or maybe before. No one knows for sure. The stories...the stories may be just that, but a truth rings through them. As the saying goes, where there is smoke, a fire is sure to follow."

"What does that have to do with Cosmin?"

"It is not meant to be taken literally, Charles."

"No, of course not. Please, continue."

"Anyway, as I said, the stories are the smoke, and the truth is a smoldering fire. So I had not heard about the girl, but indeed, Cosmin…before he became a monstrous seed of Satan…did something very bad. Very bad, indeed, so bad that his own father had sentenced him to death."

"His own father?" Charles was aghast.

"Yes, your grandfather. The stories don't say what it was that Cosmin had done, but it surely must have been horrendous. His sentence was carried out quickly. It has been said that the very day he was accused, he was handed over to the witch."

"Or sorceress."

"What is the difference?"

"Between a witch and a sorceress? Maybe the types of spells they cast. Just a thought."

"Very probable."

"Indeed."

"As I was saying," Stepan said, another slug of țuică quickly downed.

"Yes, you were saying."

"So, Cosmin was given to her and she worked her magic over him. And it is said that, at the point of death, when his spirit should have fled to Hell, for as a pagan he surely would not be admitted to the delights of a Christian Heaven, he was regurgitated from the black pit, rejected by Satan. His eternal penance would be to stalk the land, a cursed abomination whose sole task was to torment the living sinners."

"Okay," Charles said.

Stepan blinked.

"That's it?"

The Cossack tilted his head slightly. "As I said, he is a strigoi. You want more?"

"He's a vampire, not a strigoi. There has to be something else. I already knew that a witch cursed him."

"But Satan spat him out!"

"What else would Satan do? You're fucking kidding me, right? Stepan? You're joking?"

The Cossack leaned back, hands spread wide again. "What else would you like to hear? Cosmin is over one thousand and five hundred years old. There are not exactly any books written about his meager life before the witch cursed him."

"You've told me nothing, yet you said it was the key to his downfall."

"Indeed! He is Satan's reject, so the power of God will destroy him."

"Oh, is that so? How, Stepan? How will the power of God destroy Cosmin?"

The Cossack pointed an accusing finger at Charles. "Do not blaspheme Him! He is the supreme being, the father of everything. His power is boundless."

"Oh yeah? How do you know God is even a man? Anyway, the monster is here, stalking sinners and innocent alike. God hasn't done anything to rid him of the world. Maybe He doesn't have the power to destroy Cosmin!"

"You mock God!"

"I don't mock God. I don't believe he gives a rat-fuck about us, but I certainly don't mock him."

"Surely, God has provided the tools to destroy this scourge of evil. Holy water or a crucifix? A saint's relics?"

Charles frowned. "I drove that knife right into the bastard's shriveled heart. You really think the holiest water I can find will do anything?" He sensed the Cossack was a true and faithful believer, yet Stepan was still naïve in some ways.

"Saint Vasile!" the Cossack blurted out, his hand forming a cross over his forehead.

The dhampir sat back, his face twisted with shock. This is the second time he had heard of the mysterious Saint Vasile since he had come to this valley, the first being Cosmin's offhand comment the night before. "What about Saint Vasile?"

"It is said that Saint Vasile is the patron saint of sinners and of the damned."

"More fool, him."

"Before he was a saint, he was Father Vasile."

"Isn't that kind of a prerequisite to become a saint?"

"No, it's not. Don't speak foolish words. Father Vasile was Cosmin's chaplain."

"There were no Christians around this place back when Cosmin was alive, right? He's over fifteen hundred years old!"

"Not Cosmin the man, Vasile was Cosmin the Wicked's chaplain."

"See? See?" Charles smirked, a finger wagging at the Cossack. "Now I know you're full of crap. Why would a vampire need a chaplain?"

"For the same reason the castle has a chapel, of course. You can't have a chapel without a chaplain."

"There's a chapel?"

"Of course! Where else would Cosmin's knights have worshipped?"

"Cosmin had knights?"

"You know," Stepan said, his lips twisted into a droll half-grin. "You really are stupid, aren't you?"

## 11

Valea Întunecată
Early Afternoon

Vasile had been the personal chaplain of Vlad III Drăculea, the Impaler. Stepan explained that the common belief was that Vlad was just another in a long line of Wallachian rulers, and maybe he was? Perhaps one of Cosmin's aliases was Vlad II, the Impaler's father. It was impossible to know for sure. That didn't matter, though. One way or another, Cosmin had wriggled his way into the good graces of the powerful Wallachian Voivode and was confirmed as the ruler Cetatea Orașului and its surrounding estates as a mark of the vampire's power.

"Strigoi," Stepan corrected Charles.

"Whatever," Charles sneered back.

Cosmin, however, was required to keep Vasile in his employ as chaplain so that the warriors of the fortress could take communion. The arrangement worked for a time, but after Vlad's death, the Father had suddenly become expendable, and so Vasile hadn't survived a fortnight.

Soon after, miracles around the valley had been attributed to the dead priest and it was not long before he had become beatified, then canonized as shield against the region's evils. Even now, hundreds of years after the priest had been murdered, the Romanian Orthodox church within the village had a shrine dedicated to him.

"Perhaps his relics are still within the chapel? Surely Saint Vasile would have the power to send Cosmin the Wicked to hell," the Cossack offered.

It seemed as good a plan as any to Charles, and probably better than most. "How would I use the relics?"

"There are many prayers for these things. You can say a prayer and use the power of Vasile to assault the creature."

Charles frowned. "Use the power to assault him?"

"Yes, use the power of God within Vasile's relics to assault the vampire!"

"Like, how?"

"The merest touch of the Saint's relics will send Cosmin's soul quivering to Satan's embrace!" Stepan said, enraptured.

"That sounds a little far-fetched, don't you think? I need to...to *touch* Cosmin with the relic?"

"Yes! Maybe you could throw it at him."

"That seems kind of stupid," Charles groused. He wasn't keen on wasting another opportunity on something as dubious as chucking old bones at his father.

"Yes, to a stupid man, it would seem stupid. That is correct."

"Call me stupid one more time, Stepan," Charles growled through clenched teeth. "I dare you."

The Cossack gave an acquiescent nod. "I meant it in the kindest way possible. You do bring up a good point, though. Perhaps a more permanent assault would be better?"

"I could stab him with a leg bone."

Stepan laughed at the image. "If there is even a leg bone remaining. Relics have a way of disappearing with pilgrims. A stake of holly, or oak even..."

"Yeah, I thought of that. If my knife didn't do the job, though..."

"Maybe you can tie the relic to the stake and jab it into him?"

"Hmm, no. Maybe I can grind the relic up into a powder and wipe it on the stake."

"Perhaps I was too harsh, and you are not terribly stupid. Calm down, please! It was a compliment. I have it! Mix the relic's powder in some holy water, then soak the wooden stake in the mixture. Then you have three powerful objects: holy water, the relic of Saint Vasile, and a wooden stake."

Charles chewed on his lip. If anything he had experienced in the past few days made sense, surely it was Stepan's plan. Even if the holy water was just piss-tainted well water, it couldn't hurt, and driving a stake into Cosmin's black heart sure seemed to be his best strategy, even if the knife had failed. Especially a stake soaked through with the powdered remnants of Saint Vasile's holy relics.

This could be the last opportunity he would get. Charles nodded with an air of finality. "Now I just need to find his miserable body."

"Oh, that's easy. The chapel, of course."

"Wait a minute," Charles said with a smirk. "The chapel? He's a fucking vampire. Besides, I didn't see his body."

"But you said yourself you didn't see the chapel."

That was true enough. Charles had explored the crypt, but he hadn't made it all the way to the end. The strange tomb with its frigid touch had chased the dhampir away. "Why would he be there?"

"Think about it, Very Smart Charles. What better way to spit in the eye of God than desecrate His consecrated ground?"

"Fair enough," the dhampir said as he nodded with determination. "I'll see what I can find and I hope to God it works. Tell me something else."

"Anything," the Cossack said happily.

"What is this Sword of Kizağan thing you were talking about? I've heard its name before."

****

Charles's enchanted knife, according to the half-mad Russian, was a fragment of a long blade once wielded by a supposed god of the Old Turks. He was their God of War, the horrific, conquering Kizağan who slew a thousand monsters and drove them from the land, opening the way for humans to settle down. It was an ancient folktale of an ancient people from an ancient land, and one wholly unbelievable save for what Charles had experienced the past few days. Now, after all the odd and weird things that befell him, the dhampir instinctively felt that he couldn't dismiss such stories out of hand.

As Stepan's tale went, the sword had been found during one of the many ruinous wars between marauding Turks and the kingdoms of Europe, and in the process it had been wielded against the most powerful demon of all. Though the sword had struck down the monster, it had been broken in the process, its tip snapped off and the blade shattered. That same tip had supposedly become the knife now strapped to Charles's hip.

"What became of the rest of the sword?" Charles asked.

"Nobody knows. It disappeared."

"Fun story, but it sounds like bullshit," Charles said dismissively.

Stepan's brow scrunched. "Give me the knife and I will show you something."

"No. I still don't trust you," Charles squinted, the familiar distrust rising again. Stepan would surely kill Charles if he had the opportunity, even when considering their somewhat cordial conversation. After all, he was a hunter and Charles was a half-breed dhampir.

Stepan clicked his tongue. "You already let me hold it once. Besides, nobody can be trusted. Except for me."

"Uh-huh."

"If Bekhmoaram gave you the knife, then it can only be because you are also hunting. That means we are allies, you and me. We are on the same side. As the saying goes, the enemy of my enemy is my friend…"

"Just don't kiss me. Same side, huh? What side is that?"

"The good side, of course!"

Charles drew the knife. "Sometimes I wonder. Barman," he called to Tomas in Romanian. "I'm letting him hold the knife again, but I am not giving it to him. If he tries to steal my knife, he will not leave here in one piece."

"That is wholly unnecessary," Stepan said in German, the disgust in his voice betraying his basic grasp of the local language. "If anyone is to be trusted, it is me."

"Funny," Charles said, switching back to German. "All the liars say they are to be trusted. Otherwise they wouldn't be liars." He slid the knife across the table, the Cossack snatching it up as if he were dying in a desert and the blade was life-saving water. "Rest assured that *I* don't lie."

The Cossack ignored Charles's implicit threat. "You see the pattern in the blade?" he said, his finger tracing along wispy lines. "Hand forged, long ago, but not of any normal iron, and not by human hands. This metal is special. It was made before mankind began to smelt iron, a gift from the heavens to aid in the struggle against darkness. Now, I will show you the reason that I know this is the famous blade of Kizağan." He picked up the bottle of țuică and carefully tipped it, a few drops of the liquor falling on the flat of the knife's blade. He slid his finger along its length, a single fingertip smearing liquid along dull metal.

A handful of letters appeared in the iron blade, the plum brandy bringing out a distinct contrast in metals. They were some type of runes, ancient and foreign, not like any characters Charles had ever seen in his long life. He was breathless, his mouth hanging open. "What does it say?"

"I don't know. Nobody knows. But you see here, how the letters disappear under the guard? It's just a part of a longer writing. Maybe a spell, perhaps an intonation? This language is extinct. Saying it is ancient…"

"It's older than ancient," Charles interrupted Stepan. "This blade is exceptional, it's unique."

Stepan nodded. "Many thousands of years old, from long before man even discovered bronze. Before copper, even."

Charles shook his head. "Not thousands, Stepan. Millions. This iron is not of our world."

Stepan nodded. "It is special. A gift from the heavens. I've heard it said that the blade was forged using the bones of children, to infuse their blessed innocence into the iron, and that gave it power over evil. Can you believe the Old Gods would even do such a thing?"

"That sounds improbable and unpleasant."

"But there's more," he said as he handed the precious blade back to Charles, reluctant to let it go but unwilling to break a solemn promise.

"What?" Charles asked impatiently.

"It has been said that if the rest of the sword is found, then they can be married. The knife and the sword can be joined, repaired, but only by someone that is special."

"Oh Jesus-fucking-Christ, not this bullshit again," Charles said, his face shrouded with dark annoyance.

"Language, please," Stepan said in displeasure. "The words you use are filth. It means that only the one chosen by God, the one who has been blessed by God, can restore the sword of Kizağan, and only it has the power to destroy the evil spirit within. But the evil spirit is also able to wield the terrible power of the blade, and so it must be protected."

Charles smirked. "Of course, that's expected, isn't it? Cliché but expected. Why can't it ever be easy?"

"If it were easy, would it be worth doing?"

Charles ignored the Cossack. "So how does the blessed one go about fixing the sword?"

Stepan shrugged and held his hands wide. "Who knows? Only God knows, and he does not talk to me."

\*\*\*\*

## Valea Întunecată
## Late Afternoon

Stepan Ivanovic scratched the experiences into his journal. Charles had slipped out of the tavern soon after their conversation, intent on finding the tools to strike down Cosmin the Wicked once and for all. A chuckle rumbled deep within his chest, amused by Charles's contention that vampires and strigoi were different things. Everyone knows that vampires are strigoi! The only difference is, vampires don't live in Romania.

His knife, though. The Cossack was certain it was a fragment of the Sword of Kizağan. Such a weapon could give the wielder immense power! Stepan could only imagine what such a sword could do to the undead.

Louse crawled through his coarse, black hair and bit at his scalp, and the Cossack scratched at them with annoyance. He was a seasoned hunter of undead things, and though his unwashed hair and unkempt beard served a purpose, his appearance did come with drawbacks. It was a mask of sorts, and where he traveled, with what he did, having an effective mask was important. It obscured his features and made him difficult to identify, which was valuable in the event of a misstep. Not that he had many missteps. Stepan had been trained to hunt through long hours of drill in the foothills of the Carpathian Mountains. His family hadn't originated in the Russian mountains, though. They had come from the eastern steppe-land where the wicked undead and cursed creatures were few. Here, in the fastnesses of Romania's wilderness? This place virtually crawled with monstrous beasts.

Monstrous beasts are what he preyed on. He was a stalker of the supernatural, and his prey were the cursed offspring of the Rădescu line. He belonged to the fifth generation of men who had been sworn to cleanse the land of Cosmin's evil progeny, ever since his great-great-grandfather had fallen prey to one of the half-breed bastard children of the strigoi.

To Stepan's knowledge they weren't many. Only a few, and they were mostly sprinkled amongst the republics and principalities of central Europe. There had been one in Germany. A real handful, that one. Cunning, the very definition of evil. Yet Stepan had dispatched him, had removed his heart and burned it in a fire, the memory of the searing meat rekindling nauseous memories. It had been years since that incident and the stench still lingered in his mind, so powerful that he could still smell it, even after all this time. He shuddered, the memory clinging to his nostrils, his great shaggy black mane trembling as he shivered. *Cut out the heart and burn it*, his grandfather had taught him. *It is the only way to ensure the creature will not claw its way from the grave again.*

But Stepan had learned something more over the past ten or fifteen years. His grandfather didn't distinguish between the reanimated dead and the undead. Those ghouls who feasted on the living weren't vampiric. Their resurrected corpses were much easier to dispose of than the half-breeds who slithered their horrible way through the world, infecting the darkest corners of society. Dhampirs, like Charles Resseguie, the progeny of Cosmin the Wicked…those creatures were far more formidable than the ghouls. Strong and quick, cunning and ruthless, the dhampir inherited the worst of its parents. *Beware the dhampir*, his grandfather's voice rose like a mist from somewhere within Stepan's memory. *They have the memory and strength and agility of a vampire, and the foresight of a human. They blend in, they look like us, but the dhampir does not have a shred of humanity living within it. It has no soul.* Stepan remembered trembling at his grandfather's knee as he learned that lesson and many others. *Finding one is near impossible*, his grandfather had continued. *Unless you know what to look for, that is. The telltale signs of the vampiric disease which rots within them. Their skin is reddish, always flushed with blood, and they suffer from an insatiable hunger which lurks within the eye. Their teeth are pointed, like fangs, and they move silently. Pay attention to these hallmarks, boy, and learn them, because one day such detail will save your life.*

The vampire's son had visited with the Jew in Saarbrücken, but Bekhmoaram was cunning. As soon as Charles had left his home, and before the Rabbi fled Germany, he had found Stepan Ivanovic. The Cossack was Bekhmoaram's friend, and he was also an insurance policy in the destruction of the evil Cosmin, so he had described Charles in the tiniest detail. Stepan had soaked it all in. Not only that, but the Jew had also told Stepan exactly where Cosmin lurked, and though the outbreak of war had proved an obstacle, Stepan was anything if not resourceful. Through his network of contacts and his skills as a hunter, the Cossack had tracked Charles through his military postings until one of Stepan's closest agents betrayed Charles's secret mission to Romania.

What Bekhmoaram had described was not exactly what his grandfather had claimed, though. Charles's teeth certainly seemed normal, and his eyes betrayed moments of fear and confusion instead of insatiable hunger. His skin tone, though, and his wiry strength seemed to be the classic hallmarks of a dhampir.

Cosmin was the Cossack's immediate target, the focus of his singular purpose, and Charles had led Stepan to Valea Întunecată. The vampire must die, one way or another, and after Cosmin's destruction Stepan would hunt down the rest of Cosmin's progeny. Destroying these undead monsters was his life's work. Cosmin was the ultimate prize, of course, and now he knew the vampire lurked in the nearby castle that lorded over the village, deep in the wilds of Wallachia's mountains. Cosmin was the epicenter of evil, the origin of terror. If Stepan could destroy Cosmin the Wicked, then he imagined the hunt for his dhampir offspring would be so much easier.

One thing at a time, one target at a time. All the rest would fall into place as God intended.

\*\*\*\*

Cetatea Orașului

## Late night

Moonlight splashed through the window, its illumination diffused by waves in the archaic panes of glass. Cosmin surveyed his lands through that window. The vampire's domain stretched for miles across forest and village and mountain ridges, yet he hadn't seen most of it, even in all his long years. His reach was unfathomably long, but only because of the creatures that obeyed his commands. Certainly, when he transformed into the mist, he wasn't held captive to this place. But then his power was impossibly limited, and the further he went from the castle the weaker he became. The beasts, though, the creatures of the night that obeyed him and stalked the forest at night? They gave him a long reach, and his favorite creatures of all were the bats and wolves.

It wasn't limited to the living, either. All of the horrible undead things that haunted the living also heeded the vampire's desires.

Regardless, Cosmin was stuck here, for all intents and purposes. Whether he liked it or not, the mountains that hemmed in the little dark valley were realistically the boundaries to where he could range when he wasn't floating around as that damnable mist. Below the castle, deep within the promontory's bowels, lay a crack in the stone that contained a sealed doorway that led to another place, another realm.

He took his power from that doorway. It was what nourished him, what kept the vampire alive through all the long years…if "alive" was even the appropriate term.

Human blood? Fun to play with, and tasty in its own right. Maybe blood helped him to thrive, maybe it helped maintain his immense strength and his constitution. That narrow defile deep beneath the castle is what gave him his real power, though, and even if it had been sealed all those years ago, enough otherworldly power seeped through to keep him going.

It wasn't enough, though. It would never be enough. Cosmin wanted more. Acute jealousy gnawed at him. *Why did those weak, miserable humans get to inherit Earth?* he questioned his father. *What did they do to deserve this place?*

Humanity exploited the land about them. They stripped the ocean of its bounties, they raped the soil of its minerals. They even murdered each other for selfish access to those riches.

*Why does their God protect them?*

Winds of change were blowing, though. It had been just a breeze not so long ago, but that breeze had strengthened to a tempest. Soon, that tempest would become a gale, and the gale would bring with it the change that Cosmin so desired. It blew with the fires he embraced.

"What thoughts are rattling around inside that empty head, I wonder?" the hag rasped from behind him.

Cosmin groaned at her voice, though he already knew that she had appeared. He had sensed her presence, but ignored the rotten old bitch until the muddled words spattered from her spittle-caked lips. "I can't survive the light of day," he said. "But moonlight is just reflected sunlight. What is it about the moon that its reflected light doesn't harm me?"

"That is what concerns you?"

Cosmin ignored his mother. "I assumed that solar particles are what causes the pain," he continued. "Do solar particles get reflected off the moon's surface? I wonder if that is what we see when we look at the moon."

Unul Vechi gave a great, exaggerated sigh. "Nothing should surprise me anymore, yet here I stand. Flabbergasted."

"Waging war is so difficult when I am so limited. Have you figured out a way to sever my tie to Hell?"

"We must throw the doorway open so the power can course through its maw," Unul Vechi said slowly, as if she were explaining the most basic concept to a child.

"I was rather hoping there would be another way," Cosmin frowned.

"No, there is not."

"And to open the door, the Navă must be destroyed with the sword."

"Surprisingly, you are correct."

"But the sword must be reassembled."

"Again, you surprise me. It appears you have been listening."

Cosmin's hands were nestled behind his back, one cradled inside the other. He tapped an index finger against the back of his hand. *My son must reassemble the Sword of Kizağan,* he thought, not for the first time.

"Your son must reassemble the sword," Unul Vechi said, and Cosmin wondered if she were reading his mind again.

"That is true, he must do that." What remained unspoken was how Charles refused Cosmin's offer to lead the Devil's Cohort. He had flatly refused to help the vampire at all, which meant that Cosmin must rely on his own cunning.

"So it's really happening. Finally, after all these years," the hag crooned happily.

"You didn't believe me?"

"Why would I believe you? You're the worst son a mother could regret birthing. You were born with a forked tongue."

"I'm not exactly sure what you mean by 'forked tongue'. Why would I lie about something like my son?"

"You would lie about the color of my eyes if it amused you. Never mind that. The divination revealed something," she said with an uncharacteristic urgency, her liver-spotted hands wringing themselves incessantly.

Cosmin waited impatiently for a few heartbeats. He felt no twinge of heart at the death of his bitch wolf. She had served her purpose. "So…are you going to tell me what the divination revealed?"

She nodded hungrily. "It was full of confusion and contradiction. Two lives, the entrails told me. There were two lives, and one would live and one would die."

"Whose lives?" Cosmin asked. He was growing irritated with the old witch. She may be his mother, but he didn't trust the old crone as far as he could throw her. *Strike that*, he thought savagely. *I'm a vampire. I can throw the old bitch quite a long way.* He simply held no trust for his mother. She was conniving and ambitious, much like him. It was a fatal combination in his eyes.

"It's impossible to say for sure, but your son's hand seemed to tell a similar story. There were two life lines, and where they met, one ended and the other continued. I think the divination had something to do with Charles."

"Costache," Cosmin corrected the witch. "Not Charles."

"Whatever," the witch said dismissively. "His name is just a label, it means nothing. This divination, though. I am reminded of the first battle."

Cosmin's face darkened. "The first failure, you mean."

"I don't blame you," Unul Vechi said. "Much."

The first battle was a long time ago, when mankind was consisted of little more than packs of savage animals who still hunted with sticks and rocks. Cosmin knew there had been two lives then as well. Two lives that had been joined, and as a result he had nearly died.

Nearly, but not quite, though he had been cast back into Hell.

It was a rankling loss, one that took thousands of years to correct, but now they were on the edge of an abyss, and that abyss would finally lead to victory.

Or it could be yet another defeat.

"You think the divination is not fortuitous," Cosmin said.

"It's impossible to tell. Maybe it meant something else?"

"You're the witch, you figure it out. In the meantime...we have a date, don't we?"

\*\*\*\*

The young woman didn't have to wait long. Cosmin entered the chamber, his face strong and handsome, his body tall and lean. He clutched the black cloak close to his body, its burgundy fringe brushing the polished and waxed floor floorboards. With a smile perched lightly on his lips, Cosmin glided across the space, nearly floating. She returned his smile, a nervous giggle dancing on her lips.

"Regina, my sweet," Cosmin hummed as he looked her over. He knelt down next to the woman, his eyes locked on hers. "Thank you for your patience, my dear." Regina's entire short life had been spent suffering under the heavy power of others, men who used her for their own ends, men who had used her as a slave in the kitchens, and had used her as a slave in their beastly beds. Beaten, worked, and whored out, Regina had learned to survive in a world that didn't deserve her. Then Cosmin had found her weeks before, months before, even, and he had pulled her from the pit of her despair and told her there was a better way. He had told Regina that these men only deserved condemnation and death.

"But they are the power of this God-damned country," she had told him, and in that moment Cosmin knew that she would cave to his demands. He had smiled sweetly back at Regina, leaned in to hold the woman and whispered in her ear. "They don't know what *real* power is. Come with me, join me, and you will have everything you have ever dreamed of."

"Why me?" Regina had shuddered.

"I will show you something," Cosmin had replied, and he did show her. The vampire had shown Regina how the beetles obeyed his command, how the wolves came when he called. He had showed her the range of his powers.

Cosmin had shown Regina the undead beasts, as well, and he felt her yearning begin to grow. She craved power, she craved revenge, and in just a few short weeks, she now lay in his bed.

"You will have everything you have ever dreamed about," Cosmin told her. Everything she had ever dreamed about. Cosmin knew Regina's type well. Women like her had never dared to dream before. The urchins and the broken and the cast-off downtrodden had been consumed with survival, with dodging the heavy blows from slavers and masters alike, and avoiding the drunken, sweaty, grasping hands of whoremongering men.

Just like Regina.

But it was the last words he whispered that pushed her over the edge. "You will have the power to avenge your shame," he had said gruffly into her ear.

"Why me?" Regina had asked with a tremble in her voice.

"I can only do so much," Cosmin admitted. "My beasts are savage things, and they need a savage queen."

"But why *me*?"

"Why not?" the vampire shrugged. "You've been trodden upon your whole life, and now is your opportunity to right those wrongs." Cosmin had spoken truthfully, but he had held back the *whole* truth. He had his soldiers here, on Earth, but he needed more soldiers to help prepare the way for the Cohort. One could never have enough soldiers. Would she be his queen of the beasts? Cosmin didn't know, nor did he care. He only knew that she would do whatever he demanded.

And, besides, it was fun to corrupt humans.

That is why she was here, why she had agreed to come to this ruined castle in the haunted forests of the

Wallachian mountains. Now she would dare to dream, because Cosmin had given her the audacity to do it, and in her dreams, he allowed her to deal death on all the men who had tormented her. It almost made him laugh, but to do so would break his hold on her in this moment of fragility.

Cosmin held her hand lightly, lifting it to his lips to kiss her knuckles. "Are you ready, my lovely?" he purred. "Don't be afraid. What will come is a small price to pay for the power that I will gift you."

Regina nodded, entranced by his steel eyes, her head tilting back as Cosmin kissed her lightly on the lips. He moved lower to kiss her chin, then ran his fingers through hers until they became intertwined. She moaned as Cosmin ran the tip of his tongue down her neck where her life's blood pulsed. He could feel her heart beating quickly, heard the blood coursing through her veins, and then she moaned in pain and pleasure as his needle-sharp teeth slid into her skin, through the tough connective tissues and membranes of her carotid artery. Regina's heart began beating quicker, her hips bucking in pleasure as Cosmin sucked gently at her neck.

Mumbled chanting betrayed the witch's presence. Cosmin could hear the hag casting her spell in the distant recesses of the dimly lit chamber, but he knew Regina was too lost in ecstasy to notice. Unul Vechi shuffled on her stumps to cross into the candlelight, her lips and tongue forming the lost ancient words of the ancestors as she slid a blade of black glass along Cosmin's neck so that blood, thick and black and viscous, slid into a stone bowl that had been painted in loops and whorls of red ochre. The crone's rhythmic chanting rose in pitch, a keening wail that reverberated off stone walls, as she tipped the stone vessel over Regina's parted lips. Unul Vechi's keening dipped again, reverted back to chanting, and Cosmin's blood dribbled in a little stream to stain Regina's lips as she gulped it greedily down.

When Regina was spent, when the ecstasy faded and the old woman disappeared, Cosmin watched patiently as she lay on the extravagant bed. Her body was wrapped in blood-stained sheer linen cloth, and screams and moans and nightmarish dreams wracked her fevered body as she began the transformation. Cosmin watched, transfixed by the woman's descent into hell, and he hoped that when the painfully long process was finally complete, she would be powerful, far more powerful than the men who had pushed her into his satanic ritual.

Or, she would be dead.

Regina moaned in feverish agony, her body wracked by the changes, and Cosmin began to grow worried. This was the sixteenth time they had performed this particular ritual. He and his mother had tried to transform children, they had tried young, virile men and the old and decrepit. Every time, it failed. The spell was supposed to be an easy one. Their victim was to drink of the vampire's blood as he fed on theirs, and the magical words would allow the blood to meld together, to commingle until it had become a new substance altogether. Cosmin had infected her, he had imbued her with evil, and now her body was changing. She was transforming into something new, something terrible.

She was evolving.

Still, he was worried, because they had a history of failure. Was his infection too strong for mere humans? Was there anyone at all whose constitution would be strong enough to fight off the infection long enough to accept the changes?

If anyone could, it was Regina. Her hate was so palpable, it ran so deep, that her very core had been corrupted by its icy grasp.

Cosmin jumped as screams erupted from her breast, her teeth grinding together violently. He could feel her body try to force the pain away. Regina writhed on the bed, her contracting muscles causing erratic spasms which turned into violent seizures that spilled her onto the floor, and he jumped to the dying woman's side. Regina's head snapped back. Vessels in her eyes erupted, blood contaminating the whites, her vision flooded with a crimson shade. She barked at him, vomited black bile onto the floor's ancient planks, her every faculty corrupted as her body tried to fight off his infection. Regina's canines began to lengthen, imperceptibly at first, but then her teeth pushed out even longer and she shrieked in anguish.

****

Cosmin looked down at Regina's limp body in disgust. "I would describe this as a failure," the vampire seethed. "Another fucking failure, just one more in an endless parade of them. What would you describe it as?"

Unul Vechi sat quietly with her hands in her lap, one resting gently on the other. She was still and calm, a foil to her son's furiously working mind. "Something went wrong, Mother. Again! What went wrong?" he raged.

The young woman who had appeared so strong and resolute, ready to embrace her future at Cosmin's side, lay on the floor, the bed's sheet twisted around her naked body. Regina's skin, once porcelain and milky-white, had fouled into the blue-black hue of pooled blood, and her crimson lips had drawn back into a blackened, eternal grimace. Regina had suffered a foul death, one wrought with agonizingly unimaginable suffering.

Cosmin demanded answers. Regina was dead, the transformation had failed, and Unul Vechi didn't know why.

"You're so very quiet, Mother," he said with flailing hands. "I would think that by now you would have worked it out. I mean, you said that you worked it out. You said that you knew what went wrong before."

"Shut up," she snapped at Cosmin. "You know nothing of these magics."

"Apparently that makes two of us, you wrinkled old bitch! What I *do* know is that the magics have failed us again. Failed *me* again, Mother." He stalked around Regina's corpse, inspecting her body closely.

"Stop calling me that."

Cosmin ignored her. Regina wasn't a crucial cog in his plan, yet failure of any sort was a bothersome annoyance. "You need to understand something," Cosmin seethed. "My son is our future, but he is an untrustworthy son of a bitch. Even if he agrees to lead the Devil's Cohort, he will keep trying to destroy me. Do you know how I know?"

"Because he's your son?" Unul Vechi spat. "A chip off the old block?"

"Because he *hates* me, Mother! I was hoping that Regina would keep him in line, but now she is laying in a bloody pool of vomit, and my son has tried to destroy me, and still the Navă is out there, somewhere."

"We *are* getting close," the witch said firmly.

"Are we? Pray, do tell," Cosmin said lightly. Nothing seemed to be going to plan, not a thing.

"You are far too impatient, you miserable little twat. I am close to finding the Navă, I've even been able to infiltrate her dreams."

"What did she make of you?" he asked slyly. His mother was a foul-looking thing.

"I'm not the half-wit you are. I projected myself as something else, of course. Don't interrupt. With the Vessel, all we need is the Sword of Kizağan."

"My son needs to reassemble the sword, but then things can get dicey. If he decides not to play nice? Then I'll be the one at risk."

"If Charles can't be turned, then he will have to die. You'll just need to be ruthless."

"*If Charles can't be turned,*" Cosmin said mockingly. "First," he said, ticking off points on his fingers. "His fucking name is Costache. Second, if he dies, then who the hell will lead the Cohort?"

"Leave it to me," the witch said through a sly smile. "There is a Plan B."

"I hope it's a better plan than this failure. Oh, look at the time," Cosmin said, noting the distant light of dawn through a window as it woke from night's slumber. "It appears I must go. Be a good girl and clean up this bloody mess?"

"Clean up your own mess, you spiteful prick," the witch uttered angrily at her son's departing back.

## 12

Cetatea Oraşului
Early morning

Charles stood at the study window. The sky was still stained with night, but faint streaks of dawn's goldenrod rimmed mountain peaks. Soon light would lance across the land, driving the horrid things of the forest back to their dens. Back to their graves, or wherever they disappeared to. Another night gone, like the innumerable ones that had gone before, and still Cosmin infected this place with his evil filth. The dhampir's jaw clenched. *Why hadn't Bekhmoaram's knife worked?* He had killed the werewolf with it, had struck down those forest ghouls, but in the end all the knife accomplished was to irritate further an already irritating Cosmin.

Despite the iron blade having been driven through desiccated flesh and parchment skin, Cosmin still walked and talked, breathing his fetid breath all over the land.

Candles flickered from all corners of the study, wan flames casting yellow light and dancing shadows off the tables and chairs and books to tickle the dhampir's nose with greasy wax. He turned back to the window and pondered the colorful streaks of reds and purples that stained the high clouds, the new day's inexorable sun pushing back against a sullen morning darkness.

He sighed and sat heavily into one of the richly upholstered chairs. Black dragons and horned devils and other fanciful creatures had been embroidered into the cloth covering, all manner of nightmares cavorting around a pyre that scorched the feet of nuns. Charles smiled with distaste. His father celebrated the most blasphemous images, which was unsurprising. Fitting, even. Cosmin obviously enjoyed the basest and most perverse of pagan trifles.

*Where was he?* Charles thought. Those colorful streaks now began to brighten, the clouds thinning to welcome a quickly brightening sky. Last night, Charles had expected his father to noiselessly slink his way into the study and join his son, where the old bastard would get a perverse joy out of needling the dhampir. He hadn't, though. For hours, Charles had poked around, fingering ancient books and staring out into the black of night, but now that day's first light had come, the vampire would have gone back to his grave to sleep the day away. He kicked off his shoes and threw his feet onto a footstool, sinking deeper into the plush chair. If the vampire was going to stand him up, then at least he should be comfortable.

Though the sky was brightening, candlelight still glinted off the leaded glass window panes, its dancing light creating pale illusions, while the fire burned sullenly to keep the mountain chill at bay. Romania was a haunted country, he knew, its forests and valleys filled with the most gruesome of creatures and spirits, but Charles didn't know what to make of the witch and the girl, and even his father. It was all so confusing.

Charles rubbed his eyes, blanketed by a sudden weariness. He was exhausted, but that was no wonder, given he hadn't really rested in several days. A cat nap here, maybe, and a restless hour of shuteye there, but even though Charles had little need for sleep, the dhampir still needed to rest his eyes daily, if even for just for a few hours. He grumbled and stood to stretch, then stopped cold.

Window drapes had been tied back, the sun's corona not yet breaking above the distant mountains, and Charles glimpsed an apparition's reflection in the glass window panes.

A man's face. Distorted by the wavy glass and obscured by the flickering candlelight, but definitely a man's face. Old, worn and weary, with the faintest trace of hair. A priest's tonsure.

Charles knew without knowing that it was Saint Vasile, Cosmin's priest of Cetatea Orașului. The priest of the castle who had been dead for centuries.

He turned slowly, his chest tight with anxiety and unsure of what was to come. The candles flickered, giving rise to greasy soot from their weak flames, the illumination barely strong enough to push a persistent dark back to the furthest corners of the room. He craned his neck, blinking shadows from his peripheral vision.

Charles was alone.

Nervously chuckling, he sheepishly reached for the lamp. "Get ahold of yourself," he said loudly and a bit too nervously. "You're seeing things." Apparitions in the night, a figment of his overactive imagination, no doubt caused by the alarming encounter in the village and his lack of rest. "Nothing to see here," Charles laughed. "You hear me, ghosts? Nothing to see here!"

There was a distinct chill in the air, though, which was odd as the woodfire still smoldered in the study's ancient hearth. It had been distinctly warmer a few minutes before, Charles was sure of it, but now the room was cold…perhaps not *cold*, but most definitely cold*er*. There was no doubt that the room had grown colder. "It's a drafty old ruin," Charles convinced himself. "I should have stoked the fire, that's all." Grabbing hold of the fire iron, he jabbed at the smoking logs until they crackled into a reluctant flame, a small burst of heat that pushed back the sudden chill.

Charles wandered about the room to occupy his mind and to forget about the priest's face, his attention wandering to some books that had been stacked on the study's secretaire. "Arrabbiata…no, that's a pasta sauce. Aryabhatiya," Charles mumbled, his finger tracing the title of a dusty old tome. He gave a chuckle and sat down as he thumbed through the ancient book. "What does Cosmin care about astrology? Ugh, math," the dhampir grumbled in disgust. With dawn breaking over the mountains, the town below just waking, and his father having disappeared to…well, wherever he disappeared to, Charles let his eyes sink shut as the warmth of the fireplace washed over him.

Minutes passed, just a handful of minutes, and the icy fingers of cold again prickled Charles's skin. His eyes snapped open in irritation and he stretched to stumble toward the fireplace and stoke its coals back to life. Charles stopped, fire iron poised to do its job.

The logs still crackled with leaping flames, but the air grew even colder still, and he sensed that he wasn't alone in the room. Charles turned slowly, his hand raising the fire iron defensively, when an old voice cracked like dried out leather.

An elderly man stood before him, with the long brown-woolen habit and tonsure of a priest, his face long and mourning, and a massive jewel-encrusted crucifix hanging down his chest from a gold chain. Charles stumbled backward, the window's sill stopping his fevered retreat.

"Do not fall from the window, Charles," the ghost warned in old Romanian. "You are needed."

"I know who you are," the dhampir croaked. "You're the saint, aren't you? Cosmin's priest. Vasile."

"I am Father Vasile, the same," he nodded.

"What do you want?" Charles demanded, his hands clenched about the fire iron's handle to brandish it threateningly.

"The conscious mind is a barrier to the spirit realm," the priest explained patiently. "Your subconscious mind, when at rest, breaks down the barrier."

"I don't know what you're saying," Charles frowned.

A veil of exasperation fell over Vasile's face. "We can only talk when you're sleeping," he said curtly.

"Oh. I guess that makes sense." His faced screwed up questioningly. "I'm not sleeping, though." At least, Charles thought he wasn't sleeping. He felt iron in his hands and the fire's warmth at his back.

"You are sleeping, but you're not dreaming. I've summoned your conscious self and it has left your body."

Charles didn't understand what the priest was saying, not exactly. He had only closed his eyes for a minute or two, there was no way he could have fallen asleep so quickly. "My spirit left my body? Wait a minute. I'm dead?" he asked in disbelief.

"No, you're not dead," Vasile said carefully, as if he were speaking to a slow child.

"If I'm not dead, then that means you're a ghost. Either that or I'm dreaming."

Vasile sighed. "I passed away many years ago, but Our Father is not finished with me yet."

"So, you're a ghost then...for real?"

"Yes," the saint nodded with a touch of impatience. "That is one way of putting it."

"Why are you here?" Charles asked, confounded by the shade's sudden appearance. "Why now?"

Vasile's spirit fingered the crucifix as he spoke, his voice gentle and measured. "Cosmin wishes to unleash an evil which will flood the land. If he is successful, then it will be unstoppable. He is duplicitous and cunning, and if you join him, you'll be condemned to an eternity in the sulfurous pit. Forsake him, and he will do everything in his power to destroy you, just as he destroyed your grandfather."

Charles barked in anger and smacked a fist into the palm of his hand. "He killed my grandfather? That son of a bitch! Wait...who was my grandfather?"

"Your grandfather was the Voivode of Wallachia."

"Huh, that's interesting. Never heard of him."

"Vladislaus III Drăculea."

"Oh! Why didn't you say so? Anyway, I hate the prick. Why should I care about joining him?"

"He will tempt you, he will give false promises. He will tell you that humanity has failed and that a greater power awaits to take its place."

Charles fiddled with the hem of his shirt. "That sounds cliché."

"He will also tell you that his army awaits its head, and that your destiny is to lead them across the Earth."

"The horde, or whatever he said."

"The Devil's Cohort."

"Yeah, that," Charles nodded. "I don't really understand what it is, though."

"Cosmin is not what you think he is."

"He isn't an evil, terrible prick who is responsible for the everlasting damnation my soul will suffer in hell?"

"No," the priest shook his head, his brow furrowed with confusion and concern. "What are you talking about?"

"That's what I'm trying to figure out."

"This isn't about you, Charles. It is much greater than just you, but you have an important part to play in the unfolding drama."

"So my soul isn't damned?"

"No! Pay attention."

"Well, I'll be a son-of-a-bitch."

Annoyance flashed across Vasile's face. "Language, please."

"Yes, Father."

"Cosmin needs you to lead the Devil's Cohort, and…"

"What is the Devil's Cohort again?"

The priest sighed. "It is his army of demons. Millions of them, and they are in Hell. Cosmin and that witch want to open the doorway between this world and that one and the demons will flood this land under a suffocating wave of death and destruction." Vasile waved his hand and the fire reacted, flames leaping from the hearth to consume the studio in a great, screaming inferno. Charles shrieked and staggered back, arms flung across his face in an ineffective defense against the searing flames, but then the roar died into a somber silence.

The castle had been burned away into nothing, the entire landscape scoured of trees and bushes and life. What had been a morning sky of midnight blue and pastel streaks had been scorched red, the dirt under Charles's feet seared into miniscule beads of red sand. Black cliffs of basalt dropped away to a valley of red dirt and black rocks where Valea Întunecată had once sat, and sulfurous vapors hazed across the horizon and burned Charles's nose.

In its place teemed bodies of red and black and grey. Thousands of deformed bodies milled about in the valley below them, lumpen and streaming with masses of hair.

"This is the Devil's Cohort," Vasile said as he looked on. "Some of it, anyway. What you see is one of six hundred and sixty-six legions. As of now, there is a conflict in Hell, a happy consequence of the High One's absence. Just as Cain slew Abel, half of Hell's denizens are trying to slay the opposing half. I'm afraid the conflict is temporary, though. If the doorway is opened those foul beasts will be the scourge of Earth. Most humans will die."

Charles shook his head. What he saw below was a trick, an unbelievable trick. His mind couldn't fathom what he was witnessing. "Vasile," he whispered passionately. "What you are saying is impossible…"

"This is his army, Charles! This is his greater power. If Cosmin has his way, the veil will fall and the Devil's Cohort will be an unstoppable deluge that will consume the land. They will kill what they want, consume everything they can catch, and enslave the rest."

The dhampir steeled himself against the horror. "I mean, that's terrible and all, but it's not really my problem. I came to Romania to save my own soul, not...not fight *this*," he said with a wave of his hand to indicate the horde of demons.

Vasile expelled a breath of exasperation, his eyes rolling as he sighed. "If that isn't enough to get you to act, then what if I told you that Cosmin was responsible for the deaths of your wife and your children?"

The dhampir's chin knuckled at the mention of his family. Carina had been the light that illuminated his world, while the boys, Gheorghe and Petru, were a pair of whirlwinds who wrought havoc each day of their short lives. Charles loved them all, loved them more than life itself. A wan smile failed to break through his sorrow. "He what?"

"Cosmin's terrible plan requires your obedience. He saw your family as a threat."

"No," Charles muttered. "The Turks killed them. I saw it."

"You saw what your father wanted you to see."

"What I wanted to see? Like this?" the dhampir seethed, his arm sweeping across the valley's swarming demons. "How do I know that you are telling the truth? Are those demons real, is this place really Hell?"

Sadness overcame the priest, his long face drooping further. "Yes and no. What you see is what Hell is really like. Down there are demons, just like those in Hell."

"So this isn't Hell?"

"You haven't died, so I can't take you there. What you see is exactly what is in Hell, though!"

"Then you're just as bad as he is," Charles spat at Vasile. "You spout lies so that I'll do your filthy work."

Vasile nodded acquiescence. "There is a difference."

"Oh yeah? What's the difference?"

"I will readily admit when I am guilty of falsehoods. Cosmin will deny his lies until the end times. I am trying to show you what the future will be if we fail."

The dhampir stalked to the cliff's edge. He stared into the valley below, his breath held in contempt of the priest, of his father, of the whole God-damned lot of them. What had seemed a simple task just days before had spiraled out of control. Skewer the rotten old fucker, burn his heart on a brazier, and Charles's soul would be saved.

Or so he had thought.

He turned, cold eyes boring into the priest's shade. "My soul isn't at risk?"

"The sins of the father will not be borne by the son."

"I don't know what that means."

"No, Charles," Vasile said, his words heavy with gravity. "Your soul will not go to Hell. It is one of the things that Christianity has twisted for its own ends."

The dhampir nodded with gritted teeth. "I'll do it," Charles said, his eyes slits and the muscles in his jaw working furiously. "I'll kill Cosmin. Not for you, though. Not to stop his plan and not to save humanity. I will do it because I hate him, and if the miserable bastard killed my family, then I hope God guides my hand as I do it."

Charles turned back to the valley, but the hellish image faded until the light of day once again illuminated Cetatea Orașului's study. Charles looked at Vasile with a furrowed brow. "Why does he want to destroy everything? Why would he do that?"

"Because Cosmin harbors a terrible jealousy of mankind."

"What about womankind?" Charles asked as he rubbed his chin, deep in contemplation.

"That too, I suppose? Humanity was chosen by God to populate this world, and so the demons were evicted. He cast them into Hell, and ever since their banishment they have been trying to scheme their way back."

"Okay," Charles frowned in thought, his head nodding slightly. "I will send his ass to hell, but to do that, I need your relics."

Vasile tilted his head slightly. "Whysoever do you need my remains?"

"I'm going to grind them up, mix the dust in holy water, then soak a stake in it and stab him with it."

"That...that sounds somewhat reasonable, actually."

"Where are your relics?" Charles demanded. "Are they hidden somewhere? In one of the crypt graves?"

"No," Vasile began, but Charles kept talking.

"Does Cosmin have them stashed away? I bet your relics are locked up, aren't they? That conniving bastard," the dhampir spat, a fist smacking into his palm.

"My remains lie in the reliquary."

"The what?" Charles asked through pursed lips.

"A reliquary. I am a saint, after all."

"Where is the reliquary?" the dhampir asked impatiently.

"It's where all reliquaries reside, Charles. In the chapel."

"The chapel!" he shouted. "Of course it's in the chapel."

"Look in the chapel's east end. There is a memorial stone, more a slate than anything. Behind the stone is a void. That is where my reliquary lies."

Charles did smile this time, his sorrow buried under a building sense of victory. It was time.

****

Vasile's burial void was, indeed, in the chapel, safely hidden behind a stone that had sealed off the secrets within. The Saint's name hadn't been carved into the stone, but in the chapel's entire east wall, only one stone had been decorated. Faint lines had been scribed into the face of it, so faint that Charles had to squint at the stone until sunlight flashed at an oblique angle, the faint shadows cast so that a picture appeared.

It was a map of sorts, or perhaps more accurately, a sketch of the valley.

All the features had been labeled in a tight apocryphal Greek script, which Charles had once known intimately but took some effort to recall. In the sketch's faint lines, he saw a detailed castle perched on its promontory, the village nestled in its valley below, and all the mountain peaks had been labeled carefully. Part of the castle, built into its eastern fastness, was a sepulcher of sorts. Below the castle, though, was what caught Charles's attention.

Beneath the castle, deep within the stone cliff, was an entrance to the underworld, an access to the *other* side. A place to connect with the dead.

Charles chafed. "Bullshit," he griped. These things were a fantasy, they weren't real. Tilting his head this way and that, Charles was struck dumb by a lightning bolt of realization.

He spun to look at a mosaic that had been meticulously laid into the chapel's floor. Diminutive ceramic tiles had been arranged to illustrate the region, just as the stone's carved sketch had done. There was the town, and the river, and the castle itself. The chapel matched the sepulcher, the castle's promontory displayed prominently in both the mosaic and the tablet. And there, in the floor's mosaic, within the chapel, was a doorway.

But there was no doorway. There was only a passage to the crypt's dusty corridor and the main chapel door that had once served as the worshipper's entrance, but no access built into any of the other walls or even the floor. All Charles could see were ancient pews pushed to the chapel's periphery and a gigantic lectern, carved with martyrs' scenes, its oak paneling darkened with age.

Of course, it wasn't that old, and neither were the pews. Perhaps a hundred years? They were in good condition without much evidence of dry rot or even any usage. What purpose did they serve? Cosmin himself had said that the chapel had served his knights, knights who had been dead for far longer than the lectern and pews existed.

And the lectern, it was massive! Fully ten feet wide and four feet deep. More like a large desk. Charles began to inspect the intricately carved wood. Why would the rotten old vampire even need a chapel? No one ever came here. He ran his hands along the lectern's top, noting the groove carved around its edge. The top's wood was dark, very dark and deeply stained, while the groove had holes drilled down into the corners. Holes that appeared to lead deep into the lectern itself.

Charles looked closer at the lectern's sides. Here was a saintly martyr being torn apart, his face twisted with agony, while there, another martyr's entrails spilled from his abdomen. Another one being dismembered, and yet another being burned alive, his face turned up, wailing at God.

*These aren't martyrs*, Charles realized in horror. *These are sacrifices.* This is not a lectern. It is an altar.

An altar to Satan, the dhampir realized, its tremendous size concealing something beneath.

He shuddered, his heart steeled against looming evil, then leaned into the massive wooden construction, pushing with all his strength against the old wooden altar. Though it was immensely heavy, its bulk shifted against his weight. He pushed harder and it ground noisily against the mosaic floor, eventually sliding reluctantly to one side and revealing the gaping maw of a stair carved from the stone floor. A chill wind whistled up from the blackness and Charles gritted his teeth, his jaw set in determination. This was the entrance to his father's tomb, the place where the vampire disappeared to each day. He was sure of it. The more he ventured, the more was revealed. Charles was unsure of what his future held, but he knew that he had gone too far to turn back. The sinister secrets that had surfaced could not be forgotten. With one more glance into the ancient staircase, he strode across the little room to the chapel's eastern wall that held Vasile's reliquary.

Charles had no idea how thick the stone map was, but looming victory clouded his mind. With a fist clenched tight and his teeth gritted, the dhampir pulled his arm back and released a massive blow, his fist striking the stone square on its face. Over and over he struck, his fists driven on by centuries of anger and doubt, of anguish and betrayal. A roar welled up from deep within Charles's chest as the blows rained against stone, primal screams further fueling his rage and torment.

And then the stone cracked.

Each blow widened the crack more, a pile of dust and pebbles growing, until the fracture was wide enough that Charles could shove his fingers inside to grip the stone fragments, discarding the pieces until sunlight glinted off of gold and crystal.

Charles worked feverishly to remove the last of the broken stone, until he finally pulled a small casket out of the void. It was finely wrought of gold and silver, each side fit with myriad windows of the finest crystal, its fittings punctuated by large white pearls. Rubies and sapphires encrusted the reliquary's lid. The dhampir held the casket up, his face twisted by apprehension.

Charles hesitated. This moment was a culmination of his life's work, the dogged result of the search for his father. Anger and vengefulness had driven him to this point, and Charles had hoped that revenge would help him see it through, yet he was spent. All the pain he had experienced turned him numb, all the fear and loathing seemingly evaporated in his pummeling of the stone.

The vampire's son tried to muster up some feeling. He wanted to feel anger, or sorrow, or pain at the thought of the task at hand. There was simply an immense void in his heart, an emptiness cultivated by centuries of sadness, a vacuum of emotion caused by his father.

At the end of it, the only sentiment he felt was shame.

\*\*\*\*

"That's not a cock," Charles said incredulously. He held the reliquary up to the sunlight and peered through a tiny crystal window, half expecting to see a desiccated flap of skin or some kind of deflated parchment-like remains. Yet the relic was small and twig-like, mummified and misshapen.

It had a fingernail on the end of it.

"Of all the things to lie about! Why would he tell lies about this?" Now he felt the familiar burn of anger again. Whatever numbness had been caused by his outpouring of grief and pain, Cosmin's incessant lying awakened the old emotional scars. Charles would, indeed, see the task through.

Vasile's finger was light as a feather, its skin thinner than the finest vellum. Charles forced himself to touch it, to lift it from the reliquary, and the very sensation of holding the ancient, mummified finger repulsed him. He grasped the finger on either side of the second joint, took a halting breath, then pressed sharply in with his thumbs. A quiet snap, barely a sound at all, and he held the remnants in either hand. It was effortless, like snapping an old, dried-out wishbone.

After gently placing the last remains of Vasile in a stone mortar, Charles pursed his lips and sighed, then began to grind the ancient digit into dust with the blunt end of a broken broom handle he had found, the end whittled down to a savage point. It took a surprising amount of effort to reduce the relic to a fine dust, while the bigger fragments were mostly pushed around by the pestle.

The chapel's old baptismal font, which centuries before had been used to cleanse babies of sin and so be recognized by God, had filled with rain and was fouled with feathers and pigeon shit, but it was the closest thing to holy water that was available and would have to do. "Besides," Charles reasoned. "Holy water is just normal water blessed by a cretin."

He dipped a bucket into the font, doing his best to splash away the shit and feathers and so avoid the worst of the foulness, then dumped the holy dust of Vasile into the bucket's cloudy water. Charles gripped the stake and vigorously stirred the mixture, before letting the business end of the stake soak in the worst of the horrible-smelling liquid.

It was almost time.

****

Charles held his breath and stepped into the abyss, each foot probing carefully as he descended the steps, guided only by an invisible hand, for the passage was dank and black, filled with must and devoid of light. He probed with each step, silently marking the passage in his mind, the slim wooden stake balanced delicately in his hand, its sharpened tip darkened with moisture and slicked with powdered flesh. He walked a long time, the air growing noticeably colder as he descended into the blackness, until a dim light finally appeared. It flickered yellow-orange, a beacon reaching out to him, and as he moved carefully down the ancient steps the soft light grew bolder. Anticipation leapt into Charles's throat as he stepped cautiously into a great, cavernous chamber, its rough-cut roof supported by gigantic, fluted columns of black basalt polished to a sheen. Flames licked the air from braziers and candles guttered in the oppressive air, hundreds of them, the dim light of each wax stick multiplied to illuminate the temple, for that's what it was. A malevolent temple built to worship a wicked god, with forgotten prehistoric runes carved into a slick floor, the black stone polished to glitter in the blinding candlelight. Carvings of animal heads were framed by the runes. They had been gouged deeply into the floor to surround a sepulcher, a great coffin glittering golden in the flickering light, its heavy yellow lid encrusted in precious jewels and propped unceremoniously against its side.

This was the final resting place of Cosmin the Wicked. Charles crept closer, the wooden stake held high and ready to strike. There he slumbered, his father the vampire, fast asleep and waiting patiently for the sun to set. Charles stood at the sepulcher's side, eyes stabbing hatred at Cosmin, the stake's carved tip poised to drive deep into his exposed breast. He hesitated, wanting to destroy him but desirous of savoring the moment, and then his hand fell.

Sharpened wood plunged deep into Cosmin's chest to split ribs and heart alike, Charles's immense strength driving the wooden stake through flesh and bone. He willed the holy weapon to work its awful power against his evil father. Charles twisted the wood, pushing and twisting and praying that the vampire would die, that he would be cast into the deepest pit never to escape, that Cosmin's awful plans would remain forever as a foul memory.

Charles burst into tears. Pent-up frustrations released in a torrent, his body wracked with a heady mixture of relief and sorrow, and then the dhampir collapsed against the golden coffin, his hands wiping relief and weakness from his eyes.

Cosmin's eyes snapped open to stare hatefully at his son, glowering at Charles through steel-gray pupils. Though his father hadn't moved a single muscle, the dhampir's resolve evaporated. "Why won't you die?" Charles bellowed. "What the fuck do I have to do to kill you?"

Silence met his outburst, silence and the gray of malevolent eyes, and with a curse, Charles turned to flee the chamber.

## 13

Valea Întunecată
Morning

"Who is he?" Elena asked the trembling image in the mirror. *He* was the man in the market who had shocked her into the other realm. Charles, he said his name was, and the girl was still shaken by the experience though they had communicated through the æther several times. The entire experience was a jumbled confusion of thoughts and emotions. They were tied together, and he had to reassemble the sword, yet neither of them knew where it was or how to do it.

She had woken that morning having risen with the sun, her daily chores beckoning. But first, like any good Romanian girl, Elena had to make sure that her hair was braided, because that is what modest unmarried girls did.

Only she wasn't a girl. Elena was in that strange gray area between being a girl and becoming a woman, the in-between of not knowing what she was. For a few more days, she would wake to braid her hair, and then would come the Vârstă de Măritat. Soon after she would be married. Not at first, not quite, but already her parents had been searching for a suitable match. She would become a woman, become a wife, and then she wouldn't braid her hair anymore, because married women would wear the traditional naframa, that scrap of embroidered cloth that modestly covered her hair.

All of this, of course, assumed that Elena would live to celebrate the Vârstă de Măritat, and that she would become a woman, and that she would be married. Suddenly, what had seemed so certain just hours and days before had become so uncertain.

Her life had become improbable, in a way.

Elena looked in the old mirror that had become clouded with age. She had meant to work her hair into the braids, she had meant to begin the all-important morning chores such as starting the cooking fire, sweeping the kitchen out, and helping Ruxana with preparing the daily meals. She had meant to help her father, Gavriel, prepare for his day as well, because he was heading to the lower pasture to tend their sheep.

Only now, the girl with black hair stared back from the mirror, the face of a dead girl who had unexpectedly become Elena's confidant. Adina, her name was. She had been God's vessel, once upon a time, but now Adina was dead. Now being God's vessel was Elena's cross to bear, but she wasn't sure that she had the courage. She still didn't quite understand what that meant. The girl had touched Elena's temple in a dream, and then she could see the ghostly aural colors that every person radiated, she could feel their thoughts and hopes and dreams.

Dreams, not like Elena's dreams. Not like the night terrors.

She looked at the girl in the mirror, and Adina looked back, silent and unblinking, a glimpse from the spirit world superimposed on the bleak reality of Elena's face.

The girl didn't speak, she just stared.

"Who *is* he?" Elena urged, her voice quivering with tears. The man from the market, the tall one with brown hair. Charles or Costache or whatever he wanted to be called. She had seen him, he had seen her, and then there was a clap of thunder or an explosion or something.

He was there, in the gray place. Rooted as she was, unable to move or talk, only able to think, but their thoughts had connected in that strange place. It must have been a dream. It must have been a hallucination.

*Costache.*

That was what the voice had said. Costache. The blacksmith and the forge. And now the power of God was within her, and she had reached out to the man in a dream and he had answered.

Was Elena losing her mind? After everything she had experienced, she still didn't understand what had transpired, not really, and now Adina the Dead Girl stared at her from a cloudy mirror.

She wasn't just staring anymore, though. Adina's mouth began to move, lips trying to form words, but no sound came from the mirror.

It didn't matter. Elena knew what the girl was trying to say.

*He is the blacksmith. He is the blacksmith. He is the Blacksmith.*

Elena nodded. "I know," she said. "I know he is."

The girl who was becoming a woman would need to find Costache, she had to convince him that he was the blacksmith, that he had to restart the forge and mend the sword. But first, she had chores to do, and woe be the girl who neglected her chores.

\*\*\*\*

Every day, Ruxana would send Elena to the market to purchase fruit and vegetables and freshly baked bread with what few coins they could spare. She wandered down familiar alleys and streets shooting furtive glances in each window she passed, hoping to catch a glimpse of the black-haired ghost. Adina wasn't to be seen in the reflections, though. Just dusty window panes set in old wooden frames that had been fixed into ancient sandstone walls. Tip-toeing carefully along the road so that Elena wouldn't trip over the jumbled cobblestones, the girl wasn't paying much attention to the people around her.

The town market was busy that day. Bodies milled about the square, both young and old and every age in between, but Elena had stopped cold. A man stared at her, his face long and pale, his liver-spotted tonsure framed by white hair, a massive golden crucifix hanging over the brown woolen mantle that covered his thin chest. One skeletal hand held a tall priest's crozier, and he stared as if nothing else in the whole world existed but the girl. He raised his hand then, one skinny finger beckoning to Elena, then he turned away and disappeared into the milling crowd.

She choked on a breath. He had come again, this strange priest in his brown woolen smock, but something spurred the girl on and she hurried after him. Shouts followed Elena as she bowled through the crowd, the girl frantically searching left and right for the quickly retreating man. She caught a glimpse of the brown-shrouded figure sliding hurriedly down a deserted side alley, one that she knew would end at the village's boundary. The girl slid to a stop, her eyes tracking the figure as he made a turn out of her view.

*Why am I doing this?* Elena thought. *Why am I following him?* The ancient priest was unknown to her, which gave her pause. Valea Întunecată was a small town hidden in a largely unknown valley. There wasn't any reason for her not to know most of her neighbors, especially a priest clothed in strange vestments, and he didn't simply look old. He looked ancient.

The priest looked like someone who belonged in another time, another place entirely. He wasn't a resident of the village, though the people who thronged the market had ignored the man as if he didn't exist, as if he were invisible to them. Strangers invited attention in the village, yet this stranger was ignored by all. *Was he invisible?* She thought. With all the strange events of the past few days Elena couldn't dismiss the notion entirely, even if it seemed outrageous.

She stared down the twisted alley, her feet leaden and unwilling to follow the priest, the market clamor a faded memory. Elena tried her best to focus on what the old priest's appearance meant. *What good could come of this? It could be a trick of that horrible demon-creature from my dream.* She thought about that possibility for a moment, that the priest was a false spirit who would snatch the girl up, that he would abscond with her to be a plaything of the strange creatures that prowled the nighttime forests. Gravel shifted under Elena's feet as her feet shuffled with indecision. *He could be a trick of that demon-like thing, or maybe not? Why would it choose a creepy old priest to lure Elena away?* The girl grumbled, unsure what to do. The alley was deserted, it led off into the mountain's wilderness, and there were better things Elena could be doing with her time than chase some questionable priest to God-knows-where.

Elena steeled herself, her mind set firmly. Ruxana was expecting the girl back with the day's produce, and forsaking that duty meant they would all go to bed with empty stomachs. The girl spun on her heel to set off back to the market and finish the day's shopping, then stopped abruptly, a scream choked off in her throat.

He stood in her way, a stern look carved into his long features, an arm shrouded in brown wool stuck out rigidly to point her way back down the alley. Elena stumbled back, the panicked shout lodged in her throat, her thoughts a jumbled terror as she fled backwards until a sandstone wall stalled her flight so that she collapsed into a ball.

The priest closed his eyes, his lips silently quivering in a rapid prayer, his voice a crescendo that filled the girl's thoughts. *Be strong and courageous*, the voice filled Elena's mind. *Do not fear or be in dread. It is God who goes with you, Elena! He will not leave you or forsake you.*

Tears streamed down the girl's face as she cowered next to the building, her legs pulled in tight to her stomach, eyes squeezed shut and hands clasped tightly over her ears. The sound was deafening, a madness of thundering noise, and Elena willed it away.

Silence filled her head. Utter silence engulfed her, a numbness of senses devoid of market noises or chirping birds, absent even the sound of a soft breeze. Elena slowly lowered her hands and opened her eyes. Light glared from the clouds which had shrouded the sun, and gradually the day's sounds rose as morning dew.

Elena was alone in the alley.

Struggling to her feet, the girl leaned on the wall to gain her bearings. The priest had appeared, had spouted Deuteronomy directly into her mind, then disappeared again as a bolt of lightning. She was shaken by the experience, yet her resolve had grown. This man, whatever he was, had obviously not been a trick of the demon-thing. He was not a spirit sent to drag her off to some hellish place. He had beckoned to Elena, had encouraged her to follow him to some place beyond the town's boundaries, and she instinctively knew there was a purpose before her. She was the Navă, and she would see it through.

\*\*\*\*

Twisting left and right, the alley meandered on for a few hundred feet before petering out at the edge of the forest. Just beyond the trees a cliff soared up, an escarpment that lay opposite the decrepit fortress of Cetatea Oraşului that had lorded over the town for countless centuries. Doubt still nagged at Elena, but her resolve hadn't wavered. Beyond the alley's abrupt terminus a trail disappeared into the dark of the forest, and Elena assumed that somewhere out there the priest waited for her. She sucked in a breath, steeled herself against the dark woods beyond, and plunged headlong into the forest.

Rustling creatures skittered about in the ferns and bracken of the underbrush, slinking animals who remained unseen even though Elena knew they were there. Whatever beasts were out here, they weren't repelled by the light of day that filtered through the dense forest canopy. Hurrying as fast as the girl dared, she followed the narrow trail as it twisted and turned, its ambling way confusing her senses so that she lost all direction. Elena would stop and listen to the scurrying noises, breathlessly trying to judge the direction they traveled and ignoring the voice within that scolded her for leaving the town's safe confines. Many, many times Gavriel had warned his daughter of the dangers that lurked just beyond the village, and Elena had always remembered those lessons and heeded his warnings.

Today, though, the priest had beckoned, and even with the memory of her father's demands, Elena had been compelled to plunge on. Something waited for her, and courage and curiosity drove the girl on.

The trail quickly dwindled to a narrow game path, one that even deer would have trouble navigating, yet the girl pushed forward relentlessly. Nerve drove her to continue down the path, to shove her way through the clinging limbs of the game trail, and though she couldn't put her finger on exactly what it was that made her continue, she was sure the priest was somewhere up ahead.

What had started as a trail and become a game path now dwindled to nearly nothing, the pine boughs so thick and dark that the trail nearly disappeared at her feet. Elena couldn't see the natural sunlight, so overgrown was the forest in its depths. Even though the sun was nearly at its zenith, its rays fought to penetrate this far through the trees so that she thought for a moment twilight was falling. If not for a faint line of dirt in the thick ground cover, a person would never know that there had even been a trail in the first place.

Elena dropped to her knees and crawled forward as she pushed the limbs up and over her body. Under the pines, near the thin dirt trail, the girl could see lifegiving daylight just ahead. It was a clearing. She fought forward, forced nearly to a slither, and then the sun burst out.

Stones had been piled up, the boulders so thick that only sparse weeds could grow between them and the forest stood in a sentinel's perimeter, protecting this ancient ruin. What cloud cover there was had burned off so that yellow light lanced from the sun to reflect blindingly off the pile of pale rocks. Elena gritted her teeth, a hand held up to shield her sight from the glare, and then she saw him.

He stood on the pile of rocks, some stones as tall as a man, his gaunt frame slightly off-center and still shrouded in the brown wool smock, a skeletal arm extended to point at the pile's center. The priest stared at Elena the way her father did when he needed her to do some important task. The man's mouth began moving, his lips forming stern unheard words that she struggled to understand.

She saw it then.

A single stone, its carved point barely protruding above the jumble of stone.

Elena began to climb, carefully picking her way amongst the dangerously shifting boulders, the priest's mouth finally breaking into a melancholy smile. Still, he pointed at the carved stone. *Move the rocks*, he seemed to mouth. *Uncover the stela. Move the rocks, uncover the stela.* Over and over again, he repeatedly spoke the words in an unheard voice, and Elena slowly climbed toward the pillar that protruded from the boulder pile. *Move the rocks, uncover the stela*, the priest continued to mouth. Large and pointed and rough-finished, Elena could only see the very tip of the stela and she began to pull the rocks and boulders away, flinging the smaller rocks to the side while the larger boulders could only be shifted and rolled off the pile. Gradually, she uncovered the stela through tedious manual labor, barely noticing the advancing shadows as the sun traversed blue, cloudless skies.

Outlines of carved panels began to appear as the boulders rolled away, the crudely pointed stela now betraying an octagonal shape. Frantically pulling and tossing and rolling boulders away, Elena was sweating by the time the carvings themselves were uncovered. She first saw geometric symbols, esoteric markings with some unknown meaning, but then the other panels became visible as she worked. Each panel alternated with those odd symbols, and Elena's breath caught in her throat when she saw the scenes carved into the stela.

Winged people, beams of light radiating from their bodies, battled misshapen, horned beasts.

A demon-like thing with savage fangs and three eyes, his clawed hands reaching greedily towards a line of people who had been bound hand and foot, while a crone looked on with one hand clenching a knife.

An inferno, its flames consuming people who screamed out in pain and suffering.

A child holding a cup, rays bursting from its bowl.

This last panel beckoned to Elena. She reached out a trembling hand, her fingers outstretched to brush the roughly carved stone. An odd heat emanated from its surface and the girl recoiled from the stone as it seemed to vibrate against her touch.

She choked down gritty saliva, took a calming breath, and pressed her palm firmly against the carved girl's body.

Boulders began to rattle, the strangely warm stone quivering violently under Elena's palm. She snatched her hand back, but the quivering grew into a rumble and the pile of rocks quaked. Elena tried to scramble away, her hands and feet fighting to find purchase in the rattling and shifting jumble of stones, and then her feet shot out from under her and the girl tumbled backward to land in hard-packed dirt at the foot of the stela as the boulders exploded outward. Her screams were lost in the din of clattering boulders, and the rifts stretched and widened into great fissures that ran together to ring around the great stone obelisk. Boulders fractured into shards that tumbled down to lodge themselves within the ringed cleft, and slowly the clamor of stones and quaking soil gave way to a great silence.

Elena sat with her side wedged at the base of the stela, her body curled up protectively. She sensed someone nearby, a spirit emanating a cold melancholy hope, and its energy forced Elena's eyes to open and her body to slowly unfurl.

"Hello, Elena," the ancient voice rasped. "I am Father Vasile, and you are here to learn new things."

She gulped dryly and slumped against the massive obelisk, suddenly exhausted. "You are the dead priest Adina has been telling me about," the girl croaked through a throat parched by exhaustion and stress and the suddenly scorching heat of the sun.

"I am," Vasile nodded gravely. "God has graced you with an amazing ability. It is the same ability that Adina had endured. There is so much to tell you and not a terribly long time for you to learn."

"What is this place?" she asked, looking around the ring of crumbled stone with stretched around the stela in a perfect circle.

"This is an ancient place, one of a dozen that ring the valley to form a powerful wall of blessed magic."

"Is it an evil place?" she asked naïvely.

"No, no," Vasile chuckled. "Many would see it as such. This is a place from long before God's grace was brought to our valley. It was a temple at one time. All of the stones around us once made up the temple's walls, until good Christians tore it down. Yet the protective magic remains."

"What does it protect against?"

"That, dear child, is what you are here to learn. Prepare yourself for a harsh truth. For some, it is difficult to hear."

"Just tell me," Elena said, her chin wrinkled into a frown. "I already know that I'm different. I've always known."

Surprise made the priest's eyes arch. "Very well. You have more courage than I expected. This stela, and the eleven others just like it, were erected many thousands of years ago. A great battle was fought here between the denizens of Hell and the people who lived in this valley. They had come here from far away, some say they were led by their chosen god, and when those people entered this valley they knew that they had come home. Here, by the river that still flows today, the people built their village and worshipped their god."

"Who was their god?" the girl asked. "It wasn't our God?"

"No! They were a good people, but ignorant of the God of Israel."

"So who was it?"

Bony shoulders rose in a curt shrug. "One of the old gods. A false god. Does it really matter, though?"

"It does matter," Elena said, her voice hard and brittle as flint.

"Very well, very well. The people of this land would eventually call him Kizağan, but I don't have any knowledge of his name when your people settled in this valley."

"My people settled here?"

Vasile nodded in affirmation. "Yes, your people. They would come to be known as the Old Families of Valea Întunecată. Others would come into this valley, and some of them even stayed and settled here. But the Old Families made this valley their home, they are your ancestors, and it was here that they worshipped what would eventually become the pagan god known as Kizağan."

"This was Kizağan's temple?" the girl asked, her voice tainted with awe.

"At first, they worshipped him in water-meadows and other secluded natural places. Eventually they built these temples. As I was saying, a battle was fought here, in this valley. It was a terrible affair in which many, many people were slain."

"Why?"

"Why did they fight? To protect their homes."

"No, why did the things come from Hell?"

"They are greedy and foul creatures who are jealous of humanity, so they slimed their way from that place to kill and enslave!"

"How did they come here?" she asked, wide-eyed and breathless.

"There is a fracture in the ground that is a doorway to Hell. It was from there they poured forth. But your people fought back. A girl among them had been blessed with an amazing power, which we call the Navă. But being the Navă took a terrible toll on her. It is whispered that Kizağan had possessed the girl and it was her who drove the beasts back through the doorway."

"Can they come back?"

"By the grace of God the doorway has been sealed, but what can be done can also be undone. It is said that there is a power within the Sword of Kizağan that can be used to kill the devil, yet it can also be used to open the doorway to Hell."

"How can that happen?"

"Patience," Vasile chuckled. "After the battle, the girl's power ebbed. Some say she died in the battle, while others say she lived to birth many children. Who is to know the truth? Anyway, there is a natural cycle that sees the power reach its peak in five hundred year intervals, more or less. We have reached the apex of the Cycle."

"I am the Navă," Elena said numbly. "I have been seeing things, strange things that can't be explained. I've done things."

Vasile crouched to stare deeply into Elena's eyes. "Being the Navă is not a curse. It is a blessing, even with the inevitable hazards you will face."

"Will I die?" she asked nervously.

"Of course you will die! Whether that day is tomorrow or next week, or even one hundred years from now...one day you will die, just as all of God's creatures will die. Death is just the beginning of the journey, though."

"What is this...power that I have?"

"Ah, the nature of the Navă's power is one of the great mysteries. What is within you will test you, it will push you beyond your natural limits, and if you find the necessary strength, you will be victorious. Yet because of the jealousy and greed of Hell's creatures, they sense your growing power. The Navă's growing power, that is, which will itself peak when you have reached womanhood. The power has awakened their thirst for power and blood, and so it has awakened the undead that will prepare the way for their coming!"

Elena began to understand. The Old Families told tales of strange and unbelievable creatures prowling the forest, but lately a truly unknown violence had come to their valley. "It's my fault," she said.

"Your fault? What is your fault?"

The girl remembered her parents' whispered conversations during the dark of night, when they sat at the little kitchen table and sipped țuică. "People have disappeared and the flocks have been getting ravaged. If I'm the Navă, and my power has awakened these monsters, then it's my fault."

The priest shook his head. "If not you, then another would be the Navă. It is inexorable. We have reached the apex of the Cycle and nothing will stop that wheel from turning."

She had turned to look at the fantastical carving on the stela, the girl holding the cup that radiated with light. "What is this?" Elena asked numbly.

"That, dear child, is the Navă. The first Navă, who is celebrated in this stela. Each panel tells a part of the tale of that first battle." he said, indicating the carvings. "Both in pictures, as well as the language of that ancient people."

"What does it say?" she asked as she inspected the runic letters.

Saint Vasile's chin wrinkled. "It says 'He Who Destroys, Shall Be Destroyed.' It is an ancient and forgotten language. Each one of the stelae include an intonation. Taken as a whole, they create a powerful force that combine to protect the world outside of Valea Întunecată from the foul things that rise with the Navă's power."

"What comes next?" she asked, nearly afraid to hear the answer.

"The monsters are coming. To defeat them and ensure five hundred years of relative peace, you must entreat Charles to mend the Sword of Kizağan. Only he has the power to perform that deed."

"Why him?" she asked.

"Because coursing through his veins are both the blood of the Old Families, and the blood of the devil."

She shuddered. "Is he evil?"

"As all of us do, he indeed has the capacity for evil. He also has an amazing capacity for good. But to defeat the evil of Hell, you must wield the Sword of Kizağan. To do that, he must fix the sword."

"Because he is the blacksmith, and within him is the forge?" she asked, remembering the words that Adina had said.

"A little abstract, but yes. Within Charles an inferno rages, and he will need to focus that rage to unleash its power so the Sword of Kizağan can be mended."

"Once the sword is fixed, he will need to give it to me," Elena said flatly.

"Not exactly," the priest frowned. "Like as not, the inferno will consume Charles. You will need to find him and recover the sword before Cosmin does."

She gasped in a harsh breath. "What will happen if Cosmin gets the sword?"

"Then, my dear, he will open the doorway, and the Devil's Cohort will be unleashed."

"Where are the sword's fragments?"

"Cosmin hid them away. He and his son quarreled, and the sword was destroyed during their struggle. He struck down his son, who was laid to rest in the castle's crypt. What was left of the Sword of Kizağan had been stashed within the tomb."

Elena's eyes narrowed. She would have to tell Charles where the sword was, and then she would need to make her way to the castle itself. "Tell me where it is. Tell me the tomb."

Vasile's eyes matched the girl's to pierce her soul. "It is the resting place of Vlad III Drăculea."

## 14

Valea Întunecată
At the same time

"Where is he?" Charles seethed through gritted teeth. Anger burned within him, a raging inferno that threatened to engulf everything around him. Stepan had lied to him, he lied about the relic and the stake and the holy water itself.

The tavernkeeper shot the dhampir a confused look. "Who?"

"The Cossack," he growled with a flushed face and clenched jaw. Charles was furious with Cosmin, he was livid with the Russian, he was incensed with life itself. His fury was directed at the entire world which placed him in this position.

"I haven't seen him," the man responded defiantly. "And I wouldn't know where to find him."

Charles pounded the bar top with an immense strength, the hard wood of it denting under his fist. "Don't lie to me, man. You know who my father is and so you know who I am! Tell me where the Cossack is!"

The barman shook his head bravely. "I don't know where Stepan is, and even if I did…"

He howled as Charles grabbed his hand and torqued it backwards, the finger bones snapping audibly. "I'll fucking kill you," he snarled. "I'll crush your fucking head with my bare hands, you miserable son of a bitch. Where the fuck is the Cossack?"

The man sobbed as he held his mauled fingers, his face contorted in loathing agony. "For the love of Christ, I don't know! He had rented a room from a widow but I haven't seen him since yesterday!"

Charles cried out in frustration and swept his arm across the bar's worn top, glasses smashing to shards against the stone floor. "Bullshit!" he screamed so that frothy spittle flew from his lips. "Tell me where the fuck he is, you cocksucker. Tell me where he is, or I'll make you wish you did."

"I don't know," the pitiful man pleaded, his savaged hand held tight to his body, tears streaking down his cheeks. Terror had wrenched his face to deepen the crags and clefts in his features. Charles loomed over him, quivering and shaking and spouting threats against his life.

"I don't believe you," Charles raging continued. "You're lying to me, and no matter how long it takes, I'll tear the truth out of your miserable fucking soul."

Tomas began to cry harder, pitiful sobs wracking his body as Charles walked slowly around the bar top, the violent threats continuing to pour out of him. The tavernkeeper tried to retreat from the dhampir but he was blocked by the stone wall of his tavern, so he stumbled and shrunk tightly into a defensive ball. Charles stalked toward the man, his blade brandished, its keen edge glinting menacingly in the meagre daylight that penetrated the tavern's gloom. Tomas slunk back to press against the far corner as the half-breed son of the vampire loomed over him.

"Stop!" A guttural Slavic voice commanded loudly in German, and Charles abruptly obeyed. The barkeeper huddled tighter into a ball and sobbed pitifully. "Stop, Charles. Or Costache, or whatever your name is."

It was the Cossack.

Charles whipped toward the interloper, a sneer wiped across his lips. "We were just talking about you," he smiled menacingly, the German sliding easily off his tongue.

"I gathered," the Russian answered curtly. "It doesn't appear to be the most congenial of conversations. You're a poor excuse of a man, bullying Tomas like this."

"Medieval persuasion is required from time to time. It's not my preferred method, but one that is necessary."

"From time to time," Stepan said, distaste heavy in his voice, his eyes fixed on Charles's knife. The dhampir slipped his blade back into its sheath, his fingers dangling lightly on its pommel should he need to draw it quickly.

"Yes. It is necessary. Don't pretend it isn't," Charles growled through pursed lips.

"Apparently."

"You lied to me," the dhampir said flatly, his lips curving into a frown.

"Lied?" Stepan shot back, surprised anger thick in his voice. "I've lied to no one! Why would you accuse me of lying?"

"The stake failed. The holy water and the saint's relics failed."

"Impossible! If your father is a strigoi then any one of those things would have sent him to hell."

"He's not a strigoi! He's a vampire!" Charles snarled, his hands balling violently into fists.

Stepan stretched to his full height, the barrel of his chest stuck out defiantly. "You think that I'm afraid of you? I'm afraid of nothing. I've seen worse and done worse than you could ever dream of."

"I've murdered innocents, just for the opportunity to destroy my father," Charles replied, angry at his own failure. "Their sacrifice was for nothing."

"If the stake and the water and the relics didn't work, then Cosmin the Wicked is no strigoi," Stepan said through clenched teeth.

"That's what I tried to tell you, you dumb son of a bitch. Strigoi and vampires are not the same thing!"

Stepan took a step forward, his hands held out in supplication. "Obviously. I see that now. Leave the poor man alone," the Cossack said, a dip of his head acknowledging the cowering Tomas. "He knows nothing. He is simply a tavernkeeper."

Charles glanced down at the pitiful man, sobbing and cowering in the corner. The dhampir's soul was empty, devoid of any feeling. He felt no pity, nor sorrow. "He lied to me."

"He did not…"

"He did! This gristly piece of cow shit lied to me. He knows exactly where you are staying, he knows exactly where you have been." Charles looked at the sorry, wretched little man, and contemplated sliding the blade of his knife up through Tomas's ribcage, his hand twitching at the thought of cutting through skin and connective tissues to cleave Tomas' heart in two.

"Leave him alone," the Cossack snapped angrily. "He's nothing, just a poor wretch trying to earn a living for his family."

"His family?" Charles murmured, the coldness of his spirit slowly seeping away.

"Yes. His wife and children."

"How many?"

"One."

"Not wives," Charles said in annoyance. "How many children?"

Stepan laughed nervously. "Of course! I thought for a second, 'How weird! How many wives does a man need?' Six. He has six children. Two boys and four girls. But one of the boys is sick."

Charles didn't move. He didn't laugh, didn't sneer, he didn't even frown. "How sick?"

"Very," the Cossack answered gravely. "I would be surprised if he survives until the leaves turn color."

"You know quite a lot about a simple tavernkeeper."

Stepan shrugged his shoulders. "He is a nice man, and I like to take care of those who take care of me. I prefer the company of nice people and nice things. God knows, the world has plenty of people like you and me."

"Killers," Charles said flatly.

Stepan shook his head. "Bastards. Damned fools. Heartless murderers."

Charles nodded, then shifted his predatory eyes from the tavernkeeper to the Russian. "Țuică?"

The Cossack shrugged his shoulders again. "Why not? We must figure out how to destroy your father, and țuică will certainly help."

The half-breed looked down at the barkeeper, still cowering pathetically behind the dubious protection of his bartop. "Sorry about that," he said in dispassionate Romanian. "Two țuicăs, please."

****

"I kind of feel bad, you know?" Charles said in German. "Sometimes I can't help it. I've been lied to my whole life, and I just…I don't know…I just *react*."

Stepan nodded morosely. "But did you have to break his hand?"

Charles held his hands up. "In my defense, all he had to do was tell me where you are staying."

"These people hate Cosmin. They loathe him, but they think he keeps the undead things under some manner of control. They may not fight against him, but they certainly won't help him…or you…and that's understandable, is it not?"

"I tried to kill the son of a bitch! Twice!" Charles protested before swigging at the plum liquor. "Surely they can understand that."

Stepan smiled ruefully, his glass of țuică sitting untouched on the table. "Could they possibly know about your attempts to destroy Cosmin?"

Of course they didn't know, and Charles didn't need to say it. He was angry, frustrated at the townsfolk who seemed to treat him as the devil incarnate. *Which may not be far off the mark*, he thought ruefully. "What do we do now?" Charles asked, his voice edged in regret at the red failure that still rankled him.

Stepan grunted. "It's my sworn duty to destroy Cosmin. He's evil, a devourer of the innocent, a corrupter of the incorruptible."

Charles frowned, his glass of țuică empty. "Why you? Why didn't Bekhmoaram try to destroy Cosmin all those years ago? He knew where my father lived."

The Cossack fiddled with his glass, his bottom lip tucked behind teeth as he thought. "Cosmin the Wicked's offspring rivalled him in the depths of their evil," he murmured, then shot Charles a look through hooded eyelids. "Most of them, anyway. My great-great grandfather had been renowned as a trapper and hunter in the deep woods of the Carpathian Mountains, but he ran afoul of a new lord. An outsider, a man who had somehow wriggled his way into the graces of the Tsar. This new lord had my great-great grandfather executed in a most horrible manner."

"That's terrible," Charles said without emotion. "I'm not clear on what this has to do with Cosmin or Bekhmoaram, though."

"It was indeed terrible," Stepan said. "Have you ever seen someone flayed while still alive? His skin was peeled, strip by strip, from his body. *Peeled*, Charles, the way one peels a banana. This experience did not kill him, though. After enduring his skin being removed, this lord had my great-great-grandfather's eyes and tongue removed. After suffering emasculation he bled to death, but not before his lungs were removed through his back in the manner of the old Norse blood eagle."

"Jesus," Charles said, and this time he meant it as his eyes went wide in macabre fascination.

"The lord who inflicted such pain and suffering on my great-great grandfather was one of Cosmin's sons. Such is the infection that your father has spread throughout the land."

"His son did this thing?"

"Yes, his son. Your brother, a terrible creature by the name of Răzvan. For the past three generations, we have been sworn to hunt down Cosmin and all of his progeny to cleanse the land of their filth. The men in my family were born as hunters, and these skills serve us well in our pursuit for the undead."

Charles sat back in his chair. "I mean, Cosmin's a huge piece of shit, but I have yet to see him eat anyone. Or do anything remotely close to what you're describing, for that matter. If he was really that evil, wouldn't the castle be a house of horrors?"

The Cossack shook his head. "That's what you believe because that's what he wants you to believe. But, I think, deep down inside, you know the truth. Even if you refuse to admit it."

"If Bekhmoaram knew Cosmin was here, why didn't he try to destroy him?"

The Cossack gave a curt shrug. "That is a question for the Rabbi, but he won't be answering any question now."

Charles grunted acknowledgement. He harbored suspicions about his father, of course, and Cosmin was far from trustworthy, of that he was sure, but he didn't really see him as the malevolent monster that Stepan accused him of being. The Cossack signaled to the tavernkeeper, who had again retreated behind the bar, his hand immobilized by a crude splint. "Another țuică, please, Tomas?"

The barkeeper jumped to it, his remaining good hand trembling to fill Charles' glass quickly, so he could beat a hasty retreat to his haven on the far side of the cramped room.

"I have other tools in my toolchest," the Cossack mumbled. "Powerful things that are capable of banishing the worst creatures to Hell. If your stake and water and relics failed, then it's my turn."

"Good luck," Charles frowned. "You'll need it."

****

Near Valea Întunecată
At the same time

With eyes closed and a heaving chest, Elena willed her heart to slow its manic beating. Daylight stretched the forest's shadows, and with the sun having long since began its descent behind the mountain peaks, she left the ghost of Saint Vasile at the ruined temple and weaved her way along the game trail until Valea Întunecată finally came into view. Save the common trips to the sheep pastures, Elena had never been so far from the village, and even those adventures were on well-worn and well-known paths.

Now she huddled behind her parents' house, forcing her racing heart to calm, and focused her mind to conjure the image of the vampire's son. "Where are you, Charles?" she called out to him. "Talk to me, I need you!"

Elena's eyes had squeezed tight, all her concentration on his eyes and nose and mouth, on the scruff of his chin and the brown of his hair, and she heard his voice cut through the dusk air.

"What is it now?" he said boorishly.

Elena ignored the discourtesy. "Where are you? I need to see you, it's important!"

"I'm in the village," he said, and she sensed an annoyance in him that boiled just beneath the surface of his words. "What do you want?"

"You're in the village? Meet me in the market square!"

"What? No. I'm going back to the castle."

"No!" the girl exploded in fury. "No, Charles! We have to meet, now!"

"Holy Jesus," the dhampir murmured meekly. "Yeah, fine, okay. When?"

****

The very last light of the day still grasped weakly at the village square with fingers of golden dusk, and the usually crowded place had thinned noticeably. Shopkeepers had begun to pack up their wares, the carts and wagons were being hitched to horses before night's horrors befell the valley, and then she saw him.

What few people were left in the square glowed with the light colors of contentment after another long day selling their goods or buying life's meager necessities, but Charles had no glow at all. He only had the blank slate of a soulless husk. The dhampir stood stiffly, his arms crossed and his face pulled into an annoyed frown, and the girl who wasn't quite a woman hurried up, snatched the dhampir by his arm, and pulled him into a side alley so the narrow confines of sandstone walls blocked them from whatever prying eyes were left.

"Calm down, girl!" he said as he smacked her hand away from his elbow. "You're stronger than I would have thought. Taller than I remember, too."

"There's no time," she said breathlessly. "I met the priest in the forest, and..."

"Wait, wait a minute. What priest?"

"Vasile! Saint Vasile!"

"God, he gets around, doesn't he?"

"Would you shut your mouth and listen?" she spat at him, her young face taut with impatience.

"Okay, fine, what did Vasile tell you? Let me guess, it's about the sword."

"Yes, of course, but it's more than that. We need the sword to destroy Cosmin.

"I know that."

"But Cosmin needs the sword as well."

"What will he do with it?" Charles asked, his eyes furrowed with concern.

"Cosmin will open the doorway and free the Devil's Cohort," Elena said earnestly. She leaned against the stone wall, the chill of it prickling her skin. "The door to Hell has been sealed, but if he gets the Sword of Kizagan, he will use it to pry off the seal and then his demons will be released."

"All I've wanted for the past hundred years was to destroy that miserable bastard," Charles said with slumped shoulders. "And I still want to. I want to do it for my dead family, I want to do it for my mother," he whispered. "But mostly, I want to destroy him because of the hell I've gone through. Just being born to him marked me as evil." He looked up, his eyes stained with a new sorrow. "I *have* to do it, Elena. If the sword can destroy him forever, if it can utterly annihilate his rotten soul, then I have to do it. Simply sending him back to Hell isn't good enough because he'll just find a way back. He needs to be stopped…forever."

Dark shadows stretched long across the market square, the last of the vendors having led their horses and packed carts back to the paddocks before the quickly approaching nightfall fell like a blanket. Elena's heart was gripped by an anxious hand. She knew that Charles spoke the truth, but she also knew that simply reassembling the sword was fraught with risk. If they couldn't destroy the vampire with it, then all was lost on one throw of the dice. "What do we do, then?" she mourned. "He can't get hold of the sword."

"Cosmin won't," Charles reassured her. "Because I'll drive it through his wretched heart."

"No," Elena said insistently. "You have to mend the sword, but I have to wield it. That's what Vasile said."

"Did the shriveled waste of flesh say where it's at?"

"Yes," the girl said as she eyed the setting sun nervously. "He said it's in the Drăculea's tomb."

"Vlad?" Charles blurted out. "Vlad Drăculea?"

Elena nodded. "He said that Cosmin buried it with Vlad after killing him."

"Cosmin killed Vlad? He killed his own son?"

"Yes, Vlad refused to lead the Devil's Cohort, so Cosmin killed him. That's when the sword was destroyed."

"That motherfucker," Charles spat.

"Language!"

"Sorry. It's too late now, Cosmin will be awake. Meet me at the castle tomorrow morning, after the undead things have gone back to their graves. At nine o'clock, with or without you, I'm going to open Vlad's tomb and reassemble the sword."

Elena nodded quickly. "I'll be there," she croaked, her throat squeezed with fear. "Be careful," she implored as Charles disappeared into the maze of alleys. "You must wait for me! Your father can't have the sword!" If she and Charles could do it, if they could fix the Sword of Kizağan and wield it against Cosmin the Wicked, then the nightmare would end. It all seemed so impossible, but she knew that she didn't really have a choice.

Did she?

\*\*\*\*

Valea Întunecată
Early Evening

Stepan wrote for what seemed like hours, the dwindling bottle of țuică at his elbow. The Cossack's room was bare. It was all he had and all he could afford, being a man of limited means, but it had a desk and a little cot, and that suited his purposes perfectly.

His paper, that he used to keep meticulous notes of each days' events, was arranged neatly on the desk's worn top, and his pens were positioned carefully to the right of the paper, already having performed the nightly routine.

Every recollection, every minute detail was committed to paper. He knew this ritual of his was tactically unsound. Such a trove of intelligence would be a boon to his enemy, but what were the odds his notes would fall into an adversary's hands? Nil, that's what. Stepan would draft his document, read it thoroughly and commit the words to memory, then file away his knowledge so that future generations would have the tools they needed to cleanse the Earth of these horrid creatures.

The Cossack had found a loose board in the room's floor, then worried its nails until the board popped free to reveal a narrow void. It was the perfect place to secret away his precious journal and assorted papers, and when hidden in such a concealed place there was little chance that anyone would be able to find out his secrets.

He sat back in the creaking chair, satisfied at his handiwork. Everything that happened today, every word and deed that he could remember, had been recorded. The Cossack was still disturbed and a little confused after learning the truth of Cosmin's power. The stake should have destroyed him, as the holy water and saint's relics should have. Whatever Cosmin was, he wasn't simply one more soldier in the undead legions as Stepan had assumed. Charles, too, was not what he had expected. The dhampir had been scared of his father. Of that, Stepan was sure.

All of the other dhampirs that the Cossack had hunted were monstrous, they were soulless beasts who preyed on others. Charles, just maybe, was different from his brothers and sisters. There was a slight possibility that a shred of a soul lurked somewhere deep within him. If that were the case, then perhaps the Cossack wouldn't need to strike the dhampir down.

Not yet, anyway.

He smiled. Charles would have to wait. Cosmin was the game for tonight.

Pondering the circumstances that brought him to this place, Stepan lifted a cigarette to his lips, paper and tobacco perched at the edge of his mouth, one of his few vices waiting for a match to strike. Light flared briefly, a tang of sulfurous smoke that floated lazily in the room's stagnant air, and the tiny house mouse cowered for the briefest second. "Well, hello there, little friend," the Russian cooed. His companion. This was the second time the little mouse visited Stepan's temporary home, yet he was still surprised at the gumption of the tiny rodent that sat perched on the edge of the desk. Stepan had been so consumed by his notes that he hadn't noticed it climb nimbly up the table's leg. "Would you like a puff?" he giggled, holding out the pungent cigarette. The mouse's nose wiggled in surprise.

Stepan took a long drag and exhaled slowly, considering the rodent. He rather enjoyed animals. So much of his life revolved around death, around destruction and subterfuge, that he took pleasure in the innocence of simple life, and it was easy to have a soft heart for cute little mice. The tiny beast walked around hesitantly, as if expecting the inevitable blow it would receive when skulking around humans. The Cossack let it explore his desk, an amused smile perched on his lips. It sat for a moment, its tiny front paws balled, whiskers twitching. "You look like a concerned old man," Stepan laughed, and the mouse really did have an air of concern about it, as if it were someone wringing his hands anxiously. Beady mouse eyes scanned over his paper, which also amused the Cossack, as if the little thing could read his neat handwriting.

Soon, very soon, the Cossack would begin the hunt, and so he savored the last moments of this indulgence. First, though, another țuică.

\*\*\*\*

### Cetatea Orașului
### Night

"Ah!" Cosmin beamed. "The prodigal son returns. I'm fine, thanks for asking, notwithstanding the unprovoked attack that ultimately proved unsuccessful. I can't believe that not a single soul told you that wooden stakes, water laced with pigeon dung, and a miserable saint's dried-out relic would have little to no effect on someone the likes of me!"

"I thought you're a vampire. Stakes and the whole bit are supposed to work," Charles managed to force through clenched teeth. Hatred festered within him like a boil. If the girl was right, then just maybe this would be the last night he had to be subjected to Cosmin's insults.

"You see? That's your problem. You *thought*. Next time, leave the thinking to those of us better equipped for just such a pastime."

Charles glanced with thinly veiled disgust at the creature who sat still, contemplating a chessboard. The pieces had been moved, a Rook threatening Cosmin's Queen. Those words, Cosmin's queen, flooded Charles with memories.

"She was beautiful," Charles choked back.

"Who?"

"My mother. I remember suitors lined up, trying to convince her to marry them."

Cosmin grunted and pushed the chessboard to the side. "Ioana was much too smart to waste her time on those sacks of excrement."

"They were rude. She always wore black, as a widow would." Charles nodded at the board. "Who is your opponent? Another miserable bastard I assume?"

Cosmin ignored his son's probing question. "She wore black so she wouldn't be scandalized by birthing a bastard," he stated matter-of-factly.

"Did she know that you were...are...a vampire?"

"No, of course not. I appeared to her as a young aristocrat. Which I was, of course. An aristocrat, that is. We were in love."

Charles sniffed at the notion.

"We were in love!" Cosmin insisted defensively. He sighed. "I haven't completely lost my humanity, no matter what inane beliefs you have absorbed. I don't skulk around in the dead of night preying on innocents. I do have the capability for love, at least to some extent." The vampire leaned forward, his face turning earnest. "It is a kernel, this shred of humanity. Maybe it is dormant? I suppose it's dormant at times, but it can come back to life. And it *has* come back...at times."

"You're a terrible liar," Charles spat, seeing right through his father's falsehoods. "Why did she leave?" Cosmin asked.

"Leave what?"

"Romania," the dhampir said, an arm sweeping wide to take in the castle's study. "This. Why did she leave?"

"I don't know, she never said." Cosmin sat for a moment, his face betraying a hint of melancholy. "I do wish she would have stayed," he said.

Charles closed his eyes and leaned back into the old chair, memories of his mother toying at the edge of his mind.

Cosmin barked angrily. "Those were terrible days," he said. "We staked many of them up."

"I don't want to talk about it."

"About what? The violence? Or your mother?"

"Any of it. You've ruined whatever good things that ever happened to me. All my happy memories are tainted by your stink."

"Oh, come on now, it's not that bad. We've been over this! Say, you look tired. How about tea? I have Earl Gray and black."

"No," Charles replied bitterly, his eyes wet with the shame of forgotten weakness, a frown marring his otherwise handsome face. The dhampir's mind wandered from his mother to his family, to Carina and the boys, and then the words began to flow, as if Charles had no control over them. "I hated the Turks," he said. "We all did, and then the opportunity came for me to leave Bavaria and join the armies of Moldavia so we could fight the bastards. We had learned to fight them and fight them well. At Războieni we lured them into a forest and set fire to it. What a terrible thing that was! It had been a hard campaign and starvation was rampant, and the smell of the burning Turks made the soldiers' mouths water. It was a horrendous stench." Charles closed his eyes, remembering the scorched meat which had so reminded him of rendering pork fat. "King Ştefan fought wonderfully, but then the Turks' king charged into our lines and overran the town. I was captured along with others, and they held me in the fortress."

"They tortured you."

"They did," Charles nodded, the memory a taint on his soul. "How did you know that?"

"I have a long reach," the vampire said nonchalantly. "Besides, Moldavia is not that far away."

"They stretched my arms behind my back and hung me from my wrists. Such was the punishment for us wretched nobles too cowardly to die on the field of battle."

"Cowardly? No. My offspring aren't cowards, they are resilient."

Charles didn't hear his father. Instead, he felt the familiar old agony rise again, an excruciating pain from deep within his soul. The tortures he had endured as a prisoner had wrenched him unbearably from his stupor so that he had whimpered, disoriented and dangling by his wrists from the dungeon's ceiling. Bloody trails seemed to burn through the years as they trickled down his outstretched arms. Crimson drops fell lazily from his limp fingers, his lank hair matted and scabbed. "I remember the pain," he said. "It never leaves me."

"Such is the blessing and the curse," Cosmin smiled wryly. "A perfect memory."

"That whole day and night was a blur of pain and torture and anguish. Was it only a single day since the city fell? I couldn't be sure." Charles winced at the memory of lancing sunlight that stabbed down from a miniscule porthole set into the stone of the dungeon. It had been a piercing fire that blinded him, and Charles remembered his sanity fleeing with that pinprick of daylight. "I was alone in the world after that, even if I didn't realize it at the time. My tears carved rivulets through the dirt and filth that had crusted on my face."

Cosmin grunted. "Tears aren't always something to be ashamed of."

"They were tears of shame because I couldn't protect my family. I was too stupid to leave them behind in Bavaria." He could still feel the salty drops that fell from the corners of his eyes and ran hard and wet down the creases in his face. "I would let the Turks see my tears, but they would never hear my anguish. That was the fuel for my fire. Besides, any sort of sound would invite more pain from the sadist who delighted in it."

"Your family was avenged," Cosmin said knowingly.

He ignored the vampire, his mind silently grieving for his wife and boys. "I vowed that I would bathe in the Turks' blood. They would learn who I was and that fear would haunt them all of their days. But then I lost consciousness again, and I woke to a strange noise." It was a gurgling noise, like a man choking on something. Charles had been hoisted to face the stone wall, those wrist shackles cutting into the flesh of his hands. Such were the tortures that, even as a dhampir, he had lacked the energy to turn his head. Still, he listened intently at the choking, gagging racket. When the gurgling noise stopped, silence infected the cell. It was the sound of death and it permeated the dungeon. "I remember wondering where the jailer was. The smallest sound would invite his whips and knives, but I couldn't hear him. Then fear had gripped my heart. I thought that death was coming for me, but then the cell filled with a mist. It was thick and impenetrable and choking. It came from nowhere, yet it was everywhere, and then I was lifted and the chains that bound me to the ceiling were silently released. Something rose me up and then placed me gently on the floor. I thought it was nonsense, a sadistic dream of my release. Only it wasn't a dream, was it? It was you."

Cosmin didn't answer his son. He sat still, stony and silent.

"I slipped out of consciousness again, but then sometime later I jerked awake on a pile of straw in a byre." He shook his head. "My bedmate was a steer whose head had been cleaved open. I had such a headache! I saw the byre's door was open, and the courtyard beyond was an orgy of blood and gore." Charles caught his breath, a great knot of phlegm snagged in his throat. "Women lay in the dirt, dead as dead can be, but what surprised me were the Turks. Numerous Turks, a horde of them, lay bloody and tangled with the city's dead." A chuckle rumbled from Charles's breast at the memory of his reaction. "I had to look twice to make sure it wasn't staged like some macabre play. The Turks were as dead as the women, but they weren't killed by swords or spears. It was as if a pack of animals had torn them to pieces. Not a single body was whole. Most of them had their throats ripped open, their arms and legs had been torn from their bodies. It was a nightmare. I will never forget the looks on their faces. Like they had died, frozen in terror." He coughed to clear his throat and choked down the lump of phlegm. "It was the look of men who had seen their deaths and were helpless to stop it."

Cosmin sat silently, looking at his son. His wry smile had twisted into a smirk. Weak moonlight illuminated the dim room through thick curtains, their impenetrability all the better to insulate against an uncaring outside world.

Charles only shook his head, thinking of that time. Sadness came over him as he relayed the day he buried his wife. He'd found her body, the boys wrapped in her arms, all of them spattered in blood. Not even the children were saved from the Turks' wanton orgy of violence. He couldn't look at them, broken as they were, but he remembered feeling some gratitude that the end had come quickly. Others had not been so lucky.

He'd buried the bodies of his family with an old spade from a barn, the wretched graves unmarked and undecorated, yet not forgotten. Not by him, at least, though the heartbreaking labor had ended his thirst for life. For three days he sat next to the makeshift graveyard under a budding oak tree and waited for death to find him. Yet he was not fortunate enough to be granted the sweet release of eternity. He had tried to weep, he wanted to scream, but a creeping numbness had entered his soul, its icy fingers killing what remained of his capacity to feel.

Only shreds of sanity remained, and even those were a distant reminder of who he used to be.

That was the one time he'd tried to end his own life. He had stood, took one last look at what remained of his earthly ties, and walked into the lazy river that snaked across the Moldovan plain. Marshy muck had sucked at his boots as he pushed through cattails, water rising above his knees, the cold of it wicking into his cotton trousers. A languid current had tugged at his blood-soaked coat, its hem clotted with mud from his poor family's freshly dug graves. He remembered the icy touch of the water as he submerged himself completely. A difficult task, as his body had tried to float, but eventually Charles had ducked fully under the surface to suck thick, muddy river water into his lungs.

The dhampir longed for death, he wanted to join his family in whatever afterlife awaited them, and as the current pulled him downstream, he swore that he could hear Carina's laughter. Then her laughter faded, the river slowed to a sullen crawl, and Charles emerged from the river.

He found that it wasn't so easy to die.

## 15

Cetatea Oraşului
Just before dawn

Stepan crouched low so that he was hidden by the forest's underbrush. Sweat beaded his brow, the intense exertion of creeping through the wood straining his face. He was a hunter from birth, trained to stalk silently and invisibly through forests and glades, but somewhere deep inside he knew this was a fool's errand. The strigoi or vampire or whatever it was in the castle controlled the animals of the valley, from the kingly bear to the lowest beetle. Nothing escaped Cosmin's knowledge.

Still, even utilizing his skills was a comfort, and comfort was in short supply.

Especially since Charles had failed to destroy Cosmin the Wicked.

*Maybe the dhampir was duplicitous?* Stepan thought, his teeth clenched with new loathing. Every strigoi was susceptible to stakes, to holy water, and especially to saint's relics. Such blessed weapons had slayed a dozen of the undead creatures, and certainly the relics should have destroyed Cosmin. Unless, of course, Charles was right, and his father was something else entirely.

Should he face Charles again, he would pound the truth out of the half-blood man, if it came to that.

His eyes darted left and right to ensure nothing was out of place in the dark forest, though his hunter's instincts sensed a wolf trailing him somewhere in the night. During the day, the wood was so thick and dense that not even the high sun's scorching rays would reach the bracken and brambles. Weak moonlight stood no chance against the forest cover though, so Stepan crept blindly through underbrush that tugged at his ankles. The beast that followed the Cossack wasn't stalking him, rather it seemed to be shadowing Stepan, keeping him in its sight. Before long, the Cossack glimpsed another silver form slinking across a rare splash of moonlight, and then another, and another. A pack of wolves, working as one to herd the hunter forward.

It was exactly as he had expected, it was exactly what he had hoped for. The closer Stepan came to the castle, the greater the chance of being seen and tracked by the creatures controlled by Cosmin the Wicked. The Cossack had counted on this, had welcomed it, for it increased his chance to meet the monster face-to-face.

Which brought its own trepidation. He choked the fear back, swallowed it down. *My mission is a holy one,* the rote words came to flit about within his brain. *My mission is a holy one, ordained by God as the righteous path.* A smile played across his lips. Death welcomed him, and he it, for dying while on crusade was the most noble death, the highest honor, a sure path to sainthood. And what could this be called, how else could it be described, if not a crusade? His war was a holy war, to be carried against the ungodly, and the strigoi in his fastness was certainly the antithesis of the holy messenger of God. Stepan imagined that Cosmin the Wicked stunk of the devil, of sulfur and foulness, and if the Cossack's death came while driving a stake through the strigoi's desiccated heart, then it was a death to be proud of. *Charles failed,* he thought, *but where he failed, I will persevere.* His weapon had been carefully chosen, a proven tool that had struck down many of Cosmin's dhampir offspring before.

Fingers tightened around the bleached bone he held in his hand. It was long, as long as his thigh and nearly as thick as his wrist, and one end was fitted with a sharpened point of iron and birch that had been toughened in flame. It was the thighbone of one Saint Gregory. Not the dead pope, certainly, yet it was a powerful relic nonetheless, and its point had been soaked in the holiest water, it had been blessed by the Holy Father himself, and Stepan had taken the time to carve little crosses all along the smooth yellow-white shaft.

This was God's plan. Stepan was merely His weapon, a holy weapon wielded to strike down the wickedest evil that stalked the land, but then his smile turned inexplicably melancholy.

Without another thought, he burst into a moonlit meadow, the wolves ending their earnest chase. He knew they were corralling him, driving the Cossack forward as if he were a sheep and the strigoi was the shepherd. With a grunt he sprawled forward, some unseen root having caught his foot, but then rolled amongst grasses and weeds and bracken to jump nimbly to his feet, ready to face Cosmin's beasts.

Curses flew from the Cossack, his mouth hanging in disbelief. He was virtually surrounded by innumerable vermin and insects and cats and wolves, all the creatures of the night that hunted the forest. Every one of them had frozen to stand still and as silent as statues.

"Welcome," a voice hissed. It was the voice of a nightmare, it was the voice of an evil plague that infected this strange land, a voice that had haunted Stepan's dreams from his earliest days. "This is my home," it said fondly. "These are my pets."

Stepan turned to glare at Cosmin the Wicked. The creature was illuminated by silver-white moonlight and it stood stiffly, its back hunched and with hands folded behind its back. Cosmin's head was devoid of hair, brown liver-spots the only adornment on its parchment-thin pasty skin. Its bloody smile was broken by yellow-brown fangs, its jaundiced eyes squinting through foul slits.

"I'm not afraid of you," Stepan spat, steeling himself against Cosmin's icy, unblinking stare.

"Yes, you are," the creature said wickedly.

"I'm not *afraid* of you," the Russian said again, as if repeating the words would make them come true.

"You are made of fear," Cosmin said mildly through those brown-tinged fangs. "You reek of it. Fear seeps through your pores for all my beautiful creatures to smell. It's how they knew you had entered the forest. It's how they tracked you to my home. You are afraid, Stepan Ivanovic. You cannot help yourself. It is a part of you."

The Cossack's lip curled in anger, his voice rising to a defiant shout. "Believe what you want, you evil thing. I'll cast you back into the pit you crawled from." He launched himself at the vampire, his arm cocked back, ready to drive the point of Saint Gregory's bone into Cosmin's breast. The beasts howled and yipped, a billion insect legs rustling through leaves and grass to protect their master, but Stepan's only desire was to skewer the undead thing with his homemade weapon blessed by God. It was a gamble, a foolish gamble. A failure, he realized, only too late. Stepan swung his arm down to strike, and as the point of the spear plunged towards Cosmin, the foul and hunched body of the strigoi erupted into an explosion of beating wings.

Frantic flapping erupted in the meadow, a hideous din of a thousand bats screeching and diving, swooping all around Stepan as he sprawled onto the ground where Cosmin had stood a mere eye-blink before. They descended on the Cossack, smothered him, latching onto his arms and legs so that he couldn't move, then the army of ants and beetles and spiders descended onto the Stepan, and the man who had welcomed a holy death fell victim to the unholiest itself.☐

\*\*\*\*

"Where is my prisoner?" the ghoulish hag dribbled expectantly. The time of victory was nearly upon them and she could hardly contain her glee. After many millennia of failure, she could taste the steely tang of victory on her tongue.

"He is in the vault," Cosmin said. "Waiting for the Conjurer."

Unul Vechi nodded eagerly. "He will be ruthless," she grinned, spittle foaming at the corner of her mouth. "His magic will allow me to destroy the temples."

"Us, don't you mean?"

"What?"

"Us. It will allow *us* to destroy the temples."

"Yes, of course that's what I meant. Us."

"Finally," the vampire rejoiced, his lip twisted into a snarl. "I won't be confined to this damned valley."

"We will begin soon," she crooned, her face contorting with ecstasy. "What about your son? Has he agreed to become your general?"

"No, he hasn't," Cosmin frowned.

"Incompetent fool!" the witch sprayed. "Without the sword the doorway will remain sealed! We need your son!"

"You are an objectionable crone," Cosmin grumbled. "I admit, it would be easier if he would agree to stand at my side, but as long as he mends the sword we can still win the war."

"And who will lead the Cohort?" the hag spluttered at her son. "You will have far too much to do once they flood the land. You can't lead them all."

Cosmin shrugged. "I don't know, Eishith maybe?"

"Eishith!" Unul Vechi graveled. "Your whore? All she is good for is whelping vicious bastards. Na'amah would be far better."

"The point is, that can wait," the vampire spat back. "All Charles needs to do is mend the sword, and my creatures tell me that is exactly what he is going to do. The rest will fall into place."

"I know who the Navă is," the witch growled.

"So do I, Mother. You took so long to uncover such a simple thing that I had to do it myself. Elena and my son are going to come here tomorrow. They will try to destroy me, yet they will fail." Cosmin chuckled at the gawking look that she shot at him. "You say I'm incompetent, yet you are on the verge of becoming redundant."

"You little prick. Without my magics you would be lost. Never forget that!"

"Oh, I won't," Cosmin smiled, satisfied with his mother's indignant anger. Such battles of wit were hard-fought and he savored the sensation of victory. "Costache tried to kill me with a broom handle and pigeon shit."

Unul Vechi's momentary anger with Cosmin sloughed off at the revelation. "That is impossible, doesn't he know that?"

"Of course he knows it, and the miserable son of a bitch tried to do it anyway. The ingrate!"

She cackled, her laughter a guttural, choking noise, and then her old spark of contempt was rekindled. "Even if he comes around and agrees to lead the Cohort, you will never trust him. You should go another route."

"What route is that? I have Eishith and Na'amah and half-a dozen other leaping savages to lead the Cohort. It would all be simple if Costache would join me, but no big loss if he doesn't," he said, a finger wagging at Unul Vechi. "If the Conjurer can destroy the temples, then we will march to victory!" Cosmin's face shifted from one of expectant triumph to flash a hint of regret. "It's too bad Regina wasn't strong enough to make it through the transformation. Maybe she could have been one of my chosen ones.."

"Regina and Eishith and Na'amah would suffer from the same limitations that you suffer from."

"You're such an optimist, Mother. What do we do then? Pray tell."

"Forget all of them, forget them!" the witch snarled. "They are no better than animals!"

Cosmin spun on his mother, his face seething with renewed anger. "I won't wait another five hundred years! I need generals *now*! My son was supposed to be the supreme leader of the Cohort, but he has forsaken me!"

Unul Vechi ignored her son's lashing fury. "Why would you wait? Why would you? There is nothing to decree that your son will lead the Cohort, no ancient prophecy or black gospel or anything. The One Who Has Been Chosen could be a daughter, it could be anything at all."

"Is that a fact?" Cosmin snarled at her. "I am forced to hide from sunlight each day, and who knows if Na'amah or Eishith will be able to lead the Cohort? They've been in Hell for thousands of years! And even if they can, will they be able to range far from the doorway? Or will they grow weak, like me?"

Unul Vechi smiled, a wide and terrible grin full of blue gums and black teeth. "I can lead them, you dolt. You must have inherited your father's gift of brainlessness. Unlike you, I'm not bound to some place. Unlike you, I can easily move around during the day *and* the night. And, like you, I have the power to control those slavering beasts you've got stashed away in Hell. Bind your succubae to me if you must, but I can be the queen regent to your kingship!"

"Why should I think that you are any more trustworthy than my faithless son? You've betrayed me as often as not!" Cosmin said through pursed his lips, his eyes lancing thunderous lightning bolts at Unul Vechi. Did he really have a choice, though? If not his son, if not Hell's succubae, then he may need to rely on his mother. With, of course, the proper precautions. "Fine," he said at length, the foul taste of it thick on his tongue. "You have my word. Since Costache refuses to join me, then we will have to move on to your Plan B. Don't think I won't have my eye on you. Now bring me the Conjurer."

****

Guttering candlelight flickered off of dull black stone. Dozens of candles littered the chamber, its soaring dome rising far into the blackness that the candles couldn't hope to dispel. Stepan had long since ceased struggling against the leather thongs that bound him hand and foot. A thick leather strap ran from his ankles up his back to his wrists, which had been secured tightly in the small of his back so that he looked like a trussed pig.

"He is awake," a voice croaked from somewhere in the dark, the harsh sound bouncing off rough basalt so that it came from everywhere at once. "Can we begin? I want to begin."

"Not yet," came the smooth voice of Cosmin. The Terrible, the Wicked, the horribly evil creature that haunted this valley.

Stepan closed his eyes, his lips working in a silent prayer. *O Lord, have mercy on us, for in Thee have we put our trust.* He had stupidly barged through the forest, blinded by a holy duty to destroy the evil strigoi. An infantile strategy, he realized too late, and one utterly doomed to failure. It had worked before, but this creature was unlike any of the undead that Stepan had face previously. *Do not be angry with us, nor remember our iniquities, but look down on us even now.* The Cossack had survived this game for almost twenty years already, and now he saw his death approaching. Stepan didn't fear death. Instead he welcomed it as an old friend, as a lover is welcomed to his embrace, but his job was not yet done and the failure rankled him. Cosmin the Wicked still walked the Earth, and Stepan was bound like a lamb to the slaughter. *Look down on us even now, since Thou art compassionate.* Was He compassionate, though? Did Stepan deserve His compassion?

*Deliver us from our enemies.*

Deliver us from our enemies.

Stepan's eyes opened at the light swishing sound of Cosmin's approach. "I've been told that you say I am a strigoi," the vampire muttered as he crouched next to his captive, a smile playing across his thin red lips. The Cossack tried not to look at Cosmin's face, but he couldn't tear his eyes away from the jaundiced eyes and brown-tinged points of the yellow fangs. "I tried to convince the witch to let me feed, but she selfishly wants you for herself. It's all for the better. She has something planned for you. Anyway, do you understand the difference between me, a vampire, and strigoi?"

Stepan grunted through the heavy, filthy cloth that bound his mouth.

"Was that a 'no'? I'll just pretend it's a 'no'. I will keep it brief. A strigoi is an undead spirit. The simpletons in this valley believe that strigoi are ghosts that suck the life out of their closest family. Tell me, what kind of person would do such a thing? It almost seems…what's the word?"

"Incestuous?" the crone coughed, thick and phlegmy, from the fringe of flickering candlelight.

"No! Seriously, Mother? Incest is much different, and I should know. The word I was thinking of is 'depraved'. Devouring the life of your own family." He crouched lower to command Stepan's attention. "Isn't that depravity? Yes, I believe it is depravity."

The creature suddenly disappeared from the Cossack's view, that strange swishing sound of his movement disorienting. Stepan began to pray harder. *O God of spirits and of all flesh...*

"Are you listening to me? Mother, he's not listening."

*O God of spirits and of all flesh, who hast trampled down death and overthrown the Devil.*

Wrenching agony tore Stepan from his prayer. Cosmin dangled the man from the leather straps that bound his wrists, so that the Cossack was hoisted into air, his arms bent backwards painfully. Stepan could feel the muscles and tendons in his shoulders begin to give under the pressure, to tear and snap. Gleeful cackling burst out from somewhere in the darkness like dried twigs rattling in the wind.

"You better start listening to me, Stepan Ivanovic. I can make your last moments on Earth more terrible than even *you* can imagine."

The Cossack fell, released from the vampire's grasp, his body's sudden impact on stone knocking the wind from his lungs. Stepan choked air through the fetid gag, struggling to inflate his collapsed lungs.

"As I was saying before being *rudely* ignored...a vampire, as opposed to those terrible strigoi, is something entirely different." Cosmin's head bobbed around, his hands flapping as he talked. "I know, I know, drinking blood and all that. Pure strigoi, right? Well, no. I, too, drink blood. Happily, might I add." The vampire crouched down again, snapping his fingers to regain Stepan's wandering attention as his victim cried from the pain. "Where strigoi and I differ, though, is that I am not undead, not at all. My name isn't even Cosmin!" he laughed. "Isn't that funny? Everyone says that I'm some undead savage beast who preys on virgins!"

"Absurd," came the hag's ragged response. Stepan squirmed, his wrists chafing within the leather bonds.

"Absurd! Yes! Though I do like a virgin every now and then. Don't you?"

The Cossack shivered against the foul evil that had trapped him in this den of vileness.

"I thought so," Cosmin laughed again. He leaned closer to the Russian, eyes locked on his prisoner. "I have another name, an older name," the vampire whispered. "Malthus, I was once called, and will be called again."

Stepan closed his eyes in defeat, failure and despair clenching his heart in a tight fist. He was a hunter of the undead and knew the name *Malthus* from esoteric books on occult matters. Most of the tomes were fraudulent and filled with trash, but a few contained true knowledge from beyond the bounds of this plane. Malthus was one of those powerful creatures who lurked in the reaches beyond this world.

How had he found his way to Earth?

Stepan heard scratching noises from the dark reaches of the vaulted space. Thankfully, the vampire removed the squalid gag from Stepan's mouth so the Cossack could breathe easier. His shoulders still burned from the abuse he had taken, but at least the worst of the stabbing pain had subsided. "What are you, then?" the Cossack managed to cough out in Russian.

"I am happy you asked," Cosmin smiled widely as he stretched tall, with arms flung wide so that his voice echoed through the chamber. "I am the first vampire, the original evil to have befallen this land! I am the son of the Devil, I am the High One of Hell! I am a demon, and I've been bound to this body to create something *new*."

"Shut up, you twat!" the rancorous voice called from the fringe. "You're interrupting my spells."

"Sorry, Mother," Cosmin said mockingly with rolling eyes.

"You possessed Cosmin?" Stepan wheezed painfully.

"No! No! This is no mere possession, you idiot. I've melded with Cosmin, we have become *one*. I can't be cast out through simple exorcism. Don't you see? I wear his corpse as armor, so that nothing can hurt me. I am nearly indestructible in this form, Stepan Ivanovic!" Cosmin had wandered around as he talked, his hands still flapping excessively, but then he whipped around to face the Cossack once again. "They say I am evil. Am I truly evil, though? I do believe I've been misunderstood. Think about it, Stepan Ivanovic. So I kill people? Who doesn't? Even you are guilty of murder, are you not?"

"Ev…everyone I've killed…deserved it."

"That's what I'm saying!" Cosmin shouted in victory.

"Shut up!" Unul Vechi screamed back.

"Sorrrryyyy, Motherrrr. Where was I? Oh, yes. Humanity's time has passed," the vampire said, once again crouching next to the prone Stepan. "Don't you agree?

I'm not saying *everyone* will die. That's not what I'm saying at all. No, just most of them, and whoever is left will serve me and my horde."

"Your...horde..." Stepan managed to spit out, though his mouth had ran dry of saliva.

"My horde! My army. My family, Stepan Ivanovic, I am talking about my family. All four million, four hundred thirty-nine thousand, six hundred and twenty of them. No, I'm sorry. Twenty-one, my mistake. Of course, that number does not include me."

"Demons," the Cossack wheezed.

"The Devil's Cohort," Cosmin confirmed. "Your death will bring one of my most powerful followers to Earth and help prepare the way for them. Then, the girl's death will lower the veil between this world and that, even if my son..."

"Your...son..."

"That's what I said, didn't I? My son, the wayward Costache, was destined to rule alongside me, to lead the Devil's Cohort across every corner of this planet. It would have been glorious!" he shouted again, his arms thrown wide in rapture. "Except, he will not join me."

"Shut your mouth, you miserable halfwit!" the crone spat angrily. "I'm nearly finished and your insolent screeching is distracting me."

"Sorry, Mother," Cosmin said again, but this time he smiled cruelly at the bound Stepan. "It's almost time, how exciting! Aren't you excited, Stepan Ivanovic? I promise, she won't take long. You'll barely feel a pinch. Give my best to your great-great-grandfather, and don't feel bad about your failure. It appears *that* particular trait is hereditary to the Ivanovic line."

Stepan squirmed on the polished black stone of the chamber's floor. The Russian had been stripped naked, bound at both ankles and wrists, the mildewed gag replaced to muffle his cries. Frantic prayers ran through his head, and the Cossack pleaded to his God for deliverance.

Unul Vechi grinned at his suffering. "You see," she said as she stumped closer on fleshy ankles. "You shouldn't have shouted so. It's your fault that you've been silenced. Consider yourself lucky, I could have torn your tongue out, but I didn't."

"He's very lucky," Cosmin laughed.

She nodded at the bound man. "You're very lucky indeed."

He sobbed quietly, terrified at the horrid sight before him. She was living flesh rotting off the bone, her hair lank and greasy, her skin riddled with purple veins and liver spots. For the love of the living Christ, the stumps of her ankles looked as if a wild animal had gnawed the feet off her legs.

Stepan had known that his life would lead down a path that would inevitably end in his death, but could he have known such a creature as this could exist? The answer escaped him. He had spent his life hunting all manner of evil across the mountains and forests and steppes of Europe. He had hunted dhampirs and strigoi and wolfmen, even those bodies that had risen from their graves by some hideous magic.

None of those experiences could prepare him to face this bloated, reanimated corpse.

Stepan shut his eyes, tears carving grimy trails down his cheeks. He could scarce believe that he was in this position, and the Cossack prayed harder, so that God would deliver him from what would be a damnable death at the hands of the very evil he had hunted.

The hag's pendulous stomach threw her slightly off balance as she hobbled towards Stepan. Groans betrayed the relentless discomfort of walking on raw stumps, the fleshy bits of her ankles squishing against black stone. Polished rock reflected the dully flickering candlelight onto the wandering crone, and Stepan's eyes tracked her until she stopped in front of his prone form. "It never gets easier, young man," she smiled, her tongue running across the black remnants of teeth that had long since rotted away. "Are you ready? It is coming."

Stepan choked back his fear, a rancorous sob caught in his throat.

"Do you feel it? The moment is here. You lie at the Great Juncture. Today is the future, and you are at its center."

His skin was sticky from cold sweat, his heart quailing with fear. Stepan didn't know what was going to happen to him, but he feared a fate worse than death.

The old crone coughed and gagged, her ancient body wracking from the sounds. But they weren't coughs, he realized, they were words, ancient and forgotten words from bygone time, and they poured out of the witch as her tongue clicked and her mouth spat to create odd noises. Stepan tried to scream, he needed to release the terror, but he was paralyzed, as if he were frozen in a nightmare. The old woman stumped closer, her chanting growing clearer. "Do you feel it? It is here, in this room. It awaits its vessel!"

Tears poured down his face now, not a mere trickle carving streaks through the grime, but a torrent. The witch's chanting grew fevered, the voice of the ancients vomiting from her soul. She twitched, her hands held high, the loose skin of her underarms swaying with each archaic syllable, and she held his attention in the wan light, so terrible that Stepan couldn't look away. In one hand the sorceress held a small muslin bag tied with twine, its contents concealed within the fabric, and in the other was an ancient blade of obsidian, the black glass glinting ominously in flickering candlelight. Stepan realized, too late, that his fate was far worse than he could have imagined. He was a man who held the Lord in the highest regard, who longed for the day that he sat at the right hand of God, a man who adored His son, the Christ Jesus. Yet he was to become a black sacrifice. His fate was to dwell forever in the depths of Hell.

And then the screams came.

Unul Vechi fell to her knees as the black knife plunged deep into Stepan's breastbone. She leaned into him, the blade carving deeper into his chest, dull fire lancing from the knife as the old crone cackled with delight. She worked at the wound, its sharp edge opening the bloody wound in the Cossack's chest ever larger until his beating heart was exposed, then Unul Vechi yelped in triumph and seized the organ. Stepan lay transfixed, fascinated with the sensation of her cold hands as they seized his heart, its pulsing muscles still pumping blood through his arteries and veins.

Her chanting began again, in earnest this time, and the long-forgotten words of a forgotten world drew something from the æther . She sang the ancient song, she cut away the ropes that bound Stepan's wrists and feet and the gag in his mouth, and his cruel shrieking had died away as the pulsing blood slowed. Even though his consciousness had begun to fade, Stepan could still feel an infectious and intoxicating power throbbing in the vampire's cavernous vault.

Unul Vechi screamed in triumph and rapture, her bloodied hand gripping the slippery organ, its gore spilling onto the black stone, as she shoved the muslin bag into his chest's cavity. Stepan gasped for air one more time, the last of his essence ebbing, and the hag knelt next to him, her lip quivering with spittle. "It has come unto you. Your body is now the Conjurer's vessel, and it will walk the land to tear down those damned temples to Kizağan!"

## 16

Cetatea Oraşului
Morning

Looming out of the forest to tower over Elena, the decrepit castle sat as a great and stony toad, a glare from low clouds making it brood even more than usual. She had seen the citadel before, but only from a distance. Elena had never ventured through the forest to see it up-close for herself. Charles was in there, somewhere, waiting for the girl, and the thought of him being alone within the monument to evil made her shudder. She knew that he needed her, though. Charles would mend the sword, and the girl who stood on the brink of womanhood would destroy his father.

Morose clouds scudded across the sky above, and she found herself contemplating whether or not rain would fall and whether she would survive to feel its cleansing chill. Elena shook off macabre thoughts. *Such views do no good,* she reminded herself with a heart-thudding frown.

There was a great big door of stained oak and rusted hinges, the face of the monstrosity carved with all manner of twisting, snarling beasts. Elena swallowed nervously and forced herself to ignore a rising trepidation.

God had called on the girl, and she must answer Him.

The sun was traversing the sky somewhere above those heavy clouds, and that meant that Charles would be preparing himself to reassemble the Sword of Kizağan. Common sense insisted that the evil Cosmin would know of it, and undoubtedly the vampire would try to stop his son.

With another swallow, Elena mounted the castle's steps to push clammy hands against the heavy door, and she was surprised when the rusted and ancient hinges swiveled noiselessly, as if they'd been greased only yesterday.

Gray daylight illuminated the dimly lit corridor beyond. Flickering wall sconces threw off a bit of warmth, but her eyes still took a minute to adjust to the relative darkness. She slid inside quietly, though she had to suppress a chuckle at the same time. *He would already know that I'm here,* the girl realized. *The forest must be swarming with his creatures.*

If the creatures had seen her, and Elena felt certain they had, then the vampire would have been told of her presence, whether or not he slept.

Still, she crept down the hallway with the silence of a wraith. Charles had told her there was a stairwell set into one of the keep's walls, and that it descended into the bowels of the promontory, where the castle's crypt had been cut straight out of the rock. "I'll wait there for you," he had said. "But don't be late. I won't wait long."

Ignoring the incessant shiver that slid up and down her spine, Elena picked her way quietly down the dusty, flickering hallway.

"I knew you'd come," came a grating voice.

Elena gasped, her heart pounding at the ragged noise.

"I knew, because my pets told me that you'd come." The creature shuffled from a darkened alcove, a hole in the keep's wall that flowed with cold air. She was old and fat and tottered on footless ankles, with skin pasted an unhealthy color and lifeless white hair. "I am Unul Vechi, and you are the Navă ," she said simply.

"I'm Elena," the girl said through clenched teeth. "Come any nearer and I'll scream for Charles."

The witch chuckled. "It won't do you any good. If I am right, and I am, he has decided that you took too long and is in the process of reassembling the Sword of Kizağan."

"He can't!" Elena cried a little too loudly.

"Oh, hush. Of course he can. That's his entire job. It's the whole reason he exists in the first place."

"Your voice," Elena said suddenly, haunted dreams flooding her memories. "I know your voice. You're the thing from my night terrors."

"Am I? Perhaps, perhaps not. I *can* talk to people in their dreams."

"You're the thing who killed my parents!" Elena shouted, remembering the tall, thin creature with raking limbs and twiggy fingers who had savaged Gavriel and Ruxana in her nightmares.

"Now you're talking nonsense," the witch crooned through a lopsided, toothless grin. "I would never kill your parents. I have no reason to. In fact, I don't even want to kill you. I want you to live, Elena, because if you live, my son will finally be destroyed, and that would be a happy day."

****

Elena stumbled on Unul Vechi's words. The voice was the same as the one in her dream, she was certain of it, yet the old woman before her was impossible to reconcile with the malevolent thing from her dream. "Who is your son?" the girl mumbled, her fist clenched impotently.

"Some call him Cosmin the Wicked, who I'm sure you've heard of. His real name is Malthus, and he is a miserable twat who only cares for his pet project. He thinks I've been helping him, of course, because I'm his mother. But I hate him. I hate him so much it burns my stomach. If you don't believe me, though, I will show you something," Unul Vechi said, the words a panacea to the girl as the witch stumped close. "Give me your hand, and I'll show you."

"Stay away," the girl spat. "Stay away from me, you evil thing. You're as evil as Cosmin is. I can see it in your glow."

"My glow! You must mean my aura. That is a rare trick, girl! What color is my aura?"

Elena's eyes narrowed to feral slits. "You are dark as dusk. You are blue and green and purple, I can feel the evil writhing inside you like snakes."

The hag's smile grew wider, her purple gums and black teeth turned orange by the wall sconces. "I wasn't always this way. I was once a goddess. Men and women worshipped me, a long time ago, when I was perpetually young and lithe and beautiful. But then his father came to me, he whispered sweet lies into my ear, and then he put that foul creature into my womb. Look at me now! I am a *monster*."

"Who?" the girl murmured, tears filling her eyes. She was afraid to hear the truth, but forced herself to ask the question anyway.

"Satan," the witch spat. "Lucifer. The Devil. He impregnated me with that imp named Malthus, and our son sucked me dry during the pregnancy. He devoured my life, he consumed my soul! Don't you see, Elena? They destroyed me! The Devil and His son ruined everything about me! Now, though…now, I get to have my revenge. It will be the perfect revenge," she smiled delightfully with those ghastly teeth. "Now it is just the two of us, and you have a choice to make," the hag rattled after waiting a handful of heartbeats. "I have waited thousands of years for my vengeance, and now I finally have the opportunity! *You can't imagine how this feels.*"

"You're evil, though," Elena said through quivering tears. "You're just as evil as him. I can feel it."

The witch cackled with glee. "Perhaps I am! But it is a different flavor of evil. Together, you and I can destroy Malthus. My son would have Charles lead his army of mindless demons against humanity, and given enough time I'm afraid my grandson would fall victim to his charms. Thankfully, Malthus is a dimwitted idiot and an utter failure and my grandson is breathtakingly hard-headed. Be that as it may, if he is successful and his demons make it through the doorway, they will run rampant. Nothing will be able to control them, not even him!"

"Why do you care?" the girl spat, her face pinched with sorrow.

"This valley is as much my home as it is yours!" Unul Vechi shouted, a finger poking at the girl's face. "Together, we can stop my son. Think about it! Whatever undead still prowl this valley will obey my commands. I will keep them away from your family, I'll keep them away from the entire town! I will rule the night, and you'll never even know that my pets exist."

Numbness crept up Elena's spine at the prospect of allying herself to this creature. The witch's demand was a temptation that Elena considered for a moment, but then she felt waves of ambition radiate from Unul Vechi's rotting core. How long would their bargain last? Only as long as it was a convenience for the witch.

"No," Elena said with a steely voice. "I will destroy Cosmin, or Malthus, or whatever his name is. All Charles needs to do is reassemble the sword."

Unul Vechi barked with laughter. "By all means, then, descend to the crypt, but I'm coming with you. Whatever you say, you will not be able to do it alone. Don't be shocked by what you see, though."

"What does that mean?"

"Charles won't survive the forge!" she cackled, her great and pendulous belly quaking. "It is the only reason he even exists, and when he touches the sword it will consume him in an inferno. That means you must hurry, otherwise my son will get to the sword first!"

Horror enveloped the girl. Charles would die, yet their souls were supposed to be intertwined. Only together could they destroy Cosmin, that was what Vasile had said! If Unul Vechi was right, then even if Charles was able to survive the forge, even if he wasn't consumed by its power, Cosmin could still win the struggle. "But it's daytime!" Elena gasped. Daytime is when the vampires sleep, daytime is when he is supposed to be most susceptible to attack.

"You don't really believe that matters, do you? My son isn't a strigoi. He is a demon whose very essence has infected a human to meld with the living corpse. He is a vampire, girl. Sure, he can't be exposed to sunlight, but he doesn't *have* to sleep if he doesn't want to! Oh," Unul Vechi said. "It appears you are too late, though."

A scream, long and ululating and haunting, seared the very air from the stairwell's void.

****

Cetatea Oraşului
At the same time

Darkness enveloped Charles, his weak oil lamp the only thing holding back its impenetrable veil. The crypt was long and narrow and tall, and the dhampir easily found Vlad's rock-cut tomb. It was just has he remembered, the carved shield with its double-headed eagle, the clawed feet grasping a sheaf of arrows and a sword. *V D III*, it had been engraved, the letters still retaining minute traces of gold leaf. He removed the crucifixes and set them aside gingerly, his subconscious unwilling to invite disfavor from the Christian God, if He even existed.

Charles swung a massive iron hammer, its heft easily fracturing the thin stone to expose the casket beneath so that his lamp's wan and smoky light reflected off its dusty surface. The box had been pushed deep within the tomb's space, so far back that it was nearly out of his reach. "God damn it," he blasphemed, then took a deep breath and reached into the tomb, his fingers brushing away thick cobwebs while his imagination spied millipedes and spiders scuttling away from his intruding fingers.

Then he touched it. The reliquary was frigid, with a thin layer of dust obscuring precious metal. Stretching deep within the narrow cavity, Charles gripped the box and pulled, the metal chest grinding across roughly hewn rock. It was heavy and would have been impossible for any other man to remove, but Charles' inhuman strength was barely tested. The casket was made of solid gold, a fortune's worth of gold that was chased with silver and brilliant gems. Scenes of battles and hunts and saints had been crafted skillfully onto its every panel, myriad eyes set with precious emeralds and sapphires, fantastical animals studded with rubies. Charles had no eye for the riches, though. The lamp's light was glinting dully off of something else deep within the cavity. Charles reached further into the stone hole, stretching to his full length as he half climbed his way inside.

Fragments of metal had been pushed to the back of the vault. Vlad's reliquary had blocked them from view, but now Charles was grunting in the dark, laboriously retrieving each piece of the sword. Some fragments were large, as long as his arm and as wide as his wrist, but most of them were little bits of the dark iron. He began to sweat as he worked, not from exertion, nor from the catacomb's humidity, but from haunting apprehension.

Roughly arranged on the crypt's floor, the pieces of metal took on the shape of a massive sword. From point to pommel, it stretched nearly as tall as Charles himself, and the form of it was like nothing the dhampir had ever seen. An iron blade, long and heavy, was fixed to a handle of bronze, its crosspiece sweeping back towards the hand. The pommel was bulbous, a massive counterweight to the heft of the sword, and as he sat back on his haunches, Charles inspected his handiwork. All the fragments were roughly assembled, all dozen of them, except for the knife that hung heavy at his side.

"This is it, then," he murmured as he pulled the knife from his belt and stared at it. How was he going to make the sword whole without an actual forge? The hairs on his neck prickled at the thought of whatever black magic would be required. Yet he didn't know any spells or incantations to fix antique blades. With a frown marring his face and his hands gripping each end of his knife, Charles felt the electric tang of static in the air as his back flexed under immense tension. He pulled at the knife's ivory handle, hearing it crack and crumble under his massive strength, and then the blade came loose with a crack.

Whatever came next, Charles recognized that the sword was a precipice that loomed in front of him. Once it was whole, he would have to strike down the vampire. There could be no delay, no fear, and no hesitation.

Cosmin needed to die.

Charles gulped as he slid his knife's blade into its place. It was the very tip of the broken sword, the blade's crowning glory, and once the metal touched the dhampir froze in place. His palms hovered over the largest fragments of Kizağan's sword and he felt a sensation of warmth that began to build in his hands. The blade began to distort in waves under the growing heat, as if Charles stared out across a sun-scorched plain to watch the horizon dance. It was as if the metal were alive, but then the warmth bloomed red and orange and white. "It's beginning," the dhampir said in wonderment, a dazzled smile stretching his face. "I can't believe it."

He buckled under the visions that flashed across his mind, his smile twisting into an agonized scream. An orange disc rose in his mind, its long reach scorching a plain of dead grass, and Charles saw the figures in battle. One was a mass of red and black, all twisted horns and yellow eyes and steel-gray teeth. The other figure was a god, a warrior, clad in archaic bronze armor with its head crowned by massive stag antlers. Back and forth they battled, the demon's strikes parried and counter-parried by the warrior's long iron sword.

The same massive sword that now glowed in yellow and white, its molten edges flowing together under blistering flames.

Fire licked at the calves of the great warrior as it struggled against the demon's onslaught, and then a series of great swinging strikes turned the tide of battle. Charles shut his eyes tightly, tears flowing from his eyes as he gritted his teeth against the agony in his hands, the searing heat and stench of burning hair and flesh causing the dhampir to gag and cry out. Kizağan, the great war-god of the southern people, swung his sword violently at the red-skinned demon, each blow parried by the devil's spear. Those yellow eyes blazed defiantly from an evil face, but the antlered head of Kizağan bowed low as he struck out, again and again.

Blind with pain and fury and fear, Charles leaned into the raging conflagration of molten metal to suck in fiery breaths as waves of hot air scorched his throat and lungs. He saw Kizağan push forward again, attacking and counterattacking, the demon's black cloven feet and forked tail digging into the holy ground beneath his feet.

Charles's strength began to ebb, his scorched and broken body failing under the inferno's onslaught, and the demon stumbled under the war-god's attacks. At the apex of triumph, Kizağan struck, his great sword opening a cleft in the bedrock, so that an explosion of light and fire rose from liquid metal.

Howling pain erupted from deep within Charles' chest, and the demon was cast into the pit, great screams of pain rising from a thousand souls trapped within the rent ground.

Collapsing onto the cool stone with a shudder, Charles's nose burned from the noxious smell of seared hair and charred skin and bone. The demon had been defeated once, but not destroyed. It had escaped the warrior-god Kizağan, and now the sword would be wielded again to correct an ancient failure. His body began to writhe in pain, his muscles contorting and seizing, and the blackened flesh of his hand found the cooling metal of the sword's blade. *It's not supposed to end this way*, Charles thought, but then a cackling noise echoed through the crypt as darkness closed in, and the dying dhampir sucked in another painful breath.

"He who destroys, shall be destroyed," Cosmin laughed as he shuffled from the dark, his eyes winking with humor. "That's what it says. Here, along the blade. He Who Destroys, Shall Be Destroyed." The vampire gingerly lifted the Sword of Kizağan from Charles's hand, one long finger running along the runes that had been seared into the blade. "That looked awfully horrible, Costache. Thank you for mending the sword, though. It will be put to good use. All I need now is the Navă . I will place her onto the altar and ram the Sword of Kizağan through her spine, and then the doorway will be unsealed. Your sacrifice means that your brothers and sisters will be released." The vampire squatted down and patted Charles's hand, then slid the long blade across his son's charred neck so that blood ran thick and red from the bucking body. "I mean this in the most literal way possible, son," he sighed. "I couldn't have done it without you."

****

## Cetatea Orașului

They had found the chapel and seen where Charles had pushed back the massive altar, then with a grunt, Unul Vechi led the way down the roughly carved steps. Guided through the dank and musty passage by a smoking oil lamp, the witch probed each step with her fleshy stumps and Elena trailed close behind, her face gaunt and her chest clenched tightly with the memory of Charles's horribly disfigured body. The girl had screamed when she had seen him, all twisted and scorched and shrunken from the heat. It must have been an excruciating thing, what Charles had experienced. The flesh of his hands had been burned away so even the bones of his fingers had been blackened from the forge's heat.

Yet blood still pooled around his head, the dhampir's neck slashed open into a gory, grinning wound.

Unul Vechi impatiently pulled the girl onward down dark stairs. "Dry your tears, child. Charles is dead," she lectured Elena. "Moaning over him won't do any good." Now they descended the ancient stairs so that a dim light appeared below them, its brightness a heinous beacon of evil, and anticipation leapt into Elena's parched throat as they stepped cautiously into a great, cavernous chamber. The sepulcher beneath the castle was massive, so massive that Elena gawked at its roughly formed roof supported by gigantic, fluted columns of polished black basalt. Candles guttered in the oppressive air, hundreds of them, the dim light of each wax stick multiplied to cruelly illuminate the demonic temple.

For a temple is what the vampire's vault was. A malevolent temple built to worship a wicked god, with prehistoric runes and devilish designs carved into the slick floor, the volcanic rock polished to shimmer in the weak light. Carvings of animal heads were framed by the runes, which themselves had been gouged into the floor to surround an altar of glittering gold, its heavy yellow sides encrusted in precious jewels and worked into appalling scenes of hellish delights.

Cosmin sat on the altar, his eyes dancing with glee. "Hello Mother," he smiled sweetly. "And you must be...Elena? How good of you to come, although I'm surprised you aren't bound at hand and foot."

Elena choked back a gasp. Cradled in the vampire's lap was a massive sword, wholly as long as Charles was tall, its handle the yellow-orange shine of bronze. Its blade glinted of dull iron and she could barely make out strange symbols dancing along the flat of its blade, which itself had a glow about it. The girl gasped when she sensed the swirling dark greens and bright oranges, the glows of evil and good, but was it possible for the sword to have a soul? Then her eyes fixed again on the runes etched along the length of its blade. They were ancient, far older than any written tongue that still survived, and their shapes also glowed but in reds and purples and bronzes. Elena couldn't read the runes, but instinctively she knew their meaning.

He Who Destroys, Shall Be Destroyed.

Not by just anyone, though. Only the Navă could destroy this creature that sat cackling on the golden altar. How many had lived before her and not succeeded? Dozens? Hundreds, even? More? "You're Cosmin," the girl said meekly.

"No, I'm not," he smiled back at her. "This corpse that I wear as a suit? Yeah, that was Cosmin. He died, though. That's what you people do best, you die. Sometimes in entertainingly horrid ways. My name is Malthus, the High One of Hell, and through Cosmin's sacrifice I became the vampire. The first one, I should say, though I have to admit, there are some drawbacks to being a vampire. The one 'plus' is that I can't be killed. Not when I'm wearing Cosmin's corpse-armor, that is! That's what I call it," he said with a laugh. "Corpse-armor, and when I wear it, I am in-dee-fucking-structible!" He leapt down from the altar, the Sword of Kizağan swinging wickedly through the air. "Once the Devil's Cohort is amongst us I will shed this decrepit artifact that was once Cosmin and take my rightful place on the Throne of Man! I will rule over everyone! Whoever is left, that is."

"The hell you will," Unul Vechi rasped, her fingers fiddling with a stone trinket. In her hand was a Venus, an ancient and powerful talisman, and strange sounds began to pour from her mouth.

Cosmin's corpse smiled. "I knew it! My mother, the double-crossing bitch. You can't trust anyone, can you, Elena? Mother, Mother, those old tricks won't work on me." He circled wide as he talked, a predator taking the measure of his prey. "My mother is casting a spell that is *supposed* to bind me in ethereal chains. Isn't that right, Mother?"

The witch scowled, her eyes mere slits as the guttural noises continued.

"What she doesn't know, my dear Navă, is that I've taken precautions against her treachery. Now come *here*!" Cosmin jumped at the girl with a shout, wildcat-quick so that the girl couldn't flee. The vampire seized Elena, a hand clamped around her neck, and hurled her onto the golden altar that was surrounded with writhing serpents and cavorting demons and blood-drenched pagan gods. "This is the key," he snarled against her ragged screams, one hand holding Kizağan's sword so that its edge reflected candlelight. Elena's eyes widened, the vampire's grip tightening to choke off her shrieking. "And you are the lock!" Malthus roared, his words echoing from cavernous heights, the sword lifted high to strike. "And with your death, the doorway to Hell will be…what the fuck?"

Light lanced from Elena's eyes, bright rays of burning white that made black stone run like water. She shrieked in horror and pain, and more light vomited from her mouth to burn through Malthus's hand so that he leapt back, the Sword of Kizağan clattering across the black floor. "What the fuck?" he screamed again, but then his screams grew with hers as the blinding light spewed out from every pore, Elena's body exploding with searing brightness. Cosmin's skin melted, bits of flesh streaming away from the light's onslaught so that rendered fat ran in rivulets, and then Cosmin and even Unul Vechi burst into screaming, flaming totems, until the flesh had seared completely away.

Light still coursed from Elena's body, its glow as bright as the sun, and the last remnants of Cosmin's body stripped away into billowing dust. A hulking demonic frame, growling with pain and fury, unfolded to stand tall against the scorching white of Elena's light. Malthus was a towering monster with yellow eyes and twisting horns, his red-black body hung with masses of wiry black hair that waved in the streaming light, and Elena's back arched as more light poured from her slight body. He reached out one grasping hand to seize the girl, to snatch her by the neck and choke the light out of her. Snarling through teeth as gray as the sword's iron, the demon's fingers blistered and broiled in the searing yellows and whites. He pushed forward, roaring challenges against the fiery light that thundered from Elena's screaming body, then his grasping claws began to erode from the surging light. Furious screaming slipped into a shrieking agony, Malthus's skin bursting into ashy boils, his claws and horns and bones scorched to brittle carbon, and then the terrible howl twisted into mortal screams of a tortured animal.

Elena's light burst into a great and terrible explosion that consumed the air and the bodies and even the rock itself, and then its brightness receded to give way to stifling dark, and all fell silent.

## Epilogue

The timeless being surveyed the chess board, its pieces set with apparent care across worn wooden tiles. Each figure had been lovingly and painstakingly carved from the purest white quartz and the darkest of jet with the blissful smiles and terrible grimaces of angels and demons. A handful had been moved from the last time the two had met, as they often did, to play this perpetual game between old friends. It looked up at its friend's approach, the featureless face brightening noticeably. "I wasn't sure you would make it!" it said, a hint of happiness tainted with the hint of gloat.

"And why wouldn't I?" the Devil answered toothily as he adjusted his natty tie, apparently nonplussed by the setback that sat like a raw sore. Somehow the girl had bested his chosen one. A failure it was, but a temporary one. He wouldn't let it grind at him like a millstone.

"Given recent events, I should think that you would be licking your wounds," the being smiled. It was a light rebuke, but a rebuke, nonetheless.

The newcomer chuckled at the trifle of it all. "Licking my wounds? A bit unnecessary, don't you think? What happened is just a minor setback, that is all. It is all just the opening moves of our match. There are still many moves to be made."

The timeless being looked its companion over, its plain face showing a hint of distaste. "Why do you insist on wearing such extravagant clothing?"

"And what is wrong with this outfit? It's a very dapper suit, particularly when one compares it with your thrift shop castoffs." The Devil had decided to sport a bespoke suit on this particular day, paired with hand-stitched alligator skin Italian shoes, all in the purest black, its hue punctuated by a silk burgundy tie. His black hair was neatly trimmed and slicked back, his beard cropped finely into a point. He flashed the familiar, cordial grin that hid a striking serpent's tongue. "Is that an onion sack you're wearing? I would have figured that God could afford much better than burlap."

"Your clothing is cliché," the devil's companion said, its voice concealing a slight reproof. "And here I thought you were making progress, yet everything about you is cliché. You could be anything you wish, and you choose this. It's as if you stepped right out of…what are those called? 'Moving pictures'?"

"On that point, we are agreed, my friend. My suit is cliché. In fact, I believe it's something a gangster would wear. It's also tailored by one of the oldest houses in England, while my shoes are handcrafted by an Italian master. Anyway, I chose this look because, unlike you, I actually care for how others judge me. More importantly, it's comfortable."

"An angel, fallen or not, shouldn't resort to such base vulgarity. Caring for how others judge you! The only judge you should care about is me."

"Eh, whatever you say, you old goat. Whose turn, Shad?"

"Mine, I believe," Shaddai answered curtly. "I do wish you wouldn't call me that. Abbreviated names are unseemly and lackadaisical."

"Would you prefer Adonai? Or Jehovah, perhaps?"

"You mock me," Shaddai chided his companion. They both sat at the chessboard for a moment, scanning the field to plan their next moves, when the devil broke the comfortable silence.

"So," he said with a contemplating frown. "Has it been determined yet?"

"Has what been determined?" Shaddai mumbled distractedly.

"Your pawn has struck down my Bishop *and* my Queen. Yet she still has a choice to make, does she not? So, I wonder if her future has been determined. She can always come over to my side, and I believe she still will. She was tempted...but then again, you won't say. You never say," the Devil frowned, his voice thick with regret.

Shaddai smiled slightly. "Pawn? You underestimate the girl. She's a Knight at least, and I do believe she has made her decision. After all, she did take your Queen."

"A Knight! While I may underestimate her, you certainly think too highly of the girl, old friend," the devil said in wonderment. "You have been disappointed before. Many times before, I would say."

"Perhaps I have been," Shaddai smiled. "Perhaps. Or maybe you simply lack faith. Anyway, you have yet to win a single match." He pondered the board, ultimately deciding to advance a pawn. There was no need to telegraph his strategy so early in the game, and certainly not with the stakes so high. "Besides, I am not the only one who has been disappointed in the cards we have been dealt. She is absolutely *not* a Pawn, not like you treated your son, your so-called 'Bishop'. There are still moves to be played. Before long, she may even become my own Queen."

"Let us hope that is not the case," the devil replied mildly, though his stoic exterior belied a turbulent core. "C5."

"Ah," Shaddai said hwit mild surprise. "Wonderful move, a strategy reminiscent of Geller. Bravo, my friend. Xc5, Bishop takes Rook."

"Son of a bitch."

"Language, please."

\*\*\*\*

Dawn broke. Sunlight streamed into Elena's tiny room, the plaster walls illuminated by the morning rays. Elena didn't yawn, didn't stretch the night's slumber from her joints. Rather, she laid on her bed, her bloodshot eyes cruelly and morbidly contrasting with sickly, pale skin. She hadn't slept, not a bit.

It had all been a dream, she was sure. No, not a dream. It was a nightmare. A terrible trick of the mind. The past days were fantastical, they were horrible inventions of a tortured imagination, no doubt brought on by the stress of the coming Vârstă de Măritat festival.

Yet it had all felt so real, all the horrid details of her dream. She had stark memories of Charles and the witch, of the red-skinned demon covered in black hair, of the massive iron sword and the slashing light that had burst from within.

She shook her head to clear the haunting memories, but it was no use. It was as clear as day, these recollections. Though, obviously, they were too incredible to be true. The dream was as real as reflections on a duck pond…it just had to be.

"Elena!" her mother called from the tiny home's kitchen. Smells of a sizzling breakfast sat heavy in the air, a heavy scent of browning butter and egg mixed with ham and mushrooms. Such things were traditional fare, and though it was a simple breakfast that her mother prepared, the familiar smells and flavors were themselves a comfort of a sort. Though the nightmarish memories stuck with Elena, she woke at home in a warm bed, with a new day's sun rising. It wasn't much, but it was the comfort of another dawn.

It was the comfort of being alive.

"Coming, mamă," she croaked through a dry throat, her voice barely a whisper. Elena wanted to be happy. After all, the Vârstă de Măritat was only a few days away. She wanted to jump out of bed and enjoy the familiar tastes upon her tongue, the flavors of a happy childhood, but she wasn't happy. She didn't want to jump out of bed. She didn't want to start the day.

Reluctantly, Elena rose and began to get ready. She stripped off her night clothes, soiled as they were with sweat from the feverish dreams that haunted what brief stretches of sleep she had been able to snatch. Off they came, then she reached for her *ie*, the traditional shirt of Romanian women in these parts, and went to pull it over her head.

Elena stiffened from shock, a breath stuck in her throat. Her blood turned cold as a winter snowstorm and her heart seemed to stop beating. The lone mirror in her room was clouded with age, but the face looking back at her was unmistakable. Black-haired, with black eyebrows, that terrifyingly familiar haughty nose and the distinctive upturned lips.

Adina stared back at her, a ghostly visage superimposed over her own pale face, and this wasn't a dream.

She didn't cry out, though. Not a tear fell, nor a gasp or a moan. She touched the mirror, almost willing Adina to disappear, but the dead girl stared back at her, a look of sadness and terror and longing shadowing her face, and a pained sigh escaped Elena's lips.

It wasn't over. Not yet.

## Request From the Author

If you enjoyed *The Devil's Cohort*, please consider leaving a review. Reviews are the most effective way for authors, independent, self-published, and even traditional, to be found.

****

Equally important, consider sharing your favorite authors with friends and family. Many independent, self-published (and even traditionally published) authors depend on word-of-mouth advertising to grow their base of loyal readers.

**Excerpt**

A Wanderer Among the Dead:

The Vampire's Vault Book 2

Coming Soon!

\*\*\*\*

"What is your name?" he asked, his voice a rasping timbre punctuated in harsh accents. His voice was foreign to her ear, a strange and frightening prospect. There were no foreigners in this place. Where she lived was a place of sorrow, a tiny pinprick of fertility in a land where the living treaded lightly, yet he had betrayed no care for the dead or their desires because he had no sense of fear, he had no regard for the darkness. She opened her mouth, unsure what to say yet driven to respond, but he interrupted rudely. "I don't care," he said dismissively, a hand flapping away her protest, "your name no longer matters. It was a relic from a past that is now dead. From this point forward, you will be called something else."

"Something else?" she asked, her breaths growing shorter, quicker, as his fingertips brushed her neck. She was nameless, even though mankind had labeled her with innumerable descriptions. Where would she even start? Yet he didn't care, and desire welled within, her body responding unwillingly to his light touch, feathery caresses to conflict with his brusque language. A smile played on his lips. This was a man, yet unlike any she had ever met. His soul was ancient even if his flesh was not and she was powerless to resist his demands, her vulnerability causing angry bile to rise. The woman's lithe body had taken on a mind of its own, even as she screamed for release, until eventually the woman relented under the onslaught of a primal desire.

"Yes," he finally answered, and in her mind's periphery where pleasure had not yet worked its vile magic, she noted that his voice lacked conviction. She was to be his consort, his mate and life-giver. The woman had grown up here amongst the people of the shallow river-valley, but that was long ago. Her past had been forgotten, that distant memory when she was a powerful shaman within her tribe. She had grown since then. Grown in power and stature, so that man knew her as the Venus, the woman who brought life to the world. Yet under this man's tutelage she would grow to be far more powerful than even she could fathom. Hers would not be the power of a warrior, nor a huntress, but far, far greater. She would bear his children, the first of a new race of beings destined to rule the world of man.

This woman, this goddess, had not grasped her new reality. Not yet anyway. She had given in to revel in the intoxication of a forbidden delight as his fingers traced whorls down her neck and between her breasts, before dancing across her taut abdomen. He could only exist in this world in fits and starts. Dreams were his kingdom, nightmares his domain, and only on a mere handful of nights could he cross the chasm. This shaman, this woman, held a gateway to this world. A door through which his seed would pass, and through them, through his children, the world of man would be brought to their knees.

Isleman: A Novel of Scotland

Coming Soon!

\*\*\*\*

*So this is the price of honor*, the old man thought, *paid for in the blood of men.* He was irritated, the summer day causing him to sweat heavily under his mail shirt. The sun's oppressive rays made his helmet unbearably warm and he shifted it to a more comfortable position. He surveyed the field before him, inspecting the heath moorland and farms that stretched into the distance. The vast landscape was punctuated only by the village of Oldmeldrum and the small army of knights and men-at-arms led by the nephew of that rotten bastard, the Duke of Albany. *How many must die on these fields before my honor is restored?* The old man looked south and thought he could make out the small town of Inbhir Uaraidh, only a few miles distant. The horizon lay through a summer haze that rose off the boggy land. Squinting his eyes at the sun, he spat into the spongy dirt at his feet. Barely two thousand men opposed his army of five times their number. *What the hell is Robert Stewart thinking?* He spat again.

'Lord, the men are ready,' an aide said nervously. The old man smirked and turned to face his men, looking up and down the line of his Highlanders, the hill of Beinn na Ciche looming over his grand army. His ragged army. A proud pack of ruthless warriors, five or six rows deep, that stretched along the foothills. He loved them as a father loved his sons. So many of his men shared his hardships. Kin and friends alike, they rose and fell with his fortunes. They bled for him, died for him. Wrinkles at the corners of his eyes grew deeper, more pronounced, as his mouth twisted into a melancholy smile. So much death, so much pain, and yet more death and pain would be paid this day, an investment to ensure his honor was restored.

Yet the old man was uneasy. The lowland armies, when fighting against mounted horsemen, would form into bristling blocks of pikemen, the old schiltron, a fortress of flesh and blood and iron. But the men that opposed this horde had no reason to worry about a flight of horse because he had none. No, his army was of brave Highlanders, wildly charging the enemy to break their lines through fear and sheer force. What he would have given for a mere hundred heavy war horses!

Courageous as his brave Highlanders were, the old man silently worried their reckless charge would be their undoing. But ten thousand men against no more than one-fifth their number? He surveyed the battlefield, noting the slight slope down to Stewart's men. Other commanders would withdraw to higher ground and fight a defensive battle, but the old man knew such a maneuver would negate that peculiar advantage of the coarse Highlanders. No, he would move the bowmen up on the flanks, loosing arrows to keep the enemy's heads down, and unleash his horde to smash the enemy. Sweat beaded on his neck and back, causing the léine shirt to stick to his skin uncomfortably. He shrugged his shoulders to free the sticky linen and earned a temporary reprieve for his troubles.

He nodded to his sennachie to begin the exhortations. Historians of their clans, the sennachie moved in front of the Mac Domhnall contingent and raised his voice. "Sons of Domhnall! We are here to do battle against those lowland bastards across this beautiful Scottish field! Do you hear them, quaking and crying?" Hooking his hands into claws, the sennachie began shaking flamboyantly to mock their enemy before suddenly standing tall. "They know we are here! They know the name Mac Domhnall, and the sons of whores who were whelped from dogs are pissing in their boots of facing you in battle!" The sennachie's voice rose an octave, spittle flying from his quivering lip. "They know of our Domhnall, who spanked the pup of Badenoch! They fear the name of Eoin, who faced King David and didn't bat an eye! And Aonghas Óg, who fought at Bannockburn with the Bruce and sent the English bastards running home with tails tucked in fear!" This was ironic as they now faced the factions of Robert Bruce's descendants, who were cousins to the old man himself. "They know of Somhairlidh, who did what the English could not and slaughtered the Norse on the shores of our lochs!" The wild horde cheered proudly, clashing their swords and axes against their compact targe shields.

The sennachie continued to champion his clan's history while the allied clans' sennachie yelled out martial praises for the men of Mac an Tòisich and Mac Leoid, Mac Gillean and Mac Choinnich, indeed all the great Highland families who supported the Lord of the Isles. The old man allowed himself to loosen a little, and he scratched at his greasy, grey beard absentmindedly. He finally felt content and was cautiously hopeful of a swift victory over Albany's hastily assembled rabble, composed mostly of farmers and freedmen, that opposed the Highland lines. *I shall finally burn Aberdeen*, he thought to himself, not for the first time. *I shall burn it to the ground!*

Made in the USA
Las Vegas, NV
08 March 2021